Rider Down

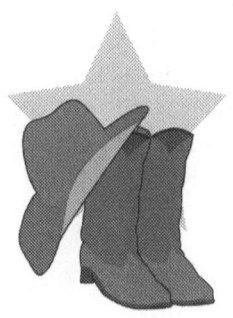

Debbie Madison

1st WORLD
PUBLISHING

Rider Down

Debbie Madison

© Debbie Madison 2006

Published by 1stWorld Publishing
1100 North 4th St. Fairfield, Iowa 52556
tel: 641-209-5000 • fax: 641-209-3001
web: www.1stworldpublishing.com

First Edition

LCCN: 2006907339
SoftCover ISBN: 1-5954-0877-0
HardCover ISBN: 1-5954-0876-2
eBook ISBN: 1-5954-0878-9

This material has been written and published solely for educational purposes. The author and the publisher shall have neither liability or responsibility to any person or entity with respect to any loss, damage or injury caused or alleged to be caused directly or indirectly by the information contained in this book.

The characters and events described in this text are fictional and are intended to entertain and teach rather than present an exact factual history of real people or events. Any resemblance to people or events are strictly coincidental.

Chapter One

The brochure had read: Enjoy the pristine natural beauty of the High Sierra's on horseback, as you herd horses and ride on trails carved out by pioneers of the 1800's. The pictures were so vivid and colorful they jumped out of the brochure and brought it to life. I was sold.

I eagerly hopped onto the crowded bus. As the doors closed a tall, well-built man with thinning white hair, stood up and faced us as he looked around the bus. "Listen up, folks," he said in a loud masculine voice. "My name is Matt." His eyes opened wide and the deep lines on his weathered face tightened as he said, "Tomorrow is going to be a very long day. I expect all of you to be up by four in the morning and on a horse by sun up."

He took a deep breath and slowly let it out as he popped open a beer and took a swift drink. Then in a much louder, deeper voice he started warning us about the obstacles and dangers that lie ahead on this four-day trip. The tone in his voice grabbed all of our attention.

As Matt's piercing voice echoed around the bus, smiles faded and looks of confusion crept onto faces. Everyone started whispering.

Was this a joke? I looked around me. No one was laughing. My heart started racing as I thought, I must be on the wrong bus! I pulled out the brochure and slowly reread it, over and over again. It didn't mention anything about getting up at four in the morning or getting on a horse earlier than I normally rolled out of bed. After all, this was my vacation and I was here to catch up on my sleep, not to lose more of it. I kept glancing down and staring at the colorful pictures in the brochure as I listened and watched him casually finish drinking a beer.

When our bus finally stopped and opened its doors, our whispers of uncertainty stopped as we stood up and piled outside.

Our campsite was nestled close to the base of a mountain and was in a valley of thick, dark green grass. Small domed tents were being erected, dotting the landscape with a splash of bright colors. The sun's fading light was bouncing off and around them. As it slowly faded behind a tall mountain range, it left a picturesque silhouette of jagged snow-covered peaks. As the last rays of sunshine disappeared, a cold breeze kicked up and sent most of us racing to find our duffle bags and a warm tent.

Horses and mules were walking around and through our campsite, casually munching on everything in their paths. None of them were tied or haltered. Two tall, young wranglers were chasing them away from the tents. The animals kept trotting away but only a couple feet and as soon as the wrangler turned their backs the animals returned.

Everyone around me was moving fast, grabbing and putting on jackets as the daylight around us faded. I grabbed my duffle bag with one hand and my sleeping bag with the other and followed the crowd towards the tents.

Two young muscular men were tossing down heavy saddles from the back of an overloaded truck. Two other men took turns catching them in midair as though they were light as a feather. A third man grabbed them and stacked them neatly, inside an old dilapidated wooden corral.

I watched them for a few minutes as I walked around looking for an empty tent. I found one and moved in. As darkness fell and lanterns were lit, I could see pockets of bright lights through my thin tent walls.

I was cold, tired, and really confused. The thought of getting up at four in the morning was still hammering away at my worn-out brain. I laid down and buried myself deep, inside the warmth of my sleeping bag.

"Dinner is ready!" a high-pitched voice shouted. "Come and get it!" another woman shouted.

As people walked back and forth past my tent, I could hear them laughing and making comments about the food they were eating. I wasn't hungry, but I figured I should venture outside and join them.

When I unzipped my tent, freezing air rushed inside. I zipped up my jacket and pushed my hands deep into the warmth of its pockets as I headed outside.

Matt was standing close to one of the bright lanterns, along-side three long tables neatly filled with food. "Listen up, folks," he said as he raised his hands high in the air to get our attention. "We're not allowed to have any fires at this campsite. So those of you who smoke need to make real sure that your cigarettes are out before you throw them down.

The light around the tables wasn't bright enough for me to make out what most of the food was. I grabbed a bag of potato chips and a very well-done hamburger.

Half of our group filled their plates and disappeared, retreating back to the warmth of their tents. The rest of us sat down together in a tight circle and tried to stay warm as we talked and ate in the darkness.

Every time anyone started a conversation Matt's loud voice would interrupt us and grab all of our attention. "When you see someone thrown from their horse, don't chase their horse and don't get off yours. Yell as loud as you can, 'rider down!' Folks, these are real animals and it takes us five or ten minutes to stop this size of a herd. If you hear anyone yell, "rider down," you carry the words forward. When they reach us on the front line we will fan out and stop the herd and send back riders to help." Matt never stopped talking about us getting hurt and or thrown from our horses.

By the end of the evening he had successfully scared us all, half to death. The way he was chugging down beer, made me wonder if he was exaggerating. For my sake I was hoping he was, especially the part about getting up at four in the morning. The night air was turning frigid and I was tired of listening to Matt, so I called it a night and retreated to the warmth of my tent.

I woke up surrounded in darkness. I could hear wranglers whistling and yelling and dogs barking. I glanced at my watch. It was barely three in the morning. I peaked outside my tent. Cold air slapped my face, sending chills up and down my spine.

The only thing I could see was the lanterns from the night before. They were still burning bright. I zipped my tent back up and retreated to the warmth of my sleeping bag. I could hear the kitchen crew. They were already up and clanging on pots and pans. I pulled the sleeping bag over my head. I had no intention of getting up. I was on vacation and I needed more sleep, a lot more.

I tried to doze back off but the whispers from the cooking crew turned into outbursts of giggling and loud laughter. And noises from tents zipping and unzipping kept me awake. I took a deep breath and a long hard look at the darkness that surrounded me. An uncomfortable feeling crept over me as I thought about all the scary things that Matt had said. What had I got myself into?

If the rest of these people can do this, then so can I. A little voice inside of me kept repeating this as I yawned and stretched my body in total darkness.

I couldn't recall the last time I was up at four in the morning. Probably twenty years ago when I was in college. I didn't want to remember. Most everyone I knew stayed away from me until at least my second cup of coffee. I don't think my brain started functioning until about noon. I was not a morning person.

"Coffee's ready," a loud, deep voice shouted. I fumbled around in my duffle bag for my insulated cup. Then I unzipped my tent and followed the voice. Gas lanterns lit my way to a couple of long narrow tables. Three women were behind them mixing, cooking, and pouring coffee. They were joking and teasing the wranglers as they showed up and asked for a cup of coffee.

All of the men were smiling, and polite. I wondered if they were putting on a show. It didn't seem natural for people to smile or joke this early. No man, woman or child I knew would be joking or smiling at four in the morning. Oh well, I thought, today is only our first day. We'll see who's smiling tomorrow at four in the morning.

"Hello, how are you this morning?" a cheery voice asked. Before I blurted out something I might regret, I mumbled "Thank you," as she poured hot coffee into my cup, then I stumbled back to the warmth of my tent. The coffee was black, thick, and bitter. I slowly drank it, hoping it would wake me up.

Last night, when I finally got to my tent, I was cold and very tired. I remember cussing under my breath as I fumbled through my neatly packed duffle bag looking for my pajamas. For the life of me I couldn't find my pajama bottoms. I must have dropped my flashlight a dozen times as I stirred my clothes around. Fatigue and sleep solved my problem. This morning I was wearing a pink pajama top, my jeans from yesterday, and to my dismay, I still had my horse-riding boots on. Well, I thought as I glanced at my pants, at least I won't have to spend much time getting dressed.

Packing my belongings in the dark was even harder. I tried to hold my flashlight in my mouth, then under my arm. My early morning temper didn't help. I finally gave up and left most of my belongings hanging out of my duffle bag and scattered around on the tent floor.

The wonderful aroma of bacon frying and an empty cup of coffee lured me back outside. In the moonlight I could see wranglers chasing and saddling horses. I could hear tent poles as they crashed to the ground. Our campsite was alive.

A group had gathered around the food tables. I zipped up my jacket and joined them. Everyone moved slow and remained quiet as they filled their plates. I wasn't hungry or thirsty. I wasn't even sure if I could eat this early in the morning. But I had a feeling that if I didn't eat now, I wouldn't have a second chance later.

I forced myself to eat thick greasy bacon and watery

scrambled eggs. I washed it down with black coffee. Neither appealed to me. I was hoping the food would help wake me up and warm my cold body.

Everyone around me was scratching their heads or rubbing their eyes. It was pretty easy to tell that none of us were used to getting up this early. I'm not even sure I slept last night. I really needed and wanted to go back to bed.

As the sun rose and warmed all of our sleepy bones, everyone's grunts and groans turned into polite, almost normal conversations. "Who are you? Where are you from?"

I made a count. There were twenty-five of us. A third cup of coffee got my brain functioning so I walked around and asked everybody where he or she was from. I was surprised to find out that there were only six of us from California.

Most everyone here was from the Midwest. And one couple came all the way from New York.

I couldn't help but wonder, Why would you fly all the way to California to ride a horse? I mean, isn't the Midwest filled with horses and farms?

"Listen up, folks, I need your attention." The sun was rising and highlighting Matt's tan leathered face as he spoke. "We've got horses saddled and waiting for you. We've assigned you horses based upon what your horse-riding skills are, or at least what you said they were on the paperwork you sent us."

He lowered his head for a second, then raised it as he lifted his hands high in the air. His voice cracked as he said, "Folks, this is real. You've all signed disclaimers, so if you get hurt, you can't sue us, and," he slowly added as he opened his eyes real wide, "some of you will get hurt. Remember to yell, 'rider down' when you see anyone thrown. Folks, this is not like the movie *City Slickers*. We're going to move one hundred head of horses and mules over one hundred miles in four days."

He spoke slowly, but you could tell by the tone in his voice, that he was dead serious. "Today is the most grueling day of all. We're going to drive this herd forty miles. We'll stop for a thirty-minute lunch. If all goes well, we should be to our night camp by 6 pm."

Wait a minute did he say 6 pm? I glanced at my watch. It was barely 6 am. Was he kidding? Was it humanly possible to ride a horse that long? Could a horse survive being ridden twelve hours? Could I survive that long? I had ridden four and five hours on a horse before but never twelve hours, not to mention on a horse I hadn't even met.

I looked around me to see if I was the only one questioning my horse-riding abilities along with my sanity. No one raised their hands or said, "Are you kidding? I can't ride that long."

As the sun rose and danced around on the hillsides, it warmed and soothed my chilled body. It slowly drained away my worries and fears. I kept reminding myself that I had paid good money for this trip and I wasn't about to back out now.

There were only six wranglers and Matt. They wore blue jeans, western hats and they all had spurs on their boots. Us tourists, on the other hand were covered in colorful matching clothes, baseball caps, and cameras dangled from our necks.

"Any of you wearing a camera," a piercing voice shouted, "must take them off. We do not stop for cameras or anything that falls down or off of your horse. Put your cameras in your duffle bags. You won't have time to take pictures anyway."

Wait a minute, I thought, I'm up at 4 am and I don't get to take pictures, because I won't have time. What's going on here? Why wasn't any of this in the brochure?

I raised my hand and boldly asked, "What do you mean, we won't have time to take pictures? I brought a small camera that fits in my pocket. Why can't I bring it?"

Everyone's eyes followed my camera as I held it up for the wrangler to see.

The wrangler walked over to me took the camera from my hands and said, "You can take small cameras," he held the camera high up in the air for everyone to see as he said, "as long as they fit inside these saddle bags." He held up a small baggie-sized satchel that had a drawstring on it. "If you need one of these, come get them now. Besides your canteen and jacket, this is the only other thing your horse will carry." He handed me back my camera along with the small satchel.

Everyone began grumbling and mumbling as they reluctantly unhooked and unstrapped expensive cameras from their bodies. You could feel the anger as they stomped away and stashed their cameras with their gear. I, on the other hand, was feeling a little smug. My cheap disposable camera fit perfectly inside the satchel the wrangler had just given me.

"Wait up," the wrangler yelled. "If you folks are wearing anything like this woman is wearing, take it off. You cannot wear anything around your waist, except a belt."

The wrangler was pointing at my waist. I was wearing a fanny pack. I had it loaded with candy, granola bars, and gum. He asked me to take it off and held it up high for everyone to see.

"I think it's a fanny pack," someone said out loud. "I haven't seen one of those in a long time," another person whispered. "I didn't know they still made those," another person added as he pointed towards me. To add humility to my embarrassment, the youngest person on the trip, a seventeen-year-old girl, asked, "What's a fanny pack?" Everyone around her started laughing.

I grabbed the fanny pack from the wrangler's hand and hurried back to my tent, where I buried it deep inside my duffle bag.

All I could fit inside the small satchel I was given was my camera, a pack of gum, and a couple of pieces of hard candy.

Wranglers were calling out names and introducing people to their horses. I took a deep breath and hurried back to my group. A tall, well-built man turned towards me and said, "Hi, aren't you Mary?" "Yes," I slowly replied. "Why?" He lifted his hat high on his forehead so I could see his face then he smiled at me and said, "They just called your name. I think that wrangler over there has your horse."

Without thanking him I raised my hand high in the air and shouted, "I'm here, I'm Mary." "If you're Mary, this is your horse over here," the wrangler shouted back. I had been dreaming about this trip for over a year. My heart was pounding as I approached the wrangler. My adrenaline was flowing and I tried not to show how excited I was. I was ready.

"Your horse's name is Tyler," the wrangler said as he handed me the reins. I studied the horse for a minute. It was black as midnight, muscular, and seventeen hands tall. He reminded me of a racehorse. I checked the saddle's cinch. It was very loose. "Excuse me," I said as the wrangler walked away, "I think my cinch is loose."

The wrangler walked back over, checked the cinch, looked me in the eyes, and said, "Yep, it's suppose to be loose." He grabbed another horse and called out another person's name.

A loose cinch on a horse didn't make any sense. I was really confused. Years ago when I had volunteered at a stable and we were dealing with a "know-it-all" jerk, we would purposely leave his horse's cinch loose. Then we would quietly bet on the side on how soon the rider would fall off, as his saddle slowly slid towards the horse's belly. Was I the jerk here? No, they wouldn't do that, would they? But if I didn't tighten the cinch, I would fall off.

I looked around me. Everyone was talking to their horses and each other. I was the only person frowning. Was everybody's cinch loose? Did anybody besides me check it? Maybe the lack of sleep had hurt my better judgment. I moved my horse away from the wrangler. And without him seeing me I got off of my horse and tightened his cinch.

"Stay back until we let the horses and mules out," a piercing voice yelled. "You folks up front move now!" Who was he talking to? I looked around me, no one was moving.

"I guess that means us," I said as a smile filled my face and I loudly said, "E-haw!" The riders around me all laughed and joined in, "E-haw!" We were off.

"You riders up front, form a line," Matt shouted as his horse caught up to ours. "You're the front line—spread out and form a line."

We all heard Matt, we just weren't sure what we were suppose to do. He kept shouting and telling us all to form a line. "You're the front row. You have to keep the herd behind you. Now spread out."

My horse was not cooperating. His ears were pinned back

and he fought me with every muscle he had. My heart was pounding as I fought to control him.

"Hey, get your horse away from mine!" a woman shouted. "He's going to kick my horse." I pulled back on my horse's reins. He wasn't impressed and he inched closer to her horse's rear end. "Didn't you hear me?" she shouted. "Get your horse away from mine!"

I yanked on my reins and pulled my horse's neck all the way back to my chest, he should have stopped in his tracks. Instead his nostrils flared and he started swinging his neck around and stomping his front legs.

I kicked him hard in the stomach. He ignored me. "Get your horse back in line!" Matt yelled as my horse leaped forward. I felt like yelling, "Help!" but I knew no one would listen. "I'm sorry," I shouted to the woman. "This horse is a little hard to handle."

Matt was watching me. He shouted, "If you aren't an experienced rider, you need to drop back to the rear. Stop your horse and let the herd pass you." He slowed his horse down and pulled alongside of me. "He'll calm down in a couple of miles," he said with a softer tone in his voice. "He's a thoroughbred and he hasn't been ridden for six months. He wants to be in front of all of the horses. Its just his nature."

My heart was racing. I tried not to look frightened. Oh my God, I thought, I'm on a racehorse that hasn't been ridden in six months. I'm going to get killed.

I turned my head for a split second to see if anyone else was having trouble with their horses. Faster than I could blink my eye, Tyler lunged forward. He stretched his neck out and took a chunk out of Matt's horse's butt.

I yanked as hard as I could on his reins as he sidestepped to my right. Matt's horse backed up and kicked out his left hind leg up at us. Luckily he missed. My horse immediately retaliated by going in for a second bite. This time we weren't so lucky. Matt's horse kicked again and his leg landed a crashing blow directly on my right ankle. It happened so fast that I wasn't sure if he had hit my leg or my horse's stomach. "Stop!" I yelled, "I've been kicked."

Matt glanced back at me and shouted, "Are you dizzy? We can't stop. There are one hundred horses and mules behind us. Are you going to pass out?"

A sharp pain shot through my entire body. I was embarrassed and frightened at the same time. As I fought back tears I said, "No, I'm okay." In a whimpering voice as tears rolled down my face I quietly said, "I think my ankle is broken." A deep throbbing pain set in from my toes to my knee. I knew my ankle was broken and I knew that if I got off of my horse right now, I wouldn't be able to get back on.

Matt wedged his horse next to mine. Both animals had their ears pinned back. "About five miles ahead we'll stop. I'll check your ankle there." He nudged his horse forward. The herd picked up speed.

"What happened?" A rider on the right asked me. "Did you just get kicked?" another voice asked. I wasn't sure what to say. In a meek voice I said, "Yes, I just got kicked. I think my ankle is broken."

The next five miles seemed like a lifetime. My horse fought me every inch of the way. He kicked and tried to bite every horse, mule, and rider that attempted to pass him. My body trembled as I strained every muscle I had, trying to control him.

As we slowed down and approached a long, closed, metal gate I caught up to Matt and said, " I'm sorry Matt, but I can't ride this horse. He's far to strong for me." I was embarrassed and in pain. My shin and ankle were throbbing and at this point in time, I wasn't sure if I ever wanted to be around or ride a horse again.

"Spread out," Matt shouted. "All of you on the front line, spread out!" A pick up truck was about one hundred feed in front of us. A short, spindly man got out and opened a long metal gate.

We parked our horses at the gate's opening and turned them sideways, forming a long line. As the herd approached us Matt shouted, "Turn them, keep them moving right." We whistled and waved our hats and reins at them. One by one they turned and headed down a steep embankment. I held Tyler as tight as

I could as he tried to bite and kick every animal that walked past him.

"Ten-minute break," someone shouted. "Bathroom break," someone else shouted. When the last horse had been turned, our group followed down the embankment.

The constant shouting had all but stopped. I'm not sure if we all were exhausted already or if we all were numb. I knew I had to make a decision on what to do.

Matt got off of his horse and walked over to mine. "I'm a veterinarian," he said. "Now let's take a look at that ankle."

Oh great, I thought. I wasn't sure how to react to the veterinarian part. I was just glad someone was going to look at it. I was too afraid to look at it myself and I knew if I took off my boot, I wouldn't be able to get it back on. I lowered my head as if in defeat and asked, "Is it broken?" "Can you feel your toes?" Matt asked as he slowly pulled down my sock. "No, I can't feel my toes." I said with a whimper, "Is it broken?"

"Your shin bone isn't," he said. "I don't know about your ankle. If I take your boot off I don't think you'll get it back on." He looked deep into my eyes and asked, "What do you want to do?"

"I'll ride," I said as I picked my head up off of my chest. "I'll ride," I repeated as I took a deep breath. Without another word, Matt turned and walked away. "Wait!" I shouted, "But I need a different horse. I can't control this one."

Everyone around me had gotten off of his or her horse. Most of them were watching me and whispering amongst themselves.

I felt sad, then excited, then very disappointed with myself. Why did I tell Matt I wanted to go on? I was an emotional wreck.

Chapter Two

"Hi, your name is Mary, right? My name is Robert, we met earlier this morning." Robert was tall and lean. He had softness in his face that I was immediately attracted to. I turned my horse towards him. "Are you the one everyone is talking about? Are you hurt? What happened?" His voice had a hint of sympathy in it and he seemed genuinely concerned. "Yes," I quietly replied, "I'm the gimp here. I've only been on a horse a few minutes and I think I've already broken my right ankle."

"I don't get it." He looked past my ankle and took his sunglasses off. "What are you still doing on a horse? Shouldn't you be going to the hospital or something?"

"Well," I said with a whimper, "I chose the, 'or something.' Besides, I can't walk, so I might as well ride." I expected Robert to respond with laughter, or some comment like "Are you crazy?" He didn't. He put his sunglasses back on and said, "Oh," as a puzzled look filled his face.

"Breaks over folks," someone shouted. "Mount up." I untied my canteen and took a sip. As I started to tie it back to my saddle, a wrangler walked up to me. "Mary this is your new horse, his name is Red. Get your gear off of Tyler and tie it on Red."

Everyone around me was already back on their horses. The herd became restless and started moving. "Front riders get in position!" Matt yelled. The tone in his voice sent my heart racing. I quickly untied all of my gear and got off of Tyler. Sharp pain shot through my ankle as it touched the ground. My leg collapsed and I fell down. "Easy missy," a wrangler said as he grabbed my arm. "Let me help you." I was embarrassed. I felt like I had become a burden and I didn't like the feeling.

"I'm all right," I said as I pushed the wrangler away and hopped over to my new horse. "I'm fine," I added in a loud voice as I tied my gear down. I wasn't fooling anybody. The wrangler didn't take his eyes off of me until I was back in the saddle.

Most of our group was already on the front line. I held Red back. My confidence was shattered. I decided it would be best for me to stay in the rear where all the inexperienced riders were supposed to be. I was on a new horse so I figured it would be a good place to introduce myself to him. Red was tall like Tyler yet very quick to respond to my every move. He ignored the mules as they kicked and vied for position. He was alert yet calm and we instantly bonded.

Now back in the rear, I wasn't sure what I was supposed to do. At first I felt like I was being punished. I was in a constant cloud of thick, choking dust. I pulled my hat as low as it would go. My bandana and sunglasses gave me some reprieve. I gave Red his reins, and he instantly responded by trotting after three mules that had broken away from the herd. The mules saw us coming and darted up a steep ravine. Red broke into a canter. "Let's get them, Red!" I shouted in excitement. We cut them off and turned them back toward the herd. "Good job!" a wrangler shouted as I caught back up with the herd. "Well done."

Red slowly rebuilt my confidence as we darted out left then right, chasing horses and mules. The throb in my ankle all but disappeared as I rode. I was glad to be riding.

I shouted and yelled at the herd until my throat went dry. Then I whistled and twirled the end of my reins at them. Red and I never stopped moving. Animals constantly broke away from the herd. Our job was to circle around them and make them rejoin the herd. This meant we never got to walk. I was constantly in a trot, bobbing up and down on Red. My bottom was slapping a hole in the saddle. I'll never make it, I thought as I tried to stretch my back. Aches and pains were setting in all over my body. I tried cantering Red; when I broke him into a run, the horses or mules I was trying to catch would spook and moved away faster. The only way to catch them was by pretending you were following them, trotting past them and then turning them back, toward the herd.

I couldn't imagine being a cowboy and doing this for a living. This was grueling work. To make matters worse, the sun was melting our bodies and frying our brains.

As the ground beneath Red's feet constantly changed, I kept a keen eye out for snakes and gopher holes as he darted around the vast open spaces.

When one horse or mule would leave the herd, a second or third animal would hastily follow them. In a matter of seconds, the herd would split off into branches. We had to think quickly and move fast.

You would have thought that by the tenth time we chased these guys back to the herd that they would have stayed there, but not these animals. If one trotted up a hill, his buddies would be right on his heels. It almost seemed as if they were playing a game of "catch me if you can" with us.

It was exciting and exhilarating. This was real. I was chasing horses and mules up and down vast, wide-open spaces. Red and I had become a team. My slightest move set him in motion. He was fast and he could turn on a dime. I thought about my first horse, Tyler. He would have thrown me by now. I'm sure glad I had switched horses.

I slowed Red down and glanced at my watch. It read 11:30 am. It couldn't only be eleven thirty in the morning—my watch must have stopped. It had to be four or five o'clock by now. I was hot, tired, and out of energy and I wasn't alone. Earlier, each time a pack of horses broke away from the herd all of us in the back would eagerly take off after them. Now we all kept looking at each other, as if to say, "Go ahead, it's your turn. I'm too tired."

The herd was slowing down and spreading out. I hollered to a wrangler a couple of horses away from me. "Why are we stopping?" "A narrow bridge," he hollered back. I had never crossed a bridge before and I was hoping my horse Red had. As the herd crowded the narrow opening, our surroundings cleared as the dust settled. A deafening, clanging noise filled the air as the horses slowly crossed the bridge. I could hear water roaring below us. "Please Red," I whispered in his ear, "be good." As Red stepped onto the bridge, two mules began fighting. They cut us off and pinned us along the edge of the bridge. I could see the raging water below me. My heart started pounding as mules surrounded us. I closed my eyes and held my breath as we crossed. Somehow, we had to get to the other side before one of the mules kicked themselves or us. I wrapped my left hand around my saddle horn and held on for dear life as we slowly crossed. A welcome sight awaited us on the other side of the bridge. Our lunch wagon was parked and tables and chairs were neatly set out in the shade of large trees. Just thinking about shade and food picked up my spirits.

"All of you folks that are not riding this afternoon stay on your horses." Matt's piercing voice got all of our attention. The herd rushed past us down to the river. "Don't worry about the herd, they won't go far. Let the riders that are going on this afternoon eat first. Stay on your horses if you aren't riding this afternoon."

Well, I thought, I guess that means I'm going on. I was starving and nothing was going to stop me from eating, right now. "Excuse me," I said as I walked Red past most of the riders. "We're going on." I said with a smile.

A wrangler stopped my horse, "I'll water him and tie him for you ma'am." he said as he tipped his hat. I wasn't sure if I could get off of my horse. I had been on him for six hours. I felt like I was glued on. I struggled to lift my right leg high enough to get it over the saddle. It weighed a ton. As my right leg touched the ground a sharp pain sliced through my ankle. I couldn't put any weight on it and it throbbed so hard it brought tears to my eyes. I grabbed the saddle horn to keep from falling.

The slinky wrangler held my horse in place as I regained my balance. "Do you need help, Ma'am?" The pain was excruciating. I fought back tears, as I said, "No, I'm fine." The pain shot adrenaline through me like lighteing. Every inch of my body responded as I twisted back and forth trying to walk. Nothing worked, I couldn't move.

"Ma'am, let me help you." The wrangler held out his thick muscular arm. "You're the one that got kicked, aren't you?" He raised his hat up and in a softer voice asked, "Are you sure you want to ride this afternoon?" "Yes," I hastily replied. "Would you mind helping me to that chair, in the shade, over there?" Without another word he braced his shoulder and arm on my right side as I hobbled over to the chair. I plopped down, wiped my watering eyes, and quietly said, "Thank you."

Everyone around me was laughing and stuffing food in their mouths. One by one they walked over to me and asked, "Are you the one that got hurt? What happened?" For some brainless, self-pitying reason, I didn't respond to any of them.

I closed my eyes and took a few deep breaths. The shade was comforting. I could have fallen asleep in a heartbeat. Matt's voice reminded me that I couldn't. "Listen up, folks, you have thirty minutes so eat up and refill your canteens. Your horses are in the clearing over there." He turned to his left and pointed toward the horses.

His voice was powerful and loud. Every time he spoke, my heart would race. I don't know why, it just did. As he walked away I stood up and hopped over to a table piled with food. As I approached it, the aroma of fresh chocolate chip cookies overwhelmed me. I grabbed a paper plate and dug in.

Our chuck wagon was only a few feet away from the table. It was a small self-contained gray trailer. It couldn't have been more then twenty feet long. Two hefty women were busily moving in and out of it. One popped her head out carrying a plate filled with hot chocolate chip cookies. Before she could put the plate down, I grabbed a handful. They barely fit on my plate.

"Hey, Mary, over here." Robert was standing close to where I had been sitting a minute ago. "I've got a chair for you. Can I get you some lemonade?" Hopping on one leg with a full plate of food was challenging enough. "Thank you," I replied, "I would love a couple of gallons of it." Everyone around me chuckled.

I've never eaten so fast and so much food in my life. I stuffed cookies in my mouth and washed them down as fast as I could with ice-cold lemonade. The cookies were sweet and the lemonade was tart, I'm not even sure I liked it. It didn't matter. The combination refueled my tired, aching body. A smile filled my face as I thought about the words, "sweet and sour." The term had taken on a new meaning in my mind.

A fast-flowing stream was meandering under the trees. It was a perfect place to cool off and re-hydrate our brains, bodies, and souls. As the water serenaded my dry swollen eyes, one of the women from the kitchen walked over and held out a small baggie full of ice cubes. "This might help," she said as she took a closer look at my leg. "Thank you," I sighed as she laid the bag on my dusty jeans. "Thank you very much."

Her kind gesture made me take a good long hard look at myself. I was embarrassed. I had been hurt in the first fifteen minutes of our first day and I realized I was feeling sorry for myself.

Robert had sensed that I wanted to be alone. He was quietly talking with two younger women who were sitting close to the water, a few feet away from me. "I'm all right," I announced as I stood up and a smile returned to my face. "Only my pride is hurt."

"So what happened? Are you going on? Can you believe this?" Everyone grabbed their chairs and gathered around me. We took turns sharing stories of how frightened we all were this morning and how much fun we were having. Our thirty-minute lunch went by in what seemed a matter of seconds.

"Refill your canteens, check your cinches. All of you that want to get on the front line go, now!"

If someone had stuffed cotton in my ears and given me a hammock, I would have slept right through Matt's commanding voice. He was all business and he sorely needed a public relations person. After all, we were paying him. Shouldn't he be saying something a little softer like, "I hope you enjoyed your lunch. It's time to get back on your horses"? The tone of his deep loud voice, along with his towering physique, set us all in motion.

The ten thousand sugar calories I had just consumed gave me a burst of energy. I thought about joining the front line.

Robert's mule was tied next to my horse. "Where are you going to ride this afternoon?" I asked him as I checked my cinch. "I'm staying at the back of the herd. Are you going up front?" I wanted to get to know him better. "No," I replied, "I'm going to the back also."

His mule and my horse stood side by side. We let the herd pass us. My horse barely lifted his neck, as the mules trotted pass and teased him.

We crossed an endless valley of white dust, dirt, and small shrubs. A hot breeze followed us and by early afternoon our visibility had dropped to less then a few feet in any direction.

The wind picked up the dust from the herd in front of us and threw it into the air, creating a cloud so thick you could cut it with a knife. God forbid any of us fall off out here. No one would even notice. Even with a bandana on I could barely breath. The dust was hot and so fine that it choked the back of my throat as it filtered through my bandana. I couldn't hear a person hollering or even whistling at the herd. We all were struggling to breath.

"Whoa, whoa!" I couldn't see anyone, but I heard the thunder of a horse's hooves getting closer to me. It scared me I couldn't see a thing. I tried not to panic as my heart raced. "It's all right, Red," I nervously said as I started patting my horse's neck. "We're alright boy, easy, easy boy." Please don't spook, I thought to myself.

The horse's hooves got louder and as I blinked to focus better, I saw a man's head and chest on top of his horse's neck. Then I heard a thud as he hit the ground. I couldn't see him, but his horse had stopped and was only a few feet away from me.

"Rider down!" I screamed at the top of my lungs. "Rider down!" I choked and coughed as I tried to take a deep breath to scream again. I stopped my horse and frantically waved my hand in the air while yelling "rider down!"

I could hear voices in front of me as my words were carried

forward. Horses and mules walked by me following the herd. I
didn't move, although I was frightened that if I didn't follow the
last of the animals, I would get left behind.

Visibility was now less then two feet in any direction. I was
using my ears more than I was using my eyes. I was down wind
of the entire group and herd.

I could no longer see the horse or rider, even though I knew
they were only a few feet from me. I was petrified and alone.
Was he hurt? Or worse, dead? The strangest thoughts flooded
my mind as I listened for any signs from people or horses.

"I'm okay," a weak voice mumbled as it coughed, "I'm
okay." "Don't move!" I shouted. "They're bringing you help." I
had no idea what I was saying, but it sounded good. And I felt
a little better knowing I wasn't out here alone.

Our silence was broken by the thunder from horses' hooves.
They got louder and louder as they approached us. "Over
here!" I kept shouting, "Over here!"

Chapter Three

Two riders appeared out of the dust. They were in a full gallop and almost crashed into my horse as they skidded to a stop. Red's ears flew up and I could feel his muscles tighten as his legs danced. "Easy boy, easy boy." My heart was racing as fast as his was. "Where?" they both shouted at the same time as they looked around me. "Right there." I quickly pointed to the right of me.

"Are you all right?" the second rider called out as he headed his horse in that direction. "Yes," a shaken voice replied. "I just can't see a thing. My horse got spooked and threw me."

As quick as the wranglers appeared, they disappeared. They didn't even get off of their horses, once the rider told them he was all right they started to trot away.

I followed their voices and made a beeline towards them. I wasn't going to be left out here again. I kept my eyes focused on their horse's tails and followed them as close as they would let me. I could hear the fallen rider's horse—they was directly behind me. As we turned and entered a canyon, the dust slowly disappeared. The herd had been stopped and was wandering all over the place. The rest of the riders were standing next to their horses wiping off their hats and sunglasses and drinking water. I was glad to be back with the herd.

"Mary, are you hurt?" I slowly got off my horse, turned around to face Robert and with a smile on my face said, "No, not this time."

"Good," Robert said as he took a step closer towards me. "We all thought it was you again. Who fell off? Were they hurt?"

I hesitated to reply. I didn't know the man's name, but I remembered his face from the bus. Yesterday I sat next to him on the ride here. I tried to start a conversation with him two or three times. He boasted he had been on this horse trip over fifteen times. I was hoping he would shed some light on what I could expect, since the brochure didn't seem to. He spoke in riddles and kept a smug look on his face. I would have moved if there had been an empty seat. I was hoping we wouldn't meet again.

His horse walked past me, as I took a sip of water. I expected him to stop and thank me or at least to say, "Hi," for staying with him, after he got thrown. He didn't. My throat was dry and raw, so I took another sip. What a jerk, I thought, serves him right. I wanted to tell the crowd around me what a creep he was. Before I could catch my breath, Matt's powerful voice sent all of us scrambling to get back in the saddle.

My face felt like sandpaper. I poured water on my bandana and wiped it off, it was cool and refreshing. I leaned forward and poured water down the back of my neck. It sent chills up my spine.

I thought about the man who had just been thrown from his horse. I couldn't help but wonder if this was the first time that he had been thrown. For some odd reason I was glad that he had fallen off his horse. My sore ankle didn't seem like such a big thing anymore.

Within a few minutes after leaving the shelter of the canyon the wind and blinding dust were back. I adjusted my hat, bandana, and sunglasses over and over again in an attempt to see better or breath easier—nothing worked.

The wind, heat, and dust were taking its toll on our horses, too. Their heads were hung low, close to the ground, and they walked without a spring in their step. Most of them dragged their feet, which thickened the dust around us.

Earlier, at lunch, Matt had mentioned that if we didn't want to ride this afternoon we could spend our afternoon at a natural hot springs. Right now, I could have kicked myself for not going. I was wondering if the people that were at the hot springs were having more fun than we were.

The last hot spring I had visited turned out to be a pool of oozing, green, smelly water, bubbling from the ground, which Mother Nature created for everyone to have his or her picture taken by. No, I thought, this has to be more fun than that. After all, we were experiencing the reality of herding horses. My ankles and knees were already mush and my body was slowly turning into a human piece of sandpaper. I kept trying to convince myself, I was having fun.

In the blinding dust I was continuously squinting or closing my eyes; my contact lenses were taking a beating. The dust moved like fog constantly changing in thickness. One minute I could see ten feet in front of me, the next I could barely see my horse's legs.

My horse and I had to rely on our hearing instead of our eyes. We listened to the hooves of the moving animals and quickly learned how to tell how many were moving away, and in what direction. I had no get-up-and-go left. I was drained and running on empty.

In the blink of an eye a rider in front of us appeared out of nowhere. Her horse turned and headed straight towards us. "What are you doing?" I yelled, as she flew past us, and I lost sight of her in the dust. Then a second later her horse came running back, charging past us. "Easy Red," I said as I tried to calm both of our racing hearts. "Easy boy." I looked up to see what was going on. Her horse slowed, then stopped a few feet in front of us. She was not on him.

"Rider down!" I screamed as I looked around me. "Rider down!" I could barely hear my own voice—it was puny and weak. I stopped Red and repeatedly yelled as loud as my dusty lungs would let me, "Rider down!"

Why was this happening to me? Where was everyone else? Where was she? My heart wasn't racing like it had earlier this morning and for some reason I didn't feel frightened. I turned

Red around and walked very slowly as I called out, "Hello, can you hear me? Where are you?"

I could see a body slumped over and curled in a ball on the ground about ten feet in front of me. It wasn't moving, and a bad feeling crept over me.

"Rider down!" I yelled again, this time louder and with a higher tone of panic in my voice. "Rider down!"

I stayed on my horse and moved as close to the body as I dared. It was the young girl that had come on this trip with her mother. The one that had asked what a fanny pack was. She couldn't have been more than seventeen or eighteen years old.

"Can you hear me? Are you hurt?" I wasn't sure why I was asking questions. I was just hoping she would respond. In between the deafening noise from the wind I though I heard something. Yes, I was sure I heard something. She was crying. She was alive.

I didn't know what to do or say. I thought about putting her on my horse,—no, that wouldn't work. I can't walk. I could tell by the way that she was bawling that she was in pain and frightened. We would just have to stay put and wait for help. I spoke loudly and never stopped talking to her. I was frightened for her. I was hoping my voice would give her some comfort. She never said a word, she just kept crying. Time seemed to stand still as we waited for help.

I was glad to finally hear and see two riders. They were the same two wranglers from this morning. "Over here!" I hollered, "she's over here." They both got off of their horses. "Hold these for us," they said as they handed me both sets of their horses' reins.

The girl's whimpering got louder as they slowly helped her to her feet. Another wrangler joined us, pulling the girl's horse behind him.

"She's okay," the youngest wrangler said in a loud voice. "She was just taking a nap." I thought about what he said, "What? A nap?" It didn't make any sense but it didn't matter. I was glad to have the company.

I got a glimpse of her face. Her eyes were swollen and her

face was bright red. She lowered her head and rubbed her eyes as one of the older wranglers whispered something in her ear.

The younger wrangler walked her horse over to her and the older wrangler helped her back on it. She was wearing a black windbreaker. She pulled the hood over her head and stopped sniffling.

"Follow us," both wranglers said as they got back on their horses. She lifted her head back up and followed the two wranglers. The third wrangler had already disappeared from my sight. I could hear his horse as he trotted away. I wasn't about to get left in the dust. I kicked Red into gear and followed them. I couldn't help but wonder if days were this crazy and long in the Old West.

This morning when I tied my bandana around my neck, it was uncomfortable, heavy, and stiff like a rope. I almost took it off, and I'm glad I left it on. Today the dust and wind were so bad I could barely breath. Wearing the bandana over my nose stopped most of the choking dust and dirt. Without it I don't think I could have breathed today. Now I know why the cowboys wore them.

We never stopped moving. By late afternoon four of our group's horses had become lame. When a horse went lame a wrangler would lasso another horse from the herd and within a few minutes he would slap the rider's saddle and bridle on it and say, "Mount up." The lame horse would limp over and join the moving herd.

As I trotted out to herd three horses back, I didn't see a hole. Red's front legs fell in it and buckled beneath him. I thought for sure I was going over his head. Somehow we worked together as he recovered his balance and got right back up and into his trot. I was glad to be on this horse. He had saved me more than once.

Earlier today when I was daydreaming I had gotten us smack in the middle of a pack of mules. Their ears were pinned back and a large black one, who was directly in front of us, was getting ready to kick Red's face. I couldn't go backwards because the mule behind me was showing his teeth and Red knew it. The mules on both sides of us closed in. They were in on the plot. Red pinned his ears back and threw his head high into the air as he charged the mule on our right. The mule leaped forward, pushing another mule out of its way, leaving us a hole to get out.

As the horses and mules headed up and down a series of rolling hills, they would disappear and reappear in front of me, as they trotted up and down the countryside. The ground beneath us was changing. It was becoming hard and rocky. It slowed our pace and the dust.

The mules chased each other effortlessly up and down steep embankments. They were enjoying our new terrain. The horses slowed their pace as they carefully picked their steps on the rocks beneath their feet.

"I'm not going up there," I said in a loud voice, as two mules dashed by me and climbed a canyon wall. "I don't care. They aren't my mules. If they're stupid enough to go up there, let them."

I don't know who I was talking to,—no one was around me. I guess I was talking to my horse or myself. It didn't matter I just knew I wasn't going up or down anything else today, especially not after mules.

Our rocky terrain opened up into a sandy beachfront and lake filled with dark blue water as far as the eye could see. The horses and mules smelled the water and picked up their pace. "Let them go!" a wrangler hollered. "Let them go." The horses neighed and made a beeline for the water. The mules were right on their tails. The animals all charged into the water and drank it like a vacuum sucking up dirt. They buried their muzzles in the water and they stayed that way for quite a while. It was a beautiful sight.

I could see the water move up their throats as they swallowed. I loosened my reins, and while keeping a safe distance from kicking mules, I cautiously walked Red into the lake.

I didn't know how muddy or slippery the shoreline was. He didn't hesitate: he walked out into about two feet of water, splashing it beneath his feet, then he lowered his head and drank.

A mustang next to us was slapping his face in the water, purposely splashing water all over himself as he drank.

A horse on the left of us was sipping the top of the water making a loud slurping noise, like sipping hot soup.

Red quietly sipped the water almost without noise. His muzzle barely touched the water.

My sunglasses were caked in dust. I tried cleaning them off with my bandana—that made them worse. Good job, I thought, now I have two layers of dirt on them. I untied my bandana and shook it out. A cloud of dirt flew off, and it felt lighter.

I was looking forward to soaking it in the cool clear water and then wrapping it around my hot dirt-laden face.

As I lowered it close to the water, I could see the front riders. They were already forming a line. The horses and mules around me were all leaving the water. Our break was over.

I stared at the soothing water for a few more seconds. I didn't want to leave. My eyes followed it as we slowly walked out, back into the dust.

We routinely stopped to check our riding equipment and to drink water. As our day passed moans and groans got louder as we struggled to get off and back into the saddle.

"My knees hurt so bad, I don't think I can ride any further," One man said. "Your knees, how about your butt?" a plump woman quipped. "It's my ankles," another rider complained, "I can't English post any more."

Everything on me hurt from my back to my toes. Listening to everyone else's complaints made me feel a little better. The throbbing in my right ankle had stopped. I guess that was good. Maybe my ankle wasn't broken. Hopefully it was just badly bruised.

This had to be the longest day of my life and it wasn't over yet. Matt was wrong. This wasn't going to be a long day—this was more like a lifetime.

When we weren't in a cloud of dust, I started taking pictures. It was a team effort, working with my horse, Red. I had to untie my satchel, grab my camera with one hand, and quickly snap a picture or two, while herding the horses. Numerous times I almost lost it as it bounced around in my hands. As our day progressed so did my, bouncing camera skills.

I brought high-speed film for fast shots; it was exactly what I needed. I had four disposable cameras, one for each day. As my confidence grew, riding Red, I snapped pictures of everything in sight.

All day we followed a tall, snow-covered mountain range that towered above us. It almost didn't seem fair. We were down here getting our brains fried out yet I could see ice-cold snow. Whenever the dust settled down, the sky opened up into a deep dark blue. We rode through endless valleys of sand, dust, and rocks.

I glanced at my watch. It was after five o'clock. I put my horse on "autopilot," I was numb. I couldn't feel my legs and my bloodshot eyes refused to stay open.

"Mary, what are you still doing back here?" Robert's voice woke me up. "I'm taking a nap," I jokingly said. "Would you like to join me?"

"How much further do we have to go? I can't feel my legs anymore." Robert positioned his mule next to Red. "And," I loudly said, "what are you doing riding a mule?"

He slid his bandana down below his chin so I could hear him. "When I signed up, it asked do you want to ride a horse or a mule? I had never ridden a mule before, so I marked the box that said "mule.""

I slowed Red down to a walk and positioned him close to Robert's mule. "Is he a good trotter?" "No, I don't like him at all. He won't trot and when he tries, he only does it in short spurts. I want to ride a horse."

"So," I said as I turned my head away to see why a mule had pushed past two other mules on my left side, "ask Matt for a horse. I told him I couldn't ride Tyler and he gave me Red."

"I have. Matt said I signed up for a mule and that is what I'm going to ride. I don't know what to do!"

"Wow, that stinks. He's tired now, why don't you try asking

him again later tonight after he's had a few beers? I know his public relations skills could use a little help. Maybe the beer will take the edge off of him."

Robert grinned and shook his head in agreement.

"Look!" I shouted. "It's finally over," I stretched my back and shook out my legs. "I don't know if I would have lasted much longer."

A short distance in front of us was a long, dilapidated, wooden corral. Pieces of it were falling off or half buried in the sand. The lead group had stopped and spread their horses out. Turning the herd toward the corral, we drove them inside.

We followed the last animals in and walked our horses into a separate corral. I wasn't sure if I could get off. I had been on this animal for close to twelve hours and my body was a big pile of mush.

A tall leathery man kept shouting, "Everyone take your gear with you. Don't forget your jackets or canteens." One by one he took our horses from us and tied them up.

I started to loosen Red's cinch, but the wrangler walked over and stopped me. "Folks, you don't need to take your horse's saddles off," he shouted. "We will do that, just take your gear."

He wasn't going to get an argument from me. I didn't want to unsaddle my horse, I just assumed I had to. "Thanks Red," I said as I stroked his neck, "Thanks for keeping me safe today, see you tomorrow."

"Mary, do you need help?" Robert saw me struggling as I limped away from Red. Right now if he had offered to carry me, I would have gladly said "yes." I had nothing else to prove to myself or anyone else today. Every inch of my body ached but for some strange reason, I felt great. I was proud of myself because I never quit.

"I would love some help," I shouted back at him. "And an ice cold beer." Robert hurried over, grabbed my gear, and held out his left arm for me to brace on. "Well I'll be darned, Mary, you do know how to smile. This is the first time I've seen you smile all day. It's quite becoming. You should do it more often."

I thought about what he said. He was right. I was being way

too serious. Somehow I had forgotten that I was supposed to be having fun today. I was on vacation.

"Can't help you with the beer, though," he said with a grin on his face as he winked at me. "Will a canteen of warm water do?" Our eyes met. "I'll pass," I said as I giggled. "Mine has more sand in it than water."

"How bad is your ankle? Or is it your leg?" I looked down at my ankle. "I'm not sure. Matt says my leg isn't broken. All I know is that it hurts like hell and I can't put any weight on it. I'm kind of afraid to take my boot off and look at it."

Robert was about six inches taller then me. His arm was strong and muscular. He was one of only a few men that made it through our first day and I was glad to have his company. Who was this stranger? Why was I so attracted to him?

Chapter Four

A small bus was parked on a dirt road down a sloping hill about a hundred feet away. "We have to walk all the way down there? I'll never make it."

Robert slowed his pace and said, "Just lean on me, Mary, I've got you." My body creaked and twitched as I walked. I felt like I was a hundred years old. I looked around me. I wasn't alone. Everyone was limping while coughing and complaining as they dragged their weary bodies to the bus. I tried to put weight on my ankle. It exploded in a pain that turned into a constant throb.

I don't know where Robert was getting his strength from but I liked it. He was practically carrying me. My head filled with questions as we walked. I knew nothing about him and he knew nothing about me. Was he married? Where was he from? We walked in silence while we constantly looked back and forth at each other.

The steps to get on the bus were steep. I grabbed on to the side rail and pulled myself up. My grip failed and my hand slid back down the metal rail as I fell straight back. Robert was directly behind me and caught me. A burst of energy shot around the bus as everyone clapped.

"I'm sorry," I said. "Are you all right?" Robert regained his balance and helped me up the second step. "Take your time, Mary," he said as he slowly let go of my waist. "That beer of yours is sounding mighty good." He helped my to the first seat in the bus where we both plopped down as everybody on the bus whistled and clapped.

"This is embarrassing," I quietly said. "I feel so stupid." I slid closer to the window and opened my canteen. The water was hot, but I drank it. I could feel the grit and dirt in my mouth as I swallowed it.

"Aren't you going to wait for that cold beer?" Robert teased as he watched me.

"Listen up folks," a familiar voice said, "It's still early, so those of you that want to go to the hot springs, can. When we get to camp pick a tent, get your gear from the trucks, and we'll leave in ten minutes.

"Not me," I said as I shook my head. "Not me, I want a gallon of ice cold water and my soft comfortable sleeping bag."

The air-conditioning on the bus slowly cooled my hot dusty body and I closed my eyes. The bus bounced us around like popcorn as it carried us up and down rocky dirt roads to our camp.

As the bus came to a stop, Matt's loud voice woke me up. "Remember, folks, we leave in ten minutes."

My head was lying on Robert's shoulder. "I'm sorry," I said as I sat up, "I must have dozed off." "Sorry for what?" Robert asked as he brushed his pants off. I hurried off the bus and hopped over to a tent. It was empty, so I threw my jacket and canteen inside.

Most of the tents around me were filled with people. They were all smiling or laughing and drinking beer and wine.

"You've got to go to the hot springs." They kept repeating, "It's great." "You mean it's not a mud hole filled with green slime?" I asked as I followed them to the chuck wagon. "Heavens no," an older women said. "It's a swimming pool and they have hot showers there." She pointed to her clean hair and added, "This morning I looked as bad as you do. Here, have a glass of wine, you look like you could use one."

I pushed the glass of wine away. I wasn't sure of what to do. I wanted to stay and drink anything that was ice cold, but I was also dying to take a hot shower. And I had less then ten minutes to find my gear and get it set up for nightfall. My ankle had me moving at a crawl. How was I going to do all of this in less then ten minutes?

"Mary, you're limping pretty bad, can I get you something?" Robert was holding a cold beer. He had taken his hat and sunglasses off. I almost didn't recognize him.

I studied his face for a second. His skin was fair except for his nose—that was red and looked sore. He had thick, brown, wavy hair and powerful deep green eyes.

"I didn't recognize you with your hat off," I teased as he walked over to where I was standing.

"I'm dying for a cold beer, but I want to go take a hot shower, too." "So what's the problem?" Robert held out his left hand and handed me a cold beer. " Why can't you take a shower?" he asked as he hit his beer can against mine in a toast.

"Because I can't walk," I hastily replied. A puzzling look filled his face. "No, I mean I don't think I can get my stuff to my tent and get to the bus before it leaves." I wasn't making any sense. I stopped talking and opened the beer.

"Are you always this nervous?" Robert asked as he sipped his beer. I thought about what he said—he was right, again. Why was I a nervous wreck? "You're right," I said as I inhaled the beer. "Thank you."

I didn't want to leave the shade of our heavily wooded campsite or the coolers filled with beer and ice, but a hot shower was sounding better and better.

"Robert, would you mind helping me carry my gear to my tent?" I asked with a serious tone in my voice.

"No," he immediately replied, "not until you have another beer and put a smile on your face." He turned away from me and headed towards the beer cooler.

"But, I've got to hurry." I shouted at him. "The bus is leaving in a few minutes."

"Here," he said as he handed me another beer, "you need this. I'll get your gear, which tent is yours?"

"Thank you," I said as a smile crept on my face. "Thank

you, very much."

"Stop saying thank you," he said as he headed down an embankment towards the trucks filled with gear. "Its annoying."

I hopped back to my tent. My beer spilled all over my hand as I hopped. I didn't care, it was cold and felt good.

My left leg wasn't going to carry me much further. I sat down on a log by my tent. I thought about not going. My tent and my fluffy sleeping bag made more sense. How was I going to get on and off the bus? How far would I have to walk once I got off the bus? Maybe I should just stay here and drink cold beer.

"We're leaving!" a voice shouted, as the buses horn blared. "Anybody that wants to go to the hot springs, we're leaving now."

"Wait!" I shouted, from inside my tent. "I'm coming." I grabbed my bathing suit and a pair of beach slippers. I stirred my clothes up again. I couldn't find my towel.

The bus's horn beeped again. "Wait!" I shouted, "don't leave without me."

Matt was standing on the steps of the bus looking outside. He saw me as I started hopping towards the bus. "Wait," he yelled as the bus started moving, "one more coming."

My arms pulled me up the steps. I was surprised to see that everyone aboard had already changed into their bathing suits. They all had towels and were carrying small bags of shampoo and soap. Their energy was high and most of them had a beer in their hands.

I sat down and looked at my clothes. I was still covered from head to toe in layers of dust and dirt. I didn't even have a towel. Darn it, I thought, I would have been better off back at camp.

Our bus stopped in front of a large adobe brick building. Cars were parked all around it. They looked out of place.

After all, we had spent twelve hours in the saddle. I had though that we were in the middle of nowhere. How did all of these cars get here?

A mother and daughter from Iowa who had befriended me at breakfast this morning were sitting directly in front of me. "Do you know where you're going?" I asked as I followed them off the bus.

"No," they both replied, "but that sign over there says showers and we're going over there." I nodded my head in agreement and followed them.

Since early this morning I had kept my head lowered hiding it from the sun, dust, and wind. It felt awkward raising it up and looking around.

Two large rectangular swimming pools filled the building. Showers were on both sides of each pool.

As I walked by the pools I noticed that everyone in the water was starring at me. I was still fully dressed in dusty horse gear from boots to bandana. I'm sure the way I was dragging my leg didn't help. I must have looked really out of place.

Oh my God, I thought, I look like a beggar or homeless person. The thought was kind of funny and I laughed out loud. It felt good to laugh. Maybe the beer was kicking in or maybe I was losing my mind.

I'm glad the mother and daughter were walking directly in front of me. I had a feeling if I had walked in here alone I would have been thrown out. It just doesn't get any better than this, I thought, as I laughed out loud again.

I was going to take a long shower then get back on the bus. The clear blue water looked so inviting, I had to stay.

In the women's locker room I took my boot off and got the first look at my injured ankle. It was swollen and black. I have had my shares of black and blue marks before but never just black. My ankle looked like someone had taken a black magic marker to it. Without the support of my boot, I couldn't walk on it.

I hopped over to the smaller of the two pools and touched the water with my toes. It was very hot. Steam was rising from it. I didn't hesitate. I slid my entire body into it. The throbbing almost immediately stopped in my ankle. I could bend and feel my toes. It was so very soothing.

The hot water washed away all of my aches and pains as I floated around in it. The pool was long and shallow and only a few feet deep. The water slowly hydrated my dry skin and body and it helped dust off my clouded brain.

"How's the water?" the blond-haired daughter asked as she dipped her big toe into it. "It's hot," I warned her. "It's real hot."

"How's your leg?" her mother asked as she joined us. "It's black," I said. "It's real black."

As our bodies and brains sucked up the moisture, I remembered that these two women were from Iowa. "I hope you don't mind me asking," I said as I sat back up in the pool. "Why did you fly all the way from Iowa to go on this horseback riding trip?"

The mother and daughter glanced at each other and almost at the same time they both shook their heads as though they didn't know and said, "After today, we aren't sure. That's all we've been talking about all day."

I thought about everything that had happened to me today. It seemed like such a long time ago. It was so surreal and yet now, for some odd reason, it seemed funny. I couldn't help but laugh at myself. My laughter was contagious. As soon as one of us would start talking, the other two would break out in laughter. Our laughter was constantly interrupted by deep dry coughs as we gasped for breath and loosened up the dust that was embedded deep inside our lungs. Watching each other cough brought on more laughter. Before we left the pool everyone around us had joined in. I've never laughed or coughed so hard in my life.

The folks back at the camp were right. This was the perfect relief for such a long grueling day. I was glad I had come.

I shook a layer of dust off of my pants and put them back on. My socks were standing up by themselves, so I decided to wear my flip-flops.

I soaked in my surroundings and watched the sun set as the bus carried us back to camp. I felt like a new person.

Our campsite was beneath tall pine trees and numerous

meandering streams. My tent was only a few feet away from running water.

I laid down on the top of my goose down sleeping bag. It curled around me and warmed my tired body. I closed my eyes and listened to the sounds of the babbling brook.

"Supper's ready!" I heard someone shout as a loud metal clanging noise rung. "Super's ready."

I opened my eyes and looked around. The sun had set and night was falling. I unzipped my sleeping bag and crawled inside.

I could hear people as they walked by my tent. They were all talking about supper. "The pork chops look real good." "Get me another glass of wine," a woman shouted.

I pulled my sleeping bag over my head and closed my eyes. My ankle had stopped throbbing and I was comfortable.

"Hello, Mary, are you in there? Hello, anybody in there? I brought you a cold beer. Are you awake?"

Robert's voice sounded different. I turned on my lantern and unzipped my tent. "How many beers have you had?" I asked as I held my lantern higher to see his face.

"Have you eaten? How were the hot springs? What are you doing in your tent?"

Robert was swaying. "I think you've had enough for both of us," I said as I zipped up my jacket. "But I'll take that one." He had a beer in both of his hands. I grabbed the one in his left hand and retreated back inside my tent.

"It's time to party. Come on, Mary, everybody's having fun, come join us."

"I'm tired and my ankle hurts and I don't want to party," I said as I zipped my tent back up.

"You're feeling sorry for yourself. You know you're not the only one that got hurt today." Robert said as he walked away.

My stomach growled as the aroma of meat cooking on an open flame filled my tent.

Robert was right. I was feeling sorry for myself. I finished the beer and put on another layer of warm clothes.

I don't know if it was the beer or the constant laughter around me, but all of a sudden I was full of energy and starving.

Somehow in my wisdom I had remembered to bring sports wrapping tape with me. It's exactly what I needed for my ankle and leg. I wrapped them up like a mummy and put my boots back on.

I left the warmth of my tent and slowly put weight on my right leg. The first few steps were excruciatingly painful as I followed the laughter.

Large blue camping coolers were sprawled out all around the chuck wagon. They were filled with numerous brands of ice-cold beer and bottles of wine. About a dozen people were sitting on folding beach chairs close by them.

Lanterns lit up the sky, along with two long buffet tables piled high with food. I grabbed a plate and didn't stop filling it until food was sliding off the sides. I had no idea if I could eat it all but I was going to try.

Everyone was eating, drinking, and being merry. I found an open spot at a picnic table and joined in.

I stuffed food in my mouth so fast I didn't have time for a conversation. I was content to just watch and listen to everyone around me.

I didn't recognize most of the people. None of them had their hats or sunglasses on. They all looked different. They actually had hair and faces.

I washed my ten-course meal down with another ice-cold beer. In a matter of minutes I consumed ten million calories. I didn't care. Today I had earned them.

When my stomach was full I joined into the conversations that were flying around the table. "Yes, she got thrown too," one woman said. "Mary, you say someone got thrown today, didn't you?" another asked. "You mean more than two people got thrown today?" I asked. "Yes, I think four or five people got hurt today."

"What about the woman that broke her ankle?" someone else asked. "That's me," I slowly replied.

Silence blanketed our table as everyone's eyes fell on me.

"I'm fine," I said as I took a sip from my beer. "And," I added, "with a few more of these, maybe I won't remember today at all."

Everybody started laughing and holding wine glasses and beer cans up in front of themselves while trading stories about what they had witnessed and been through today.

I yawned and glanced at my watch. It was nine o'clock. I had been up since three this morning and I had to be back up at four tomorrow morning. "See you all in the morning," I said as I stood up and moved away from the table.

"Mary, you're awake, where are you going?" Robert was sitting with a group of men by the beer coolers. "I'm going to bed," I said as I yawned.

"No, stay up, they're lighting a bonfire, look." I turned around. Two wranglers were piling wood and a third man was setting up folding chairs in a large circle around the wood.

My ankle was throbbing, and my brain was telling me it was time to sleep. "It looks awfully inviting," I politely said, "but my ankle is killing me and I can't keep my eyes open."

"Oh," one of the men sitting close to Robert said. "Are you the person that broke their ankle today?" "I hope not," I quietly replied as I limped away.

"Wait, let me help you." Robert stood up and held his arm out. "Thank you," I quietly whispered as I braced against him. "Why do you keep thanking me?" he asked as we slowly walked back to my tent.

Before I could answer him he tripped on a rock and flew forward. I let go of his arm and caught my balance as his knees hit the ground.

"Ouch," I loudly said, "that's got to hurt." Robert pulled himself off the ground and brushed off his jeans. "How many beers did you say you you had?" I asked as I busted out in laughter. "Maybe I should be walking you back to your tent." I hopped over to where he was standing.

"How come you're so pretty?" he asked as he turned and faced me. I quickly changed the subject and asked, "Are you all right?" He held his arm out for me to brace against. "You know," I said as I put my weight back on his arm, " I don't need another broken ankle, I've had enough fun for today."

"Here, I'll hold the flashlight in front of your feet." I took the flashlight out of Robert's right hand. "Don't worry about me, I'll follow your lead." I thought about what he had just said. I'd been married a long time and I couldn't recall the last time a man had paid me a compliment. Maybe I should have been upset. I wasn't. I kind of liked it.

"Are you going back to the fire?" I asked as I pointed his flashlight on the ground directly in front of his feet. "No," he slowly replied, " I think your right, Mary, its time for me to go to bed. I can't believe I just tripped."

"Well at least you didn't get thrown from your horse," I said as I looked deeply into his eyes. "So," he said as he looked over and grinned at me, "You do have a sense of humor, don't you?"

He pulled my closer to his chest. It felt good. "Was any of this in your brochure?" I asked as we approached my tent. "What brochure? I found out about this trip on the Internet."

"This is my stop," I teased as we walked past my tent. "Thank…" before I could finish Robert gently put his right index finger on my lips and softly whispered, "Shhh, I've heard that word enough today. Goodnight, Mary." Without another breath he turned and walked away. I watched him until he disappeared into the night.

As I put my pajamas on all of my thoughts were on Robert. I felt like a schoolgirl with her first crush. This is stupid, I kept telling myself, you're married and he was drunk. The only thing I knew for sure was, that Robert was stirring emotions inside of me that I didn't even know I had.

Earlier this evening, when I was eating dinner, a woman at my table had mentioned that if you didn't want to ride all day you didn't have to. You could take the afternoon off. If I had known how wonderful the hot springs were, I wouldn't have ridden this afternoon. All in all I was proud of myself. I had successfully driven a large herd of horses and mules forty miles on my first day and somehow I had managed not to get thrown from my horse.

My ankle reminded me about the down side of my first day, all night long. Every time I got comfortable a sharp pain shot through it, constantly waking me up. I finally gave up and unwrapped it, along with swallowing four, extra strength aspirins. Could I survive another day of this?

Chapter Five

I opened my eyes to total darkness and glanced at my watch. It was three in the morning. The top of my tent had a see-through roof on it I hadn't noticed until now. The dark sky above me was filled with bright stars that twinkled in the darkness. I could hear the water from the creek as it rushed down stream.

I stayed awake and in the warmth of my sleeping bag I continuously stretched every muscle in my body. The throbbing in my ankle was gone. So were all of my aches and pains, and I felt good.

Our tents were only a few feet apart from each other and the walls were thin. I could hear people around me as they snored and coughed.

As I stared into the stars and listened to the rushing water, I dozed in and out of sleep.

The morning air was almost warm, a pleasant welcome after yesterday's cold beginning. Even the sun seemed friendlier as it slowly rose and lit my surroundings.

A good feeling crept over me that I hadn't felt in a long time. I was excited and full of energy, and I couldn't wait to get up and back on my horse.

I wasn't alone in my enthusiasm. As I headed to get my morning coffee I passed a dozen people. All of them were smiling and moving much faster then yesterday morning. "Good morning." "Hello, good morning." It was amazing, everyone was polite and wide-awake, even the employees.

If I were an employee who had endured the grueling hours of yesterday, I would have quit. These people were a breed of their own. They definitely hadn't been influenced by corporate America.

The coffee wasn't as strong or thick as yesterday and the eggs were layered in thick, spicy cheese, full of flavor. Pancakes with hot syrup and fresh fruit filled the rest of my plate.

As I sat down to eat, a woman a few feet away from me asked, "Are you going to ride today?" "Of course," I immediately replied. "Why? Aren't you?"

"I haven't made up my mind," She replied with a sigh. "I'm still pretty sore from yesterday, maybe I'll ride half of the day." Everyone I talked to was indecisive, no one was sure if they wanted to ride all day, half of the day, or not at all.

I put my fork down and jokingly said, "I'm going to ride this morning but my afternoon depends upon how much dust I eat before lunch—yesterday filled me up." A heavy-set woman wearing leather chaps shook her head in agreement, as she said, "I coughed all night. I won't do that again no matter how much money they pay me." Everyone glanced at her for a few seconds, then we all burst out with laughter.

An older woman walking side by side with a man half her age had overheard us. "I'm not riding today and neither is my brother. We're going to play cards and get caught up on our smoking. We came here to have fun, not work."

I looked around for Robert, he was nowhere in sight. I figured he had a hangover from last night and he had decided not to ride.

Today we only had to travel thirty miles. That's ten miles less than yesterday. I was looking forward to riding hard, being a real cowgirl on my trusty horse, Red. When I dropped of my empty plate I grabbed a shiny red apple for him.

The brochure had said we could only bring one duffle bag and it couldn't weigh more than thirty pounds. My clothes were layered in dust. I brushed them off. I had brought more first aid gear than clothing and I'm glad I had. I slathered my ankle with a topical painkiller and rapped it tightly in an ace bandage.

The last bus heading back to where our horses were was honking its horn. If I was going to ride today, it was time to go.

Everyone on the bus was already hidden beneath hats, sunglasses, and protective clothing. I looked around for Robert. I didn't see him.

As I got off of the bus glare from the rising sun shot across my face, sending me scrambling for my sunglasses and hat. I looked around for my horse, Red. I didn't see him.

"Are you Mary?" a tall, thick wrangler asked as I walked around the horses. He was so big I stood in his shadow and he wasn't smiling. I wasn't sure if I should answer him. "Are you Mary?" he asked again as he approached me. "Yes," I slowly replied in a soft meek voice.

"Come over here," he said. "You get a different horse today." "No," I said as I raised the tone in my voice. "I want Red. I like Red—we bonded yesterday."

"The wrangler didn't blink an eye. He just turned towards me and said, "Your horse's name is Icky, mount up." "Wait!" I shouted as he turned to walk away. "I can't ride this horse, look at his leg, he's hurt."

Icky had a huge open wound on his back right leg. He was short with brown matted hair and he hung his head low. He's got to be thirty years old, I thought to myself. This is not fair, where is my horse Red?

"Matt!" I shouted as the wrangler walked away. "This horse is injured, he won't last thirty miles." Matt was busy assigning horses to other people. He looked up, then headed over in my general direction.

"Where is my horse Red?" I asked as he approached. "I'll help saddle him." Matt tilted his hat up so I could see his eyes. "You wore him out yesterday. And," he said in a loud piercing voice that everybody heard, "someone tightened Red's cinch yesterday and tore the muscles in his upper back. He's now lame."

"Folks, listen up. I don't want you tightening up your cinches. These animals will go lame if their cinches are too tight." As Matt's powerful voice filled the arena, everyone moved their horses away from me.

"But, what about this horse's leg?" I asked as I starred at the gash in Icky's leg. Matt examined the leg. Then without another word he stood back up and walked away.

"Good morning Mary, what's going on? Where is your horse Red?" "He's lame," I replied with a long sigh, "and they gave me a horse named Icky."

"Did you say his name was Icky?" Who would name a horse Icky?" I looked up at Robert and as a frown filled my face I said, "I don't know and I don't like it, this isn't fair."

Robert was still riding a mule. "At least I get to ride a horse," I said with a sarcastic tone in my voice as I pointed to his mule.

Robert turned his mule away from me and said, "You definitely aren't a morning person, Mary, I'll see you later." He kicked his mule in motion and headed towards a group of riders that were already forming the front line.

Everyone was talking and tying their gear onto their saddles. I was standing in the middle of the arena by myself with a frown on my face. Robert was right. I wasn't a morning person and I didn't care right now. I was very upset that I was given a new horse and that his name was Icky.

I stared at Icky for a few minutes and thought about what had just happened. Was I being punished? Was this horse's name really Icky? Who would name a horse Icky? And why?

"Mary," Matt shouted loud enough for everyone to hear, "don't do anything but walk that animal today."

This stinks, I thought as I threw my leg over the saddle. I'm finally comfortable with my horse and they take him away from me and give me a wounded horse that's named Icky. The frown lines on my face deepened as I quietly mumbled, "This is not fair, this is definitely not fair."

Icky lived up to his name. From the second I swung my leg over his saddle he gave me trouble. He stumbled and bit anything that got within an arm's length of him. He had a mind of his own and he immediately let me know it.

He was uncomfortable to ride. He was round and fat, which stretched my legs and hips. He walked so slow that I thought I would have to catch a bus to keep up with the rest of the riders.

I got some unusual looks as I spoke out loud and had a long chat with him. "I'm not in the mood," I kept telling him as I kicked him harder and harder in the gut, "not today."

When he lunged and snapped at the horses and mules around us, I'd kick him as hard as I could. Forcing him to break into a trot, I knew the faster movement made his leg hurt and I was hoping he would associate being bad with leg pain. He slowly responded. I figured since I couldn't herd horses or run that I might as well get to know my horse.

It was working and by eleven o' clock Icky had settled down and was responding to my every move, except the stumbling stuff. "Pick up your feet, old man," I repeatedly shouted over and over again, "I'm not falling off today."

It was refreshing looking up and seeing deep blue skies. Dust wasn't flying in the air like yesterday. The horses still churned it up but without the wind it stayed close to the ground.

I was bored just walking my horse. I wanted to ride hard and chase the herd. Every time a rider came close to me I quickly started a conversation, "Hi, my name is Mary, where are you from?" They would slow their horses down just enough to get a good look at Icky and I. Then one by one they would all asked me the same question, "Is that Icky you're riding?" As soon as I replied, "Yes," they would ride away. I wasn't sure if the problem was Icky or me. Everyone avoided us, even Robert. I rode alone and isolated most of the morning. I felt like I was being punished and I didn't like the feeling.

Today a husband and wife team of wranglers brought up the rear. They were in their late thirties and they both were in good shape. They rarely spoke out loud and constantly communicated with simple gestures and movements. They regularly crossed my path as they chased stray horses and mules up and down rolling terrain. I enjoyed watching them as they ran off in different directions.

The man wrangler slowed his horse down close to Icky and I. "Hey, isn't that Icky?" he asked as he tilted his hat up. I was afraid if I answered, "Yes" he would ride away like everyone else had. "Have you ridden Icky?" I asked as he moved a little closer to us. "No, I haven't," he said as he wiped sweat from his brow, "That horse stayed at my ranch all winter. He sure got fat."

"Really, then you know why his name is Icky, right?" The wrangler hesitated then said, "No, I don't know why they call him Icky." I raised my voice and said, "I do—he bites everything that gets near him, that's why."

The wrangler watched his wife trot after two unruly mules. Then he glanced over at me and nodded his head in agreement as he said, "When that animal was in his prime he was our lead horse. He got us through thick and thin, he's a fine animal."

"Then you ride him," I jokingly said as I pretended to hand him my reins. His face filled with a grin. "He's just wants to be in front. He doesn't like being back here." "Neither do I," I said as I raised my voice. "Neither do I."

Three more horses broke away from the herd. The wrangler turned his horse towards them and took off at a full gallop. Two more mules broke away from the herd and headed down a hill directly in front of me. I was tempted to chase them, so was Icky. He raised his head and followed them with his eyes. We both were bored and tired of doing nothing.

As we approached a narrow wood bridge the herd slowed down, almost to a dead stop. All of the animals hesitated as they walked across. The wood planks beneath their feet creaked and moaned as they crossed.

Icky's front feet buckled beneath him as he stepped up onto the wood. I pushed my body's weight deep into my saddle and pulled my reins back, all the way to my chest. He caught his balance and pulled himself back up. My heart was racing as we slowly crossed the bridge. "Icky," I quietly whispered close to his ear, "please pick up your feet."

He stopped dragging his feet and he raised his lowered neck.

I whispered in his ear again, "Good boy, that's it, good boy." I could tell by the way he was responding that he liked me whispering in his ear. "So you like being whispered to, you're such a handsome boy."

"What are you doing?" Robert asked as he saw me lay my head and chest on Icky's neck. "I'm whispering to Icky, he loves it," I said as I sat back up in the saddle. "Why?" he asked as he pulled his mule along side of us. "I don't know, I think we're bonding. He's my new puppy dog. "

Robert's face was hidden beneath his sunglasses and hat. I leaned forward again and threw my arms around Icky's neck and said in a loud voice, "You're my puppy dog, aren't you Icky?" He twisted his ears back towards me, "Good boy," I repeatedly said in a soft voice, "good boy."

Robert watched us for a few minutes then he turned his mule and rode away, heading back towards the front line. "I guess nobody loves us," I whispered to Icky as I watched Robert ride away.

Today our morning was passing much faster. We didn't have the hot wind and constant cloud of dust that followed us all day yesterday. We crossed two more wood bridges and before I knew it we were crossing a third bridge and heading down a sloping hill towards the shade of a cluster of tall oak trees. I could see the chuck wagon and tables neatly organized with cold drinks and hot food.

As I caught up to the front riders I could hear Matt's commanding voice, "How many of you are riding this afternoon?" Everyone was looking around back and forth at each other. "Raise your hand if you're going to ride this afternoon," Matt said as he watched us. Not one of us raised his or her hand.

Matt repeated the question, this time with a deeper and louder voice. "Raise your hand up in the air if you're going to ride this afternoon." He raised his right hand high above his head and waved it at us.

Not a person in our entire group raised their hand. One by one we all got off of our horses and tied them on a long rope tied between two trees. Everyone was dusting off their hats and sunglasses. We had all had enough.

I got a whiff of something sweet and chocolaty. I followed it to the chuck wagon. "Is that what I think it is?" I asked as a woman with a tray in her hands stepped out of the trailer. "Yes," she politely said with a smile, "I put walnuts in the brownies today."

As soon as she put them down I piled them on my plate. "Is that all your eating?" she asked as she watched me. "No," I replied as I took a bite, "I'm having a gallon of lemonade, too." Hot brownies and ice-cold lemonade, the combination was odd yet I couldn't get enough of it.

Two police cars pulled up and parked a few feet away from us on a dirt road. Matt walked over and shook one of the officer's hands as he got out of his car.

"What's going on?" I asked as I sat down next to the mom and daughter team from Ohio, whom I had met yesterday. I know they had given me their names, I just couldn't remember them. They both stared at my plate and almost at the same time said, "That's what your eating for lunch—how do you stay so skinny?" I looked down at my pyramid of brownies and jokingly said, "I think I'm turning into a sugar junky. I normally don't eat like this."

I bit off a chunk of a brownie. It was warm and melted in my mouth like butter. "These are really good," I said as I took another bite. "I don't know what you put in them but they're addicting."

"So, is Matt going to have us all arrested for not riding this afternoon?" I jokingly asked in a loud voice as Matt and two police officers headed over to where we were all seated.

"I'm sorry, I forgot your name," the mom said as she turned to face me. "I'm Mary," I said with a mouth full of food, "and I forgot your name, too. I'm terrible at remembering names." She pointed a finger at herself and then at her daughter and said, "I'm Sara and that's Beth."

"We overheard a couple of people say that the police shut down a main road sometime this afternoon so the herd can cross it." "Really," I said, "that sounds like fun. Wait a minute, no, no, I'm not walking Icky for five more hours." As I ate the brownies a little voice in side of me kept saying, "Let's go, I want to go."

Matt walked over to where we all were eating lunch and loudly said, "Folks, these officers are going to shut down the interstate so this herd can cross it. Do any of you want to ride this afternoon?"

Matt was all business and something wasn't right. So far this entire trip he hadn't repeated himself once. Yet this was the third time he was asking us if we wanted to ride this afternoon.

Everyone ignored Matt and kept right on eating as though they didn't even hear him, everyone, that is, except me.

Why had Matt repeated himself? What were the police really doing here? I had to find out. I put my plate down and followed him.

"We're still shorthanded." He said to a wrangler as the man approached him.

So that was it, Matt needed us. "Excuse me, Matt," I said in a loud voice. "I would love to ride this afternoon, but I have Icky and you said I had to walk him. Can I ride a different horse?"

Matt scratched his cheek and said, "No, but you can trot Icky." His answer wasn't good enough. "How about cantering?" I boldly asked. Matt threw both of his arms straight up in the air as though he had just lost an argument and said, "Yes, you can canter him."

Before he said another word I quickly walked away and returned back to my seat by Sara and Beth. "He guys," I whispered, "You have to ride this afternoon. Matt just told me I could run my horse."

"No way," Beth excitedly said. "Yes way," I said as my face lit up. "I'm not going." Sara said, "If you want to ride Beth, you go ahead. I've had enough today."

Beth followed me as I headed back towards the horses. "Are you sure we can run our horses?" "Yes," I replied "I asked Matt myself, he's shorthanded. He hadn't planned on everybody quitting."

Robert saw me heading towards my horse. "Mary," he shouted, "I thought you weren't riding this afternoon." "I changed my mind," I hollered back at him. "Icky misses me and we need to finish bonding."

"I think that guy likes you," Beth said. "He's kind of cute but way too old for me. Do you like him?" A smile crept onto my face as I thought about what she had just said. "Are you married?" she asked as she studied my face. "This is my horse," I replied as I purposely avoided her question. "Here comes your boyfriend," she teased as we both watch Robert catch up to us.

When Beth left to get her horse I told Robert about what Matt had just okayed. "My mule won't trot, let alone run," He complained, " I don't know if my knees can last much longer." I wanted to tease Robert about falling on his knees last night but I didn't.

"Maybe you shouldn't go, then," I said with a slow caring voice. "Matt said we would be moving a lot faster this afternoon and that's why he's letting me canter."

Robert reached his hand out and squeezed my right hand. "Thank you, Mary," he said in a soft voice, "I'm going to ride." "Hey," I said as he walked away towards his mule, "you can't say thank you, that's my line." He turned around and stared at me for a few seconds then nodded his head in agreement and disappeared in the string of horses.

Icky's head was lowered and his eyes were shut. I gently stroked his neck as I checked my gear and mounted up. A couple of other riders had changed their minds and were already back in the saddle.

Robert had stopped his mule at a chain link gate directly in front of us. Icky lunged forward and tried to take a bit out of his mule's butt. The mule retaliated and kicked his legs up and out straight back at us.

"What was that?" Robert shouted as he looked around. "Oh," I said in a calm voice, "that was Icky being well, just plain, icky." Beth positioned her horse a few feet away from me on my right. "Watch out," I warned her, "Icky bites. I thought I had him figured out this morning but I don't think he's ready to give up a lifetime of bad habits in one day." "Thanks for the warning," Beth said as she spaced her horse further from Icky.

Matt was right, riders were scarce. Beth and Robert rode away towards the front of the herd. I held Icky back and was joined by a portly woman riding a mule and the wrangler couple that I had watched earlier today. We looked around at each other as we watched the few riders left join the herd.

"Where is everybody?" the wrangler asked as we formed the back line. "I don't know," I replied, "I think everybody's tired."

It didn't take long for the horses and mules to realize that there were a lot more of them then there were of us. In a matter of minutes they started breaking away from the herd in large numbers.

"We've got this side," The wrangler's wife hollered as she and her husband trotted away chasing horses to the left of us.

The female wrangler and I were on the right side of the herd. As two mules trotted away, she took off after them. I followed her and backed her up as the animals reluctantly rejoined the herd. We took turns chasing the horses and mules, as they broke away and headed all over the countryside. Almost instantly and without a word spoken, we learned how to back each other up. We became a team.

I was hesitant to break Icky into a run. I kept him moving at a very uncomfortable trot. My ankle had been almost pain free all morning long when I had been forced to walk my horse. The minute I pushed Icky into a trot my ankle exploded in throbbing pain. This morning when Matt told me that I had to walk my horse all day I had thought that he was punishing me for overtightening Red's cinch yesterday and injuring him. Perhaps I was wrong. Maybe Matt gave me Icky on purpose, so I wouldn't hurt my ankle any further.

Icky wouldn't break into a gallop even when I continuously kicked him in the gut as hard as I could. "You stupid horse!" I yelled. "Up, pick your feet, up." I remembered how responsive he had been earlier this morning when I whispered in his ear. I pulled back on his reins, bringing him to a dead stop. Then I leaned my body forward and whispered into his left ear, "Icky's a good boy." I stroked his neck with my hand and in a soft authoritative voice I said, "Up, Icky, up."

Icky leaped forward with both of his front legs and broke

into a fast run. I almost fell off of him, sending my heart racing as I grabbed onto the saddle horn. "Easy boy," I kept repeating as I slowed him down to a comfortable canter.

I looked up and over towards my new partner. I wasn't sure if Matt had told her I could run my horse. I kicked Icky into full gear and ran up a rocky hill after three mules. My new partner backed me up and in a matter of minutes we had the mules turned around and headed back towards the herd.

It felt good. It felt real good, running up and down all over the countryside. Icky was a changed horse. All I had to say was, "up," and he would break into a smooth comfortable canter. He wasn't even tripping anymore. I think he was having as much fun as I was.

Whenever the herd settled down my partner and I would fall back and ride parallel with each other. Her name was Carol. She was a retired schoolteacher, who now bred and raised mules. She didn't talk much, but she did mention that her back was sore and she was glad that I wanted to run after and bring back the stray animals.

As we ran I pushed Icky fast and hard. He kept his ears opened and carried his head high. One hand was on my reins while the other was constantly flapping in the air, high above my head as I whistled and hollered at the animals, coaxing them to move, back toward the herd.

"Slow them down, spread out!" A wrangler repeatedly yelled as he galloped towards us from the front line.

I glanced at Carol. She slowed her mule down and positioned him along side the last couple of animals in the herd. I turned Icky around and lined him up a few feet behind her mule. The couple on the left side of the herd did the same.

"Make them walk, slow down." The wrangler forced his horse sideways into the herd. The horses and mules around him stopped in their tracks. It started a domino effect and the herd slowed to a stop.

"Mary," Carol shouted as she turned around to look at me, "sit up tall and show these city folks what we're all about."

The busy interstate freeway was directly in front of us.

Police cars had stopped traffic in both directions. Cars and trucks were backed up as far as I could see. People were standing outside their vehicles. Everyone was watching us.

I straightened my hat, brushed off my bandana, and sat tall in the saddle. I whistled and hollered at the herd as we crossed the pavement. The crowd was waving and clapping. I was tempted to wave back, but I didn't. I had a job to do. I felt proud and I never took my eyes off of the horses and mules as we crossed the road.

Chapter Six

Once we crossed the freeway, our landscape changed. It was much more pleasing to the eye, especially to my contacts. Our dry, dusty surroundings had been replaced with rolling hills filled with green sagebrush and splashes of colorful wildflowers. The ground was covered in hard, gray clay that didn't churn up dust as the horses and mules walked on it.

"Mary," Carol shouted out, "over there." I must have been daydreaming for a line of horses had left the herd and were heading down a hill directly in front of me. "I've got them," I shouted as I kicked Icky into gear.

The front line began to move a lot faster. We followed their pace, which kept us in a constant gallop. The herd enjoyed the faster pace and fought amongst themselves as they vied for position.

Icky carried me wherever I asked. Up and down hills, fast left and right turns. It was as though we had become one. When a horse or mule broke away from the herd, he knew it before I even saw it. All I had to do was gently squeeze my legs, letting him know it was time to move and he flew.

For the next couple of hours I felt no pain. I don't think Icky did either. We both were having so much fun we forgot about our hurt legs.

Patches of lush green grass and shallow pools of cool water kept pulling the animals away from the herd. The distractions were endless.

After yesterday's long day and today's faster pace, I thought that the horses would have been tired and worn out by now. They weren't. I think the faster pace was waking them up.

The mules were more restless and were kicking anything that tried to pass them. Icky knew exactly how to handle them. He would get within kicking range and then he would pull his head back the second the mules would strike. I'm sure that all of the animals that he had bitten over the years had trained him well.

The mules pinned their ears back and let you know when they were going to kick. The horses didn't, they were much more sneaky. Without warning they would grab a bite from a mule's side or butt, then they would kick the mule as they passed.

I wasn't sure who was winning the battle. I just did my best to stay out of it. When our path narrowed I tried to keep a horse in between the mules and me. It wasn't easy. Icky saved my legs from getting hit numerous times. He knew the game well.

Yesterday, as I watched the herd break away out into the wide-open spaces, I thought how much easier they would have been to control, if we had herded them down canyons or narrower channels.

I was wrong. As we approached a narrow canyon the herd came to a stop. Instead of waiting a few minutes the animals impatiently turned around and headed back straight towards us. The mules added chaos to our situation by taking off and running straight up the steep canyon walls.

I froze in my saddle as I watched a wall of thundering animals coming towards me. There were only four of us and over a hundred of them. "Move forward, move now!" I heard the wrangler and his wife yell as they ran their horses towards the charging herd. Oh my God, I thought, they're going to get killed. I expected them to pull a gun out and shoot it in the air, to turn the herd back around. They didn't. I could hear them yelling and hollering at the top of their lungs as they met the herd, head on.

"Lets go!" Carol shouted as she trotted past me. "We've got to turn them back around." I was terrified. My heart was beating out of my chest. I didn't know what to do, so I just followed her.

We whistled and yelled and waived our hats high in the air. Carol started whipping the backs and butts of the mules and they started to turn. I followed her lead and slapped their backs with my hat. Icky kept me safe as they retaliated and kicked at me. It worked. One then two then five then ten, they turned and trotted back towards the canyon.

"I wouldn't have missed this for the world," I shouted to Carol as my heart pounded, "That was quite an adrenaline rush. I can't believe I almost didn't ride this afternoon."

Carol repositioned her mule at the back of the herd. I followed her and slowed Icky down as we reformed the back line.

"Your mule doesn't like to run, does he? My friend Robert is riding a mule and he can't get it to run. Is there a secret? Or," I said as I laughed out loud, "Are they all just stubborn as a mule?"

I thought I would get a response from Carol. I had tried to start a conversation with her a couple of times earlier today. She was a woman of few words. She didn't answer me or laugh. When she did speak, her responses were hesitant and short. I felt like I was annoying her. It didn't bother me. I was doing enough talking for the both of us. And I was glad to have her company.

Here we go again, I thought as the herd once again came to a dead stop. "Let's get them, Icky," I whispered at him as we broke into a canter to get close to the back of herd.

"No," Carol yelled, "don't push them." I slowed Icky down and waited for Carol to catch up to us. "There's a river down there," she said as her mule pulled up next to Icky. "It's very steep, they need to go slow and one at a time." I didn't understand what she meant. I couldn't see the steep ravine or a river. When I did, I wanted to turn around and go home.

One by one the horses and mules slid down a steep hill carrying rocks and dirt with them as they fell. That would have been scary enough, but it got worse. At the bottom of the hill was a raging river. The water was a couple of feet below the shoreline, so the animals had to jump to get in it.

They all hesitated and wouldn't leap into the water until another animal was on their tail or attempting to bite them. They were splashing and bobbing their heads up and down, trying to swim against the fast current as it carried them downstream.

The only thing I knew about horses and water was giving them a drink. I've never seen a horse in water and these animals didn't look like they were having fun. When they reached the other side they were slipping and sliding on the muddy shoreline as they pulled themselves out of the water.

I hesitated at the top of the steep embankment. I can't do this, I thought, I'll get killed. This wasn't in the brochure. This was like something from the movies and it was real.

"Go Mary, go!" Carol nudged her mule forward, almost touching Icky's tail. I didn't want to go; neither did Icky.

A mule was directly in front of me only a couple of feet away. He twisted his head back towards us. I wasn't sure if he was going to turn around and run back up the hill like I wanted to, or if he just wanted to kick Icky.

"We're waiting for that mule," I shouted as I glanced back at Carol. "Move," she yelled. "Get that mule moving."

"Get up!" I hollered. I took my hat off and waved it back and forth at him. "Move you stupid mule, move." I yelled as he pinned his ears back. A bad feeling crept over me as I realized that Icky and I were pinned between two mules.

To make matters worse, the ground was giving way and we were sliding downhill. I tried to calm my racing heart. "Get up you stupid mule!" I screamed in a panicky voice. "Move it!"

Icky was more concerned about his foot holdings then he was about the mule in front of him. His front legs locked as they slid down the crumbling soil.

"Get up, get up!" Carol yelled in a deep masculine voice. I

was terrified. Icky's head was only a few inches from the mule's tail and there wasn't a thing I could do about it.

The mule heard her Carol and turned his head around, looking up. Icky's face was in his tail. I slapped it as hard as I could with my hat. My knuckles were turning white as I held onto the saddle, waiting to get kicked. The mule leaped forward and jumped into the fast moving water.

It was my turn. No, it was Icky's turn. We both stared down at the water. I should have been frightened and worried about drowning or dying. I wasn't. For some stupid reason all I could think about was getting my expensive boots wet. I lifted my legs up and draped them over Icky's neck.

"Put your feet back in the stirrups," Carol shouted, "or you will fall off when your horse jumps."

Icky wanted nothing to do with the river. I though about turning around and running back up the steep hill. Then what do you do? a little voice inside of me kept asking. His feet danced as the ground crumbled around them. I don't know who was more nervous, him or me.

Carol was on our tail. I leaned forward and as calmly as I could, I said, "We can do this Icky." Then in a louder voice as I kicked him hard I said, "Up, get up!"

We flew over the edge and crashed into the water. My legs and boots were submerged. I don't know whose heart was racing faster Icky's or mine. The water felt good—it was refreshing. A few seconds later my teeth started chattering. The water was freezing.

Icky didn't like it. His nostrils flared; he didn't want to swim. His legs were all over the place as he tried to find a solid bottom to walk on. We bounced up and down as he pushed himself up off of the bottom of the river.

"Come on Icky, swim, and stop trying to walk, swim, "I kept saying." Let's get out of here." He acted like a cat that had been thrown in the water. He was doing everything he could to get out.

The river wasn't wide. It was just cold, deep and moving fast. As he swam I could hear his labored breathing; he was doing all of the work. I held on and encouraged him to keep on swimming.

The shoreline was torn up from all of the horses and mules ahead of us. It was a mess of soft slippery mud. Getting out was just as scary as jumping in.

Each time Icky thought he was out of the water the ground beneath his feet gave way, sending his front legs crashing back down into it. We were being carried further and further down-stream. I was scared stiff and knew I had to do something.

I tucked my chest as close to his neck as I could and I yelled, "Up, Icky, up!" Then I kicked him hard in the ribs. Water was splashing everywhere. He dug his front feet into the slippery mud and pulled us out. I kicked him again and held on tight as he lunged forward and broke into a trot. The muddy ground beneath his feet flew up and slapped me as he plowed through it, heading straight up a hill.

The herd was spread out in a small valley of greenery and tall trees. They were casually munching on their surroundings. The wranglers were filling canteens and drinking water.

Robert and Beth were sitting in the shade of a large oak tree. I rode over to them and got off my horse. My body was trembling and my heart was still pounding. Icky immediately pulled and ripped up the grass beneath his feet.

"Now that was fun," Robert said as he took his sunglasses off and wiped them with his bandana. "I had just about enough of the dust. Thanks for talking me into riding this afternoon, Mary, that was worth this entire trip." He took off his dusty hat and slapped it against his wet pants.

"You mean you enjoyed that?" I asked as I looked at the mud on my clothes. "Yeah," Beth, replied, "That was pretty awesome. I wish I had some pictures of me in the river, that was really wild."

Robert walked away and headed to the river. "What did you do take a mud bath?" Beth asked as I sat down in the grass next to her. "That scared the crap out of me," I said as I took a drink of water. "My heart is still racing."

"Mary, you know that Robert's got the hots for you, don't

you?" "What? What are you talking about?" We both lowered our voices almost to a whisper. "He must have asked me a hundred questions about you. It was kind of funny because I don't know anything about you." As Robert walked back from the river, Beth winked at me as I changed the subject.

"You really liked that?" I asked Robert as he sat down next to both of us. "Liked what?" A grin filled his face as he said, "You should see your face, Mary, it's filled with mud." He handed me his bandana. "Here its clean. I just washed it off in the river." Beth winked at me again as he handed me the bandana.

"How did you get so much mud on you? Did your horse fall?" "No," I slowly replied as I took a layer of mud off of my face, "I was the last one out of the river. You guys left me a pool of mud. I was scared to death that we wouldn't make it up that hill."

"You should have seen Robert's mule." Beth pointed at him and said, "He swam like a fish. He was much faster than my horse. My horse tried to walk across the river." "So did Icky," I said as I took a drink of water. "He didn't want anything to do with that water. He was breathing so hard I was afraid we weren't going to make it."

My boots, socks, and pant legs were soaking wet. I didn't mind. They offered me some cool relief from the hot sun. I was more worried about my new leather boots. If they shrank I was in trouble, I didn't have another pair of shoes. No one told me we would be herding horses through raging water. This definitely wasn't in the brochure.

I handed Robert his bandana back. He slowly accepted it while he held on and squeezed my hand for a few seconds. He didn't say a word he just kept staring at me. I though about what Beth had said and I thought about how much fun I had with him last night. I wanted to spend more time with him.

The front line had already formed. As quickly as I had gotten off my horse I had to get back on, the herd was moving.

Beth pulled alongside of Icky as I got back in the saddle. "So, what are you going to do about it?" She quietly asked. "Do about what?" I asked as my face lit up with a smile. She winked at me and whispered, "He's hot, go for it."

Encouragement I didn't need. Robert intrigued me. I liked being around him and I was looking forward to seeing him tonight.

Over the next couple of hours we crossed three more bodies of water. None of them were as deep or as fast as our first and by the third crossing, it became routine.

The late afternoon sun was blinding. I could feel it burning my face. Now I knew why cowboys' skin looked like leather. The elements out here were incredibly brutal.

Yesterday I had covered my face with sun blocker and the dust and the dirt stuck to it like glue. By the end of the day my skin was two shades darker, layered in dirt, and it felt like sandpaper.

I was regretting not having it on today. I kept my head lowered, letting my hat shade my face. The sun seemed brighter today, probably because we weren't constantly in a cloud of dust.

"Mary, stop!" Carol yelled. "Don't move a single step." I stopped Icky in his tracks. The tone in her voice sent adrenaline rushing throughout my body. "Don't move!" another deep voice shouted as a wrangler approached me. I looked around me. I saw nothing. I listened for a snake—no Icky would have gone berserk if it were a snake. What was wrong? My heart raced as the rider approached.

"Back up," he shouted, "Back your horse up, now." I hadn't backed Icky up before. Without hesitation I lowered my reins and pulled him back. "That's far enough," the wrangler said in a calmer voice after only a few feet. "You've got to look where you're walking," he said as he pointed towards the ground. "That's barbed wire. It's real nasty stuff. It will get you in all kinds of trouble."

I looked down at it. Icky's legs were only a few feet away. A long strand of barbed wire was strung out, lying close to the ground, half buried in the sand.

"These stupid ranchers need to clean this crap up," he added as he rode away.

"Thank you," I shouted, as I kept staring at it. How could

I have missed it? Perhaps because of the sun's glare or maybe because I was too tired to see it. Either way, I was glad to know that someone else was watching out for me.

The sun started to set as we moved the herd down a long gently sloping hill. The green valley below us was filled with tall trees, horse corrals, and barns.

We headed the herd towards a large open corral at the bottom of the hill. I could tell by the way everything looked that this was a private ranch. Fences were all painted in white and the grounds were manicured. Trees dotted the landscape and opened up into areas with huge arenas and grassy horse padlocks.

The horses were well groomed and quietly basking in the sun. There were no flies and I didn't even see a pile of manure. The grounds were postcard perfect.

Matt got off of his horse first and said, "We've got hot showers and appetizers for you folks. Grab your gear. We've got camp set up at the end of that dirt road." He pointed down a long narrow road.

Today we had been on a horse for over twelve hours. Longer than yesterday and yet we only drove the herd thirty miles. That's ten miles less than yesterday.

My legs felt like rubber and my ankle hurt. I looked down the dirt road, it seemed like a mile long. My legs looked down it and said, "No;" The allure of hot showers and cold appetizers kept me moving.

I felt like a baby taking his first steps. I knew I had legs—I just wasn't sure if they remembered what they were supposed to do. My first few steps were really awkward. I stopped and stretched my arms high in the air, straightening my back.

"Does that help?" Beth asked as she caught up to me. "No," I replied. "I hope they have some hot water left, I'm dead." "Don't look now," She said as she glanced behind her. "Here comes your boyfriend." "Stop calling him my boyfriend," I said in a stern voice. "I'm married and so is he." "So what, I thought this was California, don't you all play around here?" I straightened my back out as best I could and stood tall, as I said, "No."

"Wait up," Robert shouted. "I can't walk any faster, wait up." Beth and I stopped and waited. Everyone around us or that passed us was limping and walking crooked.

Robert threw his left arm around my shoulder, offering me some support as I walked. I threw my left arm around Beth's. We looked like three very drunk people as we slowly walked down the dirt road, leaning left then right, into each other as we took turns moaning, groaning, and hearing different parts of our body pop.

"Can you imagine doing this every day?" I said as I stretched my neck out and heard it crack. Robert stopped us and while slapping a layer of dust off of his clothes he said, "Now I know why cowboys didn't live past thirty years old."

"Really?" both Beth and I said at the same time. "Are you sure?" "Yes, they lived very hard lives. If they weren't killed or maimed at a young age, then Mother Nature wore them out early."

As we walked, Robert went on and on, talking about the Old West. I had been in the saddle only two days and I felt a hundred years older. I was beginning to understand how hard these peoples' lives were. I was gaining a more realistic perspective of what the western frontier was really like.

"Look at that," Beth stopped us and pointed towards a line of horse corrals. "I'm impressed, can you see how clean those horses are? Why, I would bet you a dollar they're cleaner than we are."

We glanced at each other's clothes, then at our own. I had splotches of dried mud everywhere, from my gloves to my boots. I started to laugh as I said, "I won't take that bet, I know I'll lose." As we walked past the clean horses we kept pointing at them and back and forth at each other's clothes. None of us could keep a straight face; we all kept busting out with laughter.

Beth giggled like a teenager, quietly and almost under her breath. All I knew about her was that she was from the Midwest. I never asked her how old she was. I was guessing she was in her late twenties. She wasn't very tall and she spoke with a hint of uncertainty in her voice.

She seemed to be enjoying our company, even though both Robert and I were about twenty years her senior. I found her refreshing and was glad she was walking with us.

Our dirt road narrowed and curved to the right as it opened up into a clearing of tents and people. Everyone was zipping and unzipping their tents as they put their belongings and then themselves inside.

As we turned the corner, Beth's mother spotted us. "Beth," she shouted, "over here. I've got your stuff already in this tent."

Beth headed towards her mom and Robert and I went off in different directions looking for an empty tent. He whispered something to me as I walked away. I was too sore and too tired to turn back around and listen. I kept walking.

Most of the tents were taken, already filled with the rest of our group that had gotten here, earlier this afternoon. Everyone was casually walking around with clean clothes and gleaming hair.

I desperately wanted to join them. All I had to do was find an empty tent. Then find my gear and then figure out where the showers were.

A tent close to the pile of duffle bags was still empty. I threw my jacket and canteen inside and limped over to the heaping pile of duffle bags. I lucked out. My gear was easy to find. It was on the ground at the side of the tall pile. I grabbed it and moved into the tent.

Somehow I had managed to find enough room inside this small bag to bring a stash of face and body wipes. They took up a lot of valuable room and I pondered long and hard if I should bring them. They turned out to be invaluable. The cool moisture and fresh smell almost instantly took off enough layers of dust to nearly make me feel human again.

My sleeping bag was soft and very inviting. The allure of a hot shower and fresh food kept me from lying down.

There were no signs pointing to where the showers were, so I followed a trail of clean people and asked, "Where are the showers?" A woman who still had a towel wrapped around her head replied, "Their over there." She pointed past a thicket of mature trees. "Wait," she shouted as I headed in her opposite direction, "you need special coins. You get them from the cook by the chuck wagon, over there."

I followed her finger as it pointed past all of our tents. "Way over there," I said with a long sigh. "g-r-e-a-t." I would have paid a hundred dollars for someone, anyone, to walk over and quickly bring me back some coins. My ankle was barely letting me put weight on it and I didn't know if it would carry me all the way over there and then all the way back here again.

Everyone around me was in good spirits. That is, every except for me. I was tired,—no, I was exhausted and in a lot of pain. The chuck wagon was only a couple hundred feet away from me but it seemed like miles as I slowly limped towards it.

"How is your ankle?" "How was the afternoon ride?" Was it fun crossing the highway?" Everyone I walked past had a question. I thought about what they were asking. Crossing the highway, which seemed like days ago, so much more had happened today. As the memories came flooding back, so did a surge of energy along with my smile.

Ice-cold beer and potato chips with thick, spicy dips lured me away from the showers. The chips were really salty and I washed them down with an icy beer. Together they were a perfect combination.

Everyone around me was chitchatting and looking refreshed. It was hard to believe these were the same people that were too tired to ride past noon today.

I was tempted to grab another beer and a handful of chips and just go back to my tent.

"Here are your tokens," a wiry man with an overgrown mustache said as he handed me two nickel-sized pieces of metal.

"How many minutes per nickel?" I asked as I tossed them around in my hands. "I don't know," he replied while scratching his head.

"Can I have ten more?" I asked as the smile from my face faded.

"I'm only supposed to give you two," he replied as he looked into a small box filled with coins. "Please," I said in a long sad voice, "I'm terribly dirty." I hung my head down as though I was really sad.

He pushed his hand deep into the box of coins and quickly scooped out a handful. He dropped them into my open hand and quietly said, "Okay."

I winked at him as I turned around and headed toward the showers. Shame on me, I thought, as I walked away. I hope this doesn't get him in trouble.

Without a towel I had no idea of how I was going to get dry. All I knew for sure was that I desperately needed a shower and that I had enough coins to stay in hot water for as long as I wanted. I carefully opened my hand and counted my loot.

The evening air was warm and balmy. I eagerly threw half of my belongings into a plastic bag and headed towards the showers.

There were four women standing in line waiting for the showers. I reluctantly joined them. I was impatient. I had ridden longer and harder then any of them today and I wanted to be next. I opened my hand to look at all of my coins. A woman getting out of one of the shower stalls noticed them. "Where did you get those?" she asked as her face lit up. "Thank you, thank you very much," she said as she daintily took a few coins from my open hand. Then she made a beeline back into the same shower.

Everyone heard her and started talking to me. The coins disappeared from my hand in a flurry of "Thank you's."

When I realized I only had two more coins left and at least a half more hour wait in line, I gave up and handed my last two coins to the woman directly behind me.

There were two sinks in the bathroom and no one was around them. I got out of line and decided that ice-cold water splashed on my face would be the best that I was going to get tonight. I turned the hot water faucet on. It flowed out hot and fast. Without hesitation I stripped to my underwear and washed every inch of my aching body. I looked like a bird taking a bath as I splashed water all over the sinks and mirrors. I didn't care who was watching me or what they were thinking.

The hot water and steam rejuvenated and soothed every inch of my body. Women were patiently waiting in line and still thanking me as I left the bathroom. All of my thoughts were on Robert. Was I going to see him tonight?

Chapter Seven

Darkness was falling, so I headed back to my tent. I dried myself off with my last clean cotton shirt. I slowly brushed my hair as I took some long deep breaths. I felt like a new woman.

As I unzipped my tent the wonderful smell of meat cooking on an open grill grabbed my attention. Lanterns were lit and shining bright on a line of hungry people circling the chuck wagon.

I joined them and while waiting in line I thought about everything that had happened to me today. Was I one of the lucky ones? How many more people were thrown from their horses today? How come nobody wanted to ride earlier this afternoon?

"Here, I though you could use this," Robert said as he handed me a cold beer and joined me at the back of the line. His hair was shining and his clothes were clean. He was wearing a large silver belt buckle that I hadn't noticed before. Light from the lanterns reflected off of it, drawing it to my attention. "Is that what I think it is?" I asked as I bent down to get a closer look at it.

"It's real," he said as he looked down at it, "but it's not mine, it was my dad's. He won the national championship in bronco riding. I brought it with me for good luck on this trip."

"It's beautiful," I said as I studied it. The buckle was large about the size of a baseball. It was gold and silver and had a lot of inscriptions in it which were too small to see in the dark.

"Has it brought you luck?" I asked as my fingers touched the cold metal.

I looked up at Robert's face, waiting for him to answer. "You're blushing," I whispered close to his ear as I took my finger off of the buckle.

"Ma'am, how do you want your steak cooked?" I turned around and held out my empty plate. "Do you have any rare?" I asked as I listened to the meat sizzle. "Yes, ma'am," he replied as he slapped a steak on my plate. "Do you have anything smaller?" I looked at the size of the steak—it must have weighed two pounds. "Nope," he said as he picked up another steak and slapped it down on Robert's plate.

I didn't eat a lot of meat and the steak on my plate looked like the side of cow. Oh well, I thought as I stared at it, I worked hard today. I guess I deserve this.

Four well-fed cooks never stopped moving. If they weren't preparing or serving food they were putting it away or washing dishes. I walked up to one and asked which coolers had cold beer in them. She smiled at me and said, "The three closest to that tree over there." Then she surprised me by saying, "I've never seen one person eat as many brownies as you did today." She looked at my steak and added, "What's your secret? How do you stay so slim?"

I shook my head as though I had no idea. I didn't think she would believe me if I told her I never ate like this at home.

"I know why the cowboys died so young," I said to Robert as we headed over to the beer coolers, "if they ate meat like this," I looked down at my steak, "then they probably all died of heart disease."

As Robert bent down to get two beers out of the cooler, I looked up. The moon was full and the sky was clear. A warm inviting breeze followed us as we walked over and sat down on folding beach chairs neatly set out in a large circle.

"It's about time you two showed up," Beth said as I sat next to here. "Where have you been?" "I gave up waiting in line for a shower," I said as I plopped down into the low chair.

"Does anybody want half of my steak? "I asked in a loud voice. "I'll take it," Robert said as he held his plate out, "Why aren't you hungry, Mary?" "I'm starving," I replied, "but this is way to big for me and I've got to save some room for dessert."

"I dare you to eat it," Beth said as I cut it in half. Sara was sitting next to her daughter Beth. She bent forward in her chair and threw her voice past her daughter as she asked, "Is it true that you guys ran your horses all afternoon, or did Beth and that wine she is drinking make it up?"

I glanced over at Robert to see if he was going to answer her. I was hungry and my mouth was full. He was facing away from us and talking to three men sitting next to him on his left.

"Tell her," Beth said as she raised her voice. "My mom doesn't believe me, tell her." I swallowed a half-chewed chunk of meat and took a couple of big gulps from my beer, as I said, "Oh yes, we ran our horses all afternoon." "You mean you trotted," she said. "There is a big difference between trotting and running."

I looked at Beth at the same time she looked at me and we both said in loud excited voices, "We weren't trotting, we were running." "Up and down steep ravines," I added. "They weren't steep," Beth said as she sipped her wine. "What about that first river?" I said. "I suppose you didn't think that was deep?"

"What river? You got to cross a river?" Sara kept interrupting us as Beth and I reminisced about our wild afternoon.

A well-dressed woman who looked like she just came out of a salon from Beverly Hills walked by us. "Did you say that you ladies were running your horses today?" she asked as she slowly picked up a chair and sat down next to us. "Beth and I grinned at each other and said, "Oh yeah, we ran all afternoon." "Are you sure?" she asked as a puzzled expression filled her face. "Yes," we both said in a loud voice, as we nodded our heads in agreement.

"Don't get me wrong," she replied with a slight uppity tone in her voice. "You're both inexperienced riders. I was told that experienced riders were to stay on the front line and that inexperienced riders were to stay in the back and eat dirt and dust all day."

I couldn't help but laugh as I thought about what she had just said. She was right. Matt had told me to fall back after I had gotten kicked yesterday. She was right about the dust and dirt, too. The part I thought was funny was the part about walking our horses.

Yesterday I walked my horse a little bit but most of the day I was trotting. This afternoon Icky and I never stopped running. I didn't have the energy to argue or explain what I thought was funny, I just kept laughing.

I put another piece of meat in my mouth to keep me from saying something I might regret. The woman kept her eyes glued at my face as though waiting for me to respond to what she had just said. She was articulate and frowning and her fingers were manicured. I had no intention of tangling with her.

I kept stuffing meat into my mouth and giggling under my breath in between quick sips of beer.

As she stood up to leave I turned toward Robert and while tapping his shoulder to get his attention I purposely said in a loud voice, "Robert, did you walk your mule today?"

He turned to face me and said, "No, that stupid mule I was on, wouldn't run. My knees and ankles are killing me from trotting all day."

"Oh, hello, my name is Robert," he politely said as the stylish woman sat back down and listened. He glanced towards me and said, "I want a horse like yours, Mary, so I can run like you did today."

"I don't think you would like Icky, he's a handful. He bites anything that tries to pass him, and," I added as I took another sip of beer, "he trips and he doesn't like water."

"Wait a minute," I said in a louder voice, "how did you know I was running my horse today? You couldn't have seen me. You and Beth disappeared in front of us once we crossed the freeway."

"I know," Robert said as he moved his chair a foot closer,

"We didn't plan on it. Beth and I just started chasing horses and somehow we ended up in the middle of the herd. The horses wouldn't stay together. Beth and I had planned on falling back and rejoining you. Every time we let some of the animals pass us they constantly broke away from the herd and we found ourselves chasing them over and over again."

I put down my fork, and said, "Do you realize that we paid good money for this? I've never worked so hard in my life."

Beth moved her chair closer to us and we started reminiscing about our afternoon's adventure.

"I was sure I was going to drown in that water," I said as I glanced first at Robert, then at Beth. "Weren't either of you worried or frightened when your horse jumped in?"

"I didn't have time to be worried," Beth said. "Worried—it was great!" Robert said as his voice filled with excitement. "That is what I came on this trip for."

Everyone within hearing distance had moved his or her chairs closer to us. Robert, Beth, and I teased each other as we talked and relived the excitement and fears of our long afternoon.

"Excuse me," a polite tiny voice asked. "When did you go through water? And what do you mean you ran your horses all afternoon?"

"Wow!" another woman said, "I want to go to the back of the herd with you guys tomorrow." "It's not fair," an angry voice added. "How come I didn't get to run my horse today?"

My plate was empty and I was out of breath. I stood up and headed towards the chuck wagon. "How was it?" one of the cooks asked as she stopped washing metal plates for a second.

"That was the best steak I've ever eaten," I replied with a smile. "Thank you for all the wonderful food you made. I've really enjoyed it."

"Goodnight," I added as I tuned around and headed towards my tent, "thanks again."

"Wait!" she shouted. "Aren't you going to stay up for the dance and music?" "What music?" I asked as I turned back around to face her.

She pointed to a white van that was parked just past and outside our circle of chairs. "Have another beer," she said. "Those guys are really good."

"Besides," she added as she dropped a plate into the soapy water, "tomorrow you only ride fifteen miles and you don't have to get on your horse until eight o' clock. The night is still young and the beer is still cold."

I thought about what she said—it all sounded great to me. A lot more sleep, cold beer, and live music, yes, this part of the brochure I remembered.

"Thank you," I said again as I turned back around and headed towards the beer coolers. I grabbed two and headed back over to where Beth and Robert were.

I noticed that one of the wranglers had a shovel in his hand. He walked over to about the middle of our circle of chairs and started digging a hole. As fast as he scooped dirt out another wrangler threw wood in. A third wrangler I hadn't seen before was laughing out loud and dancing around both of the other men. He was carrying a can of barbecue lighter fluid. The two wranglers working seemed annoyed by him and repeatedly asked him to leave. Those of us who saw him started egging him on by shouting, "You go dude, light it up!"

As he danced, he sprayed the lighter fluid on the wood. Most of us were a safe distance away from him so we just laughed as he emptied the entire can.

He threw the lighter fluid can over his shoulder and stepped a few feet back. Then he lit matches and launched them in the air at the wood. He had a captive audience. "Awwww," we all said when the matches fell to the dirt or missed hitting the wood. On his fifth attempt the match hit its target and exploded in flames.

Everyone watching started clapping. Matt appeared from behind the illumination of the flames. He threw his hands high in the air and in his loud voice said, "Listen up, folks. Tomorrow is an easy day. You can sleep in until six o' clock. We ride at eight." He lowered the tone in his voice and continued, "There are plenty of cold drinks and these characters are going to serenade you.

A thin, heavily bearded man stepped out in front of Matt and said, "I don't take requests unless you have money." The crowd roared. He lifted up a fiddle and started to play.

A second younger man opened up a long black case and pulled out a guitar. He draped a strap over his neck and started tapping his right foot as he said, "One, two, three." They both tapped their feet in harmony and music filled the air.

Hands were clapping and toes were tapping as everyone joined in. The fire was dancing to the music and the full moon illuminated the ground around us.

Wranglers grabbed us and one by one they made us stand up and dance. Everyone was laughing as we sang and repeated, "And around and around you go with a doe see doe." This was like a scene from a good western movie, only it was real.

"Get up, Mary," Beth yelled as a wrangler pulled her out of her chair. "No way," I yelled back, "I would love to dance but my injured ankle won't let me."

One of the women from the chuck wagon stopped twirling in front of Robert's chair and held her hand out. "Go get her," I said as I pushed on his back encouraging him to get up.

He stood up and took hold of her hand as he glanced back at me. Beth was out of breath and plopped down in the chair next to mine. "Hey, Mary," she said in a loud voice as she slapped my shoulder, "I saw you touching Robert's belt buckle, what's that all about? You told me you were married, have you changed your mind?" "How many glasses of wine have you had?" I asked as I put my index finger to my lips and said, "Be quiet, Beth, he can hear you." She leaned close to me and in a quieter voice she said, "You can't hide it, Mary, I can tell, you really like him." I nodded my head as though she was right and clapped to the music while I watched Robert as he danced and twirled his partner around in circles. Beth was right, I did like him and I wished that it were me up there dancing with him. My feelings were growing for him and I didn't know how to stop them.

The music and the energized crowd helped all of us realize that we weren't as tired and worn out as we thought we were.

As our enthusiastic clapping and dancing slowed down, two women from the chuck wagon walked around and served us cake and ice cream. "Aren't you glad you stayed up?" one of them asked as she dropped a scoop of ice cream on my cake. "How come I haven't seen you dancing?" the other one asked as she handed me a napkin. "Oh, it's you, aren't you the woman who ate a plate of my brownies?" Here, let me get you another scoop of ice cream." "No," I said, "I mean, yes, that was me, I mean, "No thank you, I have plenty.""

My eyes were getting heavy and opening slowly as I watched and listened to the clapping, singing, and dancing around me. I glanced at my watch It was ten o' clock. I had been up since three thirty this morning and I had ridden on a horse for close to twelve hours today. As I thought about my day and everything that had happened to me, it all seemed surreal.

My ankle quickly reminded me how real everything had actually been as I stood up and limped back to my tent.

"Wait up, Mary, let me help you." Robert was right behind me and I heard him. I just wasn't sure if I should stop and wait for him. I was drained and worn-out and all I wanted to do was to dive into my sleeping bag.

"I'll see you in the morning," I said as I waved my hand high in the air, acknowledging that I had heard him.

What I didn't see was a cluster of small rocks directly in front of me, hidden by the shadows of the tall trees. As I put my arm down my left foot smashed into them, sending me off balance. My right leg flew forward, trying to keep me from crashing to the ground.

As the weight of my body pounded on my right ankle, it gave way and I flew forward. I had no idea what had happened. All I knew for sure was that my ankle was exploding with pain and that I was lying on the ground flat on my stomach.

"Are you all right?" Robert asked with a panicky voice, "Mary, are you all right?"

Tears were forming in my eyes. I tried to hold them back. "No," I replied as I started to cry, "no, I'm not all right."

"Hear let me help you," he hurried over to my side and

tripped on the same pile of rocks that I had just stumbled over. He lost his balance and flew forward straight towards me. I had managed to pull my self up, into a sitting position as he landed hard on his knees a few inches away from me.

"You're a lot of help," I said as my tears turned to laughter. "Didn't we do this last night? I've got to stop meeting you like this."

"I think your crazy, Mary," Robert said as he gently wiped the tears from my face. "Yes, I'm crazy all right," I said in a softer, quiet voice. "I'm crazy for having believed the stupid brochure for this trip."

Robert wrapped his arms around me and pulled me close. He slowly and softly kissed the tears that were rolling down my face. My heart pounded as his hand gently lifted my chin up so I could see his face. our eyes met.

"What am I going to do with you?" he whispered as he stroked my hair.

As I looked into his eyes all of my aches and pains seemed to disappear. I quietly replied, "What am I going to do with you?"

I wrapped my arms around his waist and pulled myself tightly to his chest. He smelled fresh and he was wearing a cologne that enticed me.

"How long have you been married?" he asked as he kept stroking my hair. "A little over two years. How about you?" "Close to three years."

How could I be this comfortable in a man's arms that I've only known for two days? Many questions flooded my mind as we held each other tight. I felt like I had known him forever—everything about him felt right.

In the darkness of the night we listened to the music and laughter from the crowd as we quietly gazed at the moon and each other. Neither of us wanted this moment to end.

"Can you walk?" Robert asked as his soft hand caressed my neck. "I don't know," I said. "Do you believe in fate?"

"Robert looked deep into my eyes and whispered in my ear, "I use to." Then he slowly and tenderly kissed my cheek. His lips were warm and soft, I wanted more. I turned towards them as he kissed me again.

"What are you two doing sitting in the dirt?" Both Robert and I recognized Beth's voice as a flash of bright light crossed our faces. "Oh, its you two, I know, I know," she said as she walked away, "your both are married and you're just good friends. I think you should go for it and get a room."

Robert and I were both blushing like two teenagers who got caught making out. I cleared my voice and said, "I think it's time for me to go to bed. Would you mind helping me back to my tent?"

"The gleam in Robert's eyes disappeared as he said, "I'll help you back to your tent if you help me figure out how to stand back up. I haven't sat on the ground in I don't know how long." His frankness brought a smile to my face.

"Deal," I said as I pulled myself up onto my knees. I held tightly onto his left hand and locked my wrist as I pushed my arm up into the air, helping him stand up. I couldn't help but think about what I was doing.

"You know," I said as I started to giggle, "we look pretty old, right now." I looked up at Robert and asked, "How old are you?"

"I'm forty-two," he said as he pulled me up. "How old are you?" "You're kidding," I said as I stood back up. "We're the same age—wow, that's a coincidence."

My ankle wanted nothing to do with me. "I'm sorry," I said as Robert braced his leg helping me to walk, "I really don't like being dependent on anyone, it makes me feel old."

Robert stopped walking and turned towards me as he said, "Mary, you're the prettiest and smartest woman I've ever met. Where were you three years ago when I got married?"

I didn't know how to answer him. He sounded so serious, if I didn't know better I would think that Robert was falling in love with me. The thought scared me and at the same time it made me felt warm all over.

The music has stopped and tents around us were being unzipped. We both knew it was time to go to bed.

"Mary, I,…" "Goodnight," I whispered in his ear as I softly kissed it. "I'll see you in the morning."

I turned around and fell to my knees to unzip my tent. Robert stood and watched me until I closed the opening.

A feeling crept over me that I didn't know how to control. It was a good feeling yet at the same time I wasn't sure what it was.

Was I falling in love with Robert? Part of me said, "Yes." A voice in side of me kept repeating, "You're married, what are you doing?" And my ankle kept reminding me that it was time to take some aspirin and get a good night's sleep. I couldn't sleep. My thoughts were on Robert.

Chapter Eight

Light from the early morning sun danced across my face and woke me up. A strong wind had played havoc with our tents last night. It had howled and screamed all night long. My tent walls had flapped so violently I thought my tent was going to fly away. I must have woken up a hundred times and heard the pounding of tent stakes and wranglers yelling back and forth at each other.

The air was still this morning and the birds were chirping. Maybe it was a bad dream, I thought, as I unzipped my tent and peaked outside.

The bonfire was still smothering and the folding chairs that once surrounded it were in pieces and scattered all over our campsite. Mother Nature had picked up and thrown anything and everything that wasn't tied down. Our campsite was blanketed with debris and looked like a city dump.

Wranglers and cooks were already moving fast and picking up everything in their paths as they hurried to clean up the mess.

I'm glad we hadn't had that kind of wind on the trail yesterday—it would have blown us into another state.

I laid back down and thought about last night as I watched sunlight reflect and bounce all around my tent. I remembered tripping and falling and how embarrassed I was. But most of my thoughts kept drifting back to Robert's tender touch and warm lips.

A feeling of guilt crept over me as I thought about my husband, Steven, and my two children. Steven was a great husband who had openly accepted my teenagers along with all of the mayhem that they constantly threw at us. He was the most patient man that I had ever met. I missed him and my children.

I thought about both Steven and Robert as I taped up my ankle. It was puffier and more swollen then yesterday and I noticed new bruises on my knees and shin. My right leg looked like it had been through a battlefield. I was glad I could hide it under a pair of pants.

Outside of my tent I stretched my arms up high in the air and cracked my back.

The sky around me was layered in hues of dark blue with some of the prettiest aqua colors I had ever seen. There wasn't a cloud in sight and the air was crisp and clear.

A young wrangler walked by me. He was carrying a hammer and wearing a deep frown on his face.

"Long night?" I asked as he stopped in front of my tent. "I hate the wind," he replied as he bent down and pounded on the metal stakes that kept my tent from blowing away.

I nicknamed him; "the tent man." To me he had the toughest job of anyone here. Daily he had to tear down thirty or forty tents and fold them tight enough to fit back inside the small nylon bag that they were originally shipped in. Then he had to reset them back up at a different location, along with loading and unloading all of our other camp gear from duffle bags to sleeping bags.

He wasn't a very big man. He looked more like a young kid fresh out of high school. He had come to my rescue yesterday morning when every attempt I made at deflating my air mattress failed. Who ever invented them is getting the last laugh, at everyone who tries to get them back inside the tiny bag they originally came in.

I punched on it, sat on it, and even tried to lie on it as I rolled it up. I had the bottom half in once but it popped out like a cork out of a bottle as I let go to grab the other side.

My sleeping bag presented the same problem. It was made of goose down feathers and was as soft as any bed I had ever slept in. Getting it to shrink back into the size of a pillowcase was a frustrating, almost impossible challenge for me.

Whenever the tent man heard me cursing under my breath or punching something he would come over and watch me for a few minutes, then he would work his magic. He was quiet and had the patience of a saint. I envied him that as I watched him calmly fold, shrink, and twist everything and anything back into it original tiny package.

Tents opened slowly. Cheery, "Good mornings," were scarce. The long windy night had taken its toll on everyone. I even heard the tent man mumbling under his breath as he helped me shrink my own air mattress.

Even the cheerful cooks weren't smiling today. I helped myself to a cup of thick, black coffee. Nothing smelled good this morning. It didn't matter. I wasn't hungry. My ankle was aching and I was tired. All I wanted to do was go back to bed.

I passed by the bacon and eggs and stopped in front of half a cake left over from last night. I sliced two large pieces off and covered them with sweet strawberry sauce. I'm turning into a sugar freak, I thought, as I ladled another scoop of strawberry sauce on top of the cake. Out of the corner of my eye I could see the cook that I had gotten the brownies from yesterday. She was talking to the other cooks and pointing at my plate.

"Do you have any nonfat milk?" I asked as I slowly limped closer to where they were standing. Their eyes were locked onto my plate. I glanced down at it and for some reason, the cake looked a lot bigger on my plate then it had back on the table.

"You want nonfat milk?" one of them asked as a smile returned to her face. "Please," I replied as I licked a finger full of strawberry sauce. "It's in that cooler over there," she replied with a giggle. "You're the one who likes Ann's brownies, aren't you?"

"Yes, I am." I said as I walked away and headed towards the cooler. It took me a few seconds to realize why they were giggling at me. It hit me once I read the word, "nonfat" on the milk carton. My plate was filled with a thousand—no, a million fat calories and I was asking for nonfat milk. The thought brought a smile to my face.

Wranglers had recovered some of the folding chairs and had put them back in a neat circle around the smothering fire. Bodies were scarce this morning and most of the chairs were still empty. I didn't see a person I knew.

I sat down and quietly ate by myself. The cake was sweet and the milk was cold. It was exactly what my body was craving. When I went back for a second glass of milk I noticed that the cake platter was already empty. It made me feel good knowing that I wasn't alone on a sugar binge. I grabbed two pieces of bacon and sat back down.

As the early morning sun touched my face it burned and hurt. I had worn a hat, a bandana, sunglasses, and sun blocker all day yesterday but our long day and hard ride had taken its toll out on me. My body was worn-out and the skin around my eyes was bright red and swollen.

I decided that I was going to take the afternoon off. My mind kept trying to talk me into riding all day but my body said, "No." I had been in the saddle for almost twenty-four of the last forty-eight hours, a feat in my wildest dreams I wouldn't have thought was possible. Yes, I deserved and badly needed a break.

"Where did that wind come from? I don't think I slept a wink." Sara caught me by surprise. I hadn't even noticed her or Beth until they sat down next to me. I must have been daydreaming. I was tired and my body was letting me know it.

"So...." Beth said as she took her sunglasses off and winked at me, "how was he?"

"How was who? What are you talking about?" her mother asked. "I was talking about the wind last night, wasn't it horrible, Mary? Did it keep you up all night?"

Before I could answer her Beth said, "No, mom, it wasn't the wind that kept Mary up all night, but I know who did."

Beth was dying to find out what happened between Robert

and I last night. I did my best to ignore her as I held a conversation with her mother about the bad weather and our lack of sleep last night.

"I'm not going to ride this afternoon," I said as I touched my swollen face. "I've had enough, my body says, I quit."

"That's what Beth and I were discussing earlier," Sara said as she slowly cut up a piece of bacon. "I thought you two were crazy riding yesterday afternoon."

Sara had thinning hair and looked a little older than me. It was nice to know that I wasn't the only person here who was too tired to ride all day today.

"I bet Robert isn't going to ride this afternoon either," Beth said as she raised her eyebrows. "Are you two planning on eloping?"

"What are you talking about?" her mom asked in a slow serious voice. "Who is Robert and what do you mean 'elope'?"

"He's Mary's new boyfriend," Beth said in a flirty girlish voice. "I caught them making out last night."

Sara's fork stopped before it filled her mouth as she said, "Oh, I thought you were married."

"She is," Beth said, "but she's from California." "Oh," her mom said again as she resumed eating her breakfast.

I didn't need or want any part of this conversation and I wasn't going to have it. I stood up and walked away.

The sugar in the cake and the caffeine in the coffee were slowly kicking in, waking up my tired body and brain. I walked back over to refill my cup.

Robert had the coffee pot in his hand. At first I felt awkward and I didn't want to be around him. He turned to face me and with a soft, tender voice said, "Good morning, Mary, I didn't sleep very well last night. I need a lot of this stuff this morning, may I pour you a cup?"

His soft, caring voice melted away my fears. "Please," I replied as I held my coffee cup out. Why was I afraid of him? What was wrong with me?

"Have you had breakfast?" he asked as he carefully set the

hot coffee pot down. "Yes," I said as a smile crept into my face, "I ate half of the leftover cake from last night and washed it down with fat-free milk."

"That's an interesting combination," he said as he picked up a plate. "I've got to sit down," I said as I turned and walked away, "my ankle is killing me."

A little voice in side of me said, Mary, keep walking, and don't look back, stay away from him, he'll only cause you trouble. My heart was telling me a different story, saying, Mary, you know this feels right, don't fight it, he's your dream come true.

I was too tired and physically exhausted to figure anything out right now. All I could think about was having the afternoon off and taking a very long nap.

Matt's piercing voice lifted our weary heads as he loudly said, "Folks, I hope you had a good time last night and as I promised you, today will be an easier ride. Finish up your breakfast and head down the road to the stables."

As he turned and pointed his hand towards the stables a middle-aged man asked, "Where do we go if we don't want to ride today?"

Matt turned back to face him and said in a deeper more authoritative voice, "Today everybody rides, there is no half day ride today. Today is a full-day ride for everyone."

Moans and groans filled the air. "This isn't fair," I said as sat back down next to Beth and Sara. "I finally admitted defeat and I still have to ride. I don't think I can do it. Every inch of me is swollen or bruised."

I wasn't alone. Everyone around me was complaining. They had all planned on taking the afternoon off and a few of them had hoped not to ride at all today.

"What going on?" Robert asked as he sat down next to me. "Everybody looks upset."

"We all have to ride today," I said as I let out a sigh, "all day. No one can take the afternoon off."

"You want to trade that icky horse of yours for my mule?" he asked as he gobbled his breakfast. "I don't think my knees will last another day."

"Mine either," Sara said as she touched hers. "This is your fault, Beth," she said as she raised her voice. "You're the one that had to come all the way to California. The men just aren't good enough for you back home, you've dragged me all the way to California, for what?" She looked around the crowd and continued. "I don't see any men. I told you there weren't going to be any more men here than there are back home. Why, I could have stayed home and taken a boat ride with Terry, that would have been a lot more fun."

Robert and I listened to Sara as she complained and yelled at her daughter. Beth had her sunglasses on but we could tell by her body language that she wasn't listening or caring much about what her mom was saying to her.

Beth had just gotten divorced and came to California looking for love. She dragged her mother along promising her that California offered every amenity she had always dreamed of, from back massages to a pedicure.

"She must have gotten on the wrong bus, too," I joking, whispered to Robert. We both took a careful look at her. Her hair looked like a hurricane had blown threw it and her clothes were wrinkled and dirty.

I glanced over a few times at Robert. I could tell by the expressions on his face that he though the scolding was funny. I couldn't have agreed with him more.

"How bad are your knees?" I asked as I watched him rub them. "Did you get hurt last night when you fell?"

. "If I fall tonight," he said with a grin, "there's one small area that isn't bruised yet. I'm sure I can hit it."

I liked Roberts's sense of humor, he spoke with confidence and he wasn't afraid of making fun of himself.

"Beth is spreading rumors about us." I whispered close to his ear as I carefully looked around me to make sure that she wasn't watching me.

"I don't care," he quickly replied in a loud voice, "we're both adults. Now," he said as he rubbed his knees again, "Are you going to let me ride that horse of yours or not?"

"No," I replied purposely raising my voice. "I've got Icky

trained and I don't ride mules." I stood up and slowly headed towards the stables.

"Wait up," I heard Beth and Sara yell at the same time. I stopped and watched people as they passed me. Everyone was frowning and looked worn-out, perhaps from the party last night or maybe from the wind. They were all dragging their feet and their heads were hung low. I was glad that we only had to ride fifteen miles today. I rubbed a thick layer of sun blocker on my face as the hot sun touched and irritated it.

"Were still trying to decide if we want to ride in the front or back today," Sara said as she and Beth caught up with me, "Where are you going to ride, Mary?"

"I'm going to stay in the back," I said as I put my gloves back on, "as long as I don't have to eat that terrible dust, that almost killed me." Both women nodded their heads in agreement.

"Where's Robert?" Beth asked as she looked around. "I told you," her mother said in a reprimanding voice, "leave them alone. That's none of your business." Beth kept quiet as her mother continued. "I apologize for my daughter, she shouldn't meddle in anyone else's business. I raised her better than that."

Beth picked up her pace and hurried away from us towards the stable. I had enjoyed her company but right now I was getting a little annoyed with her childish comments about Robert and me.

Sara and I leisurely walked to the stables as we traded stories about our lives. Just about everyone in our group past us as they headed towards the horses. I wasn't in a hurry and with the way my body was feeling right now I really didn't care if they left without me. I had a feeling that Sara felt the same way.

"Mary," I heard a wrangler loudly yell as we approached the horses. "Which one of you is Mary?"

Oh no, I thought not another new horse. "Please, no," I quietly mumbled, as I slowly raised my hand and without an ounce of enthusiasm in my voice said, "I'm Mary."

"You ride Icky today." He said as he pointed towards a horse's tail. "He's that salt and pepper horse over there."

I let out a sigh of relief. At least I got to ride the same horse today. I was glad I wouldn't have to start all over with a different horse. I don't think I would have had the energy.

As I tied my jacket to the back of my saddle, Matt rode up and stopped his horse a few feet from me. He was riding a different horse than I saw him on yesterday.

"Mary," he asked as he watched me finish tying my gear down, "how did Icky do yesterday?"

"He stumbled a lot," I replied as I looked up at him, "but he's a good horse, thank you Matt, I like him."

He scratched his chin and as a puzzling expression filled his face he said, "Go figure that. You like Icky but you didn't like Tyler. Go figure that."

I wasn't sure what he was talking about. I was just glad to have the same horse for a second day.

"Are you sure his leg is all right?" I asked as I bent down to look at it. Matt didn't answer me. He had already moved away and was busy in a conversation with two other riders.

This morning there wasn't an enthusiastic rider amongst us. We all moaned and groaned as we mounted our horses. None of us complained about what horse or mule we were riding or even raised a question about our cinches or stirrups needing to be adjusted. We all just wanted to get the day over with.

Icky didn't wait for me to get into the saddle to start in with his bad habits. As soon as I untied him he pinned his ears back and started walking towards the butt of a mule about ten feet away from us. "Stop it!" I yelled as I pulled back on his reins, "stop it." I swung my leg over the saddle and yanked his reins back, as hard as I could. "I'm not in the mood," I shouted as I yanked back on his reins again.

The rider on the mule heard me and turned around to see what was happening. It was Robert. He wasn't wearing his sunglasses and his nose was already red.

"You look terrible," I said as I studied his face. Where are your sunglasses?"

"I don't know," he hesitantly replied. "I had them at breakfast and then I went back to my tent to finish packing and I lost them.

Robert was talking slower and he was different, less confident than he had been the last couple of days. He didn't have the gleam I saw in his eyes last night.

"I see you still have your favorite mule," I said with a smile as he hid his face under the shade of his hat.

"I see you still have that biting horse," he replied as a grin crept onto his face. "What did you say his name was?"

"Icky," I said as I pulled on his reins when he lunged at Robert's mule again. "And," I said with a long sigh, "it looks like I'm going to have to start all over with his training today."

Icky was determined on being the boss today. He refused my commands and kept his ears pinned back. As he fought me I repeatedly kicked him hard in the gut. Matt and Robert were watching as I wrestled with him.

Everyone else's animals were calm and quiet. I forced him into a trot and kept him running in circles, first left then right. I don't need this, I thought as I strained my muscles getting him to respond.

When he finally gave in to my commands I stopped him and looked around. Matt was moving the front riders into position to let the herd out. It was time to move.

Chapter Nine

There were less than a dozen of us who stayed behind. We positioned our horses in a long tight line blocking off the dirt road we rode in on, yesterday. Riders bringing up the middle of the herd fell back and whistled and waved their hats at the horses and mules, forcing them through a narrow gate a couple animals at a time.

Most of the herd followed the other animals down a long dirt road. Others weren't as compliant; they turned towards us and charged our horses as they tried to break free.

What amazed me was how quickly we worked together, as a team, in silence. When a horse or mule tried to force us to move out of its way, we would immediately, without a spoken word, back each other up, forcing the animals to turn and head back towards the herd.

If one of our horses moved too far right or left leaving an opening for the herd to pass through, another one of us would immediately wedge our horse in the open space, closing the hole in a matter of seconds. It was impressive.

I didn't see Robert, Beth, or her mom Sara. They must have moved to the front line earlier, when I was preoccupied going in circles with Icky. I was hoping Robert was going to stay on the back line with me today.

Since we only had fifteen miles to ride today, I was looking forward to getting to know him a little bit better and hopefully sorting out some of my very confused feelings.

I recognized most of the riders except for two of the women. They didn't look familiar to me at all. If I had met them at camp I sure didn't remember them.

I looked around for the wrangler, Carol, who I rode with yesterday. I didn't see her. I still hadn't thanked her for saving me from the barbed wire yesterday. I owed her and I was looking forward to talking and riding with her today.

"Are you Mary?" one of the women asked as she positioned her horse close to Icky.

"Be careful," I said as Icky pinned his ears back, "my horse bites." My warning didn't deter her. She moved closer to me and said, "My name is Jane. I overheard you last night when you were talking about running your horse yesterday."

"My friend Gloria and I have been on the front line for the past two days and were really disappointed. We're both experienced riders and we want to run and ride hard, like you did yesterday. Do you mind if we ride with you today?"

"No, not at all," I replied. I studied her face for a minute and racked my brain as I said, "I don't remember seeing you at camp, is it me?" She laughed out loud and yelled, "Gloria, get over here! Come tell Mary where I was last night." Jane had shoulder-length thick brown hair and was thin as a rail. She was tall and in good shape. I guessed she was in her early thirties.

"You're Mary, right?" her friend asked as she trotted over. "I've got to warn you," she said as she raised her voice. "Don't listen to a word that woman says, she's crazy."

"Last night she sneaked out of camp and partied all night long with a bunch of good-looking cowboys." She stopped her horse a few feet from me and in an angry voice said, "Boy am I pissed at her, she didn't even invite me."

"Oh, hi, I'm Gloria," she said as she turned around to look at me. "You did say your name was Mary, didn't you?"

I didn't know anything about these two women but I liked them. "Yes," I replied nodding my head, "I'm Mary."

We slowly moved the herd back up the same hill that we had

come down from yesterday.

Gloria trotted off chasing strays up and down the hill.

Jane and I walked our horses side by side as we watched Gloria. Although she was a lot younger than me, her face looked tired and her head was hanging as low as mine was.

"I bet you had more fun than I did last night," I said as I lifted my head up just high enough to see her face. "I doubt it," she slowly replied. "I came to California to play hard and maybe get lucky. I haven't seen a cute cowboy yet."

She raised the tone in her voice and said, "You've got the best looking guy here. If he was twenty years younger I would have grabbed him up in a heartbeat. Why, he's got the tightest ass I've seen in a long time. How is he in bed?"

"What are you talking about?" I asked as a puzzled look filled my face.

"You know who I'm talking about," she said, "that guy you've been hanging out with, the one with the gold belt buckle. "You have got to be kidding!" I replied. "Are you talking about Robert?" "I don't know his name, is that his name?" she asked.

Jane and I rode side by side all morning long. We took turns spilling out our hearts as we watched Gloria run up and down hills, chasing strays. They both were single, and had no intention of ever having children or getting married, and they both had come here, all the way from New Mexico.

Whenever Gloria would slow down long enough to join us, we would loudly share stories about the crazy things that we had done in our lives. After listening to each other, we would burst out in laughter and yell, "What were we thinking?"

These two women seemed fearless and they both had a, "bring it on" attitude. They brought out the kid in me and I wanted to join them and be crazy, young, and single again.

I couldn't believe how well Icky was behaving. Jane and I rode only a couple of feet apart and side by side, yet Icky never tried to bite her horse once. He kept his head lowered and his ears up and he obeyed my every command.

I think he was as tired as I was and we both were quite

content at watching everybody else chase and move the herd today.

I kept the brim on my hat lowered, almost touching my eyebrows in an attempt to keep the sun off of my face. I could feel the heat as it ate through layer after layer of sun blocker. The sun was brutal. Every time I lifted my head up it attacked me and burned deeper into my already pink skin.

It was hard to believe that today was only the third day of this trip. Last year when I fell in love with the brochure for this trip I was disappointed that it wasn't for a longer length of time. Now I knew why.

If we had to endure these conditions for much longer I would have rebelled, and quit, and by the looks on everyone else's face this morning, it would have been a full-on mutiny.

What amazed me was the stamina of these horses and mules. Most everyone was still riding the same horse or mule that they had started out on three days ago. The way they climbed and fearlessly jumped into moving water was remarkable. There were numerous breeds here, from mustangs to thoroughbreds.

My stable horse at home wouldn't have been able to keep up, even at a walk. These animals were athletics, in great shape and thick from neck to hoof.

Today we followed a range of gently sloping hills that constantly fed down into long valleys of dark green grass.

Dust and dirt were replaced with soft grass and dark red clay. The hard ground gave way to a loud clip-clop noise as the horses marched on it. The noise echoed around the valleys as we drove the herd up and down the hills.

Trees sprouted up and partially shaded us as we moved the herd in and around them.

Matt had kept his promise. Today was an easy ride and our surroundings were pristine and picture perfect.

About mid-morning the pain in my ankle and my back had nearly disappeared. I'm not sure why, maybe because of the constant slower movement on my horse today. Or perhaps from the soothing greenery that my eyes had been feeding on all morning. Either way it was a welcome change.

Streams of gently running water followed us all morning long. They snaked and flowed into shallow pools, dotting the plush green valleys below us.

As we headed down a rocky ravine the noise from our horses' hooves was drowned out by rushing water as it cascaded down the rocks on both sides of us, racing to the bottom of the hill. I watched it as it jumped from rock to rock and splashed playfully on everything near and around it.

I could smell the moisture and feel the cool mist as I headed Icky down the hill. If this ground had been a little bit more level I would have stopped and taken a very long nap.

All the riders in from of me must have been thinking the same thing. They were facing and watching the water instead of the horses and mules moving around them.

"Wake up people!" A deep loud voice shouted. "Keep those animals moving." The horses and mules must have felt like we did, for they were stopping and sipping the water and watching it as it splashed their muzzles.

As our path narrowed we headed down much steeper and rockier hills. Water was still following us, splashing and running along both sides of our path, wetting the rocks around us as we crossed them. Icky hesitated a few times as he repositioned his feet on the slippery ground.

The herd came to a dead stop and we had to fall into a single line formation as our decent steepened.

Mules became impatient and broke away from the herd by climbing up steep canyon walls almost effortlessly. The rocky and narrow path made it impossible to run or even trot after them.

"Mary," I heard Jane shout from a couple of horses back, "get those mules."

"I'm not that crazy," I hollered as I glanced back at her, "Thet're all yours."

Icky was carefully picking his steps and I gave him all the time in the world to do so.

"Yahoo!" I heard Jane and Gloria shout with a high shrill. They yelled and hollered as their horses caught up to me. They weren't on the path and the ground underneath their horses' feet was breaking loose and sliding down the hill.

"You guys are crazy!" I shouted as I nervously watched them. "We'll show you how it's done," Jane shouted as she passed me on my left. "Chicken," Gloria yelled in my direction as she passed me on my right.

"You'll get killed!" I screamed in a panicky voice. "Let them go—its not worth it."

Icky's ears flew up as they passed me. "Oh no you don't," I yelled as I pulled back on his reins. He fought me and pulled his reins forward as far as he could as we started to slide down the embankment. His neck was already fully extended and he knew how hard it would be for me to pull it back up at this steep of an angle. I couldn't stop him.

The harder I pulled back on the reins the scarier my situation got. His front legs were already slipping on the rocks and when my reins pulled his head up, he couldn't see the ground in front of him. He kept slapping his feet down hard on the rocks as he tried to find a level or even surface to walk on.

I gave in and loosened the grip on my reins. My heart was pounding so fast I thought it would fly out of my chest as he took off, down the hill. I held on for dear life and threw my weight back as far as I could in the saddle.

"Slow down!" I kept yelling as I jerked back on his reins. I could hear laughter from Jane and Gloria, and then I heard a blood-curling scream followed by terrified voice shouting, "Rider down!" The fear in the voices sent goose bumps up and down my spine.

Icky was fighting me so hard I was sure I would be the next, "rider down."

"No!" I kept yelling as I hit his head with my reins. "I'm not falling off, you stupid animal, slow down!"

A few seconds later I heard a panicky, high-pitched voice yell, "Help me! Somebody help me!"

Another frightened voice screamed, "Watch out!"

I was so busy trying to stay in the saddle I didn't have time to look up or think about anybody else. I had my own problems. I was grabbing and holding on to my saddle as Icky slipped and slid and pulled me down the hill.

"Mary!" somebody shouted. "Your saddle." My saddle had shifted off of my horse's back and was slowly sliding down his left side, towards his stomach.

"Please don't let me die," I prayed as I shifted as much of my entire body's weight as I could to the right, trying to pull the saddle up, back onto my horse's back.

My weight was still deep in the saddle and my left hand started to shake as my fingers tightened their grip.

Icky's reins were all over the place as my right hand kept jerking on them in an attempt to slow him down.

My body was bent over so far backwards that the hair on my head was almost touching his butt. I had his reins pulled back all the way to my chest; they were so tight that they forced his head straight up, high into the sky.

He violently shook his head at first to his left and then to his right in an attempt to free himself from the death grip my right arm had on his reins.

"Loosen up the reins!" I heard a familiar voice shout. "Let him go!" It was Matt. I immediately followed his instructions and slowly loosened my grip.

I expected Icky's to lung forward and get us both killed. He didn't. He slowed down and stopped fighting me.

My saddle was still sliding down off of his back, heading for his stomach. "No!" I yelled in a panicky voice. "I'm not dying today." I stood up as high as I could in the saddle and as my heart raced, I leaned my entire body to the right and pushed every ounce of weight I had down, hard, onto my right stirrup.

I could feel the saddle as it slowly moved and shifted up towards the center of Icky's back—it was working.

Pain shot through my right ankle as I forced my weight, hard, back down on it again.

The saddle stopped sliding. It wasn't level with his back but I was glad I was still in it and alive.

I gave him his reins and held on as he charged down the hill.

He only slowed down when a mule or horse blocked his descent.

In a matter of minutes we were down and back on flat ground. My adrenaline was still flowing and my heart was still racing as my body shook from fear.

Matt hurried over to were we had landed. I tried to calm my racing heart as he approached me. I thought he was going to yell at me.

"Mary," he said in a loud voice, "I thought you said that you liked that horse." I didn't understand what Matt was trying to say. I was still trembling and I'm sure that my face must have been as white as a ghost. I looked at Matt and caught a glimpse of a grin filling his face as he turned and without another word walked his horse away.

In the past three days I hadn't see Matt smile once. I wasn't sure if he was teasing me or if he was just glad I had gotten down the hill in one piece.

Chapter Ten

The last two days we had been served lunches fit for a king. Today was different.

Earlier at breakfast, bread, lunchmeat, fresh fruit, and a large bag of hard candy were neatly arranged on a long table beneath the shade of a tall tree.

We were instructed to make our own lunches and put them in a brown paper bag, after we penciled our names on it.

The meat was thick and fresh and I almost made a two-pounder sandwich out of it.

My sweet tooth was getting the best of me and I settled for a peanut butter and jelly sandwich with the emphasis on the jelly. I stuffed my bag with anything and everything that had sugar in it. I passed up the fruit and grabbed a handful of hard candy and a brownie. I felt a little guilty and walked around the table one more time and picked up an orange.

A mule that had been carrying large plastic bottles of water was going to carry our brown bag lunches today. He had bulky, square, dark green canvas packs draped across both sides of his back. We took turns dropping our lunches inside of them.

Last night at the bonfire, when Matt had our undivided attention, he told us a few disturbing stories, about getting dehydrated and hallucinating. I wasn't sure if anyone believed him. But he sure convinced us that we needed to drink water and lots of it all day long, especially today because we were headed up to an elevation of over ten thousand feet.

I untied my canteen and took a few sips of water. It helped to calm my racing heart.

Everyone around me was lining up by the mule that had carried our lunches. A wrangler was calling names out as he held the brown lunch bags up.

Food, sugar, they both sounded awfully good to me. Putting my feet on the ground and not moving for a while sounded even better.

I slowly got off of Icky. His saddle slid down towards his stomach as I put my weight on my left stirrup to get off. I jumped off before I slid under his stomach. He didn't mind the unusual dismount, but my right ankle did.

It started to throb so hard it brought tears to my eyes. For a second I wanted to get back in the saddle.

I looked around for Jane and Gloria. I didn't see them or Sara or Beth. The only person I saw was Robert. He was in line patiently waiting for his name to be called.

I limped over to a tall pine tree and tied Icky to a thick branch in the shade beneath it.

I wanted to yell out and ask Robert to grab my lunch or to help me walk, but my pride wouldn't let me. I slowly and gingerly limped over to where the lunches were being given out.

"That's it, folks," the wrangler said as he closed the satchel. "Wait a minute," I said, "where is mine? I made a lunch, where's mine?"

The wrangler reopened the canvas pack and looked inside. "Oh," he said as he pulled out a wet, empty bag. He wiped off the water as he read the name on the bag and said, "Mary, is that your name? Is this yours?"

I was at a loss for words. Everyone else was already sitting on logs underneath the shade of trees and unwrapping food.

"What happened to it?" I said in a sad voice as he handed me the torn, empty bag. "Where's the food?"

He stretched his neck and looked down deep inside the dark pack, being careful not to get stepped on by the mule it was still strapped to.

"Is this yours?" he asked as he pulled out a plastic baggie that had a gooey flattened sandwich inside that looked like a pancake.

His hand dug around for a few more seconds as he said, "How about this?" He pulled out another plastic baggie with a brown flattened square inside it.

"Yes," I said with a sigh, "that was my brownie." My body was running on empty and my brain was craving sugar. "Thank you," I said with a sad tone in my voice as I took the food and headed for the shade.

I stopped for a minute and looked around for Robert. Where did he go? Where was everybody? My ankle was throbbing. I gave up looking for my friends and limped over to an inviting shady area that had water running through it.

The shade and the babbling brook were a perfect combination. I took a deep breath and slowly let it out as I sat down. I was tempted to take my boot off and let my ankle rest in the water. I settled for a few quick splashes of icy water on my face. It was refreshing, so I moved a few inches closer to the water's edge.

I almost fell in as I splashed more and more of it on my neck and arms. I don't think the rest of my body would have minded a bit if I had fallen in.

The creek was only a few feet across and it wasn't very deep. It was almost hidden by the thick green shrubbery that grew around it and followed it as it flowed down hill.

I knew we only had a half an hour to eat lunch, yet for some strange reason I wasn't hungry anymore.

I took my bandana off and soaked it in the cool water. When I tied it back on around my neck, the cold water dripped onto my back and sent chills up and down my spine. It was a good feeling and I could have stayed here for the rest of the day.

"Hi, my name is Sandy. Do you mind if I join you?" A woman startled me as she sat down in the shade a few feet away from me.

I didn't look up or answer her. The cool water was like a soothing ice pack on my swollen eyes and face. I had to blink a couple of times to pull myself out of whatever trance I was in.

"Sure," I slowly replied as I opened my eyes and lifted my head away from the water. "This feels so great I wouldn't mind staying her all day." I turned my neck around to see who she was.

I didn't know her, although I had seen her numerous times over the last three days. She was very young and was riding on the front line with Matt.

She had a girlish chubby face and she smiled at me as I turned to face her. "I heard that they lost your lunch," she said as she held out an orange for me to take from her hand. "I have some candy if you eat candy," she said as she dug her other hand into her brown bag.

My slow responses must have made her feel uneasy for she said, "Are you sure it's all right for me to sit here?"

"I'm sorry," I said as I lowered my head down, "it's me—the cold water feels so good I don't want to move. Please, sit down, I could use some company."

Sandy was shy and looked like she couldn't have been more than twenty years old. She was slim and showed no sign of aging or sunburn. She spoke in a tiny soft voice and for some odd reason she made me feel old.

"That was some awesome riding," she said as she handed me a fistfull of hard candy.

"What are you talking about?" I asked as I shook my head as though she was wrong. "I almost got killed coming down that hill. I've never been so frightened in my entire life. I'm still shaking inside."

"I thought you did great," she said. "I would have been underneath that horse as he slid down that hill. That was really gutsy standing up and using your body weight to pull the saddle back up onto your horse's back. I've never seen anyone do that before. Where did you learn to do that?"

I wasn't sure what to say. It sure made me feel a lot better hearing someone tell me that I had done a good job with my icky horse. I moved a few feet closer to her and listened to her as I stuffed food into my mouth.

"Why aren't you riding in the front with us experienced riders? You know you don't have to eat all of that dust. You're a great rider, why don't you join us on the front line?"

I didn't answer her. My stomach growled out loud and suddenly I realized how hungry I actually was. I kept eating.

The orange was sweet and juicy and it helped me wash down my dry, flattened sandwich.

Two other young riders joined us. The three of them shared their experiences from this morning with each other. They all had tiny high voices and their energy was flowing as they used body language to paint a picture of what had happened to them. Watching and listening to them was quite entertaining. I quietly sat there and finished my lunch.

"Oh, you're their friend," one girl said as she glanced over at me. "Are they all right?" another girl asked. "I think so." A tiny voice answered.

I heard them talking, but I really wasn't paying any attention to what they were saying.

My ears were being serenaded by the noises from the water in the creek as it splashed and ran downhill.

With food in my stomach and cold water on my face, I halfway felt like a human being again.

All that was missing from this place was a hammock. It was a perfect place for a picnic and a long snooze. If they would have had hammocks set up here, I would have been tempted to forget about everything that had happened to me. I would have signed up again.

"It's time to go!" a loud piercing voice shouted and echoed around us. "Let's go, people, lunch break is over." The voice jolted me awake and instantly smashed and shattered all of my, "I love this trip," thoughts.

Sandy offered to help me to my feet. I pretended I didn't hear her. I was already feeling old enough for today. I squirmed around on the hard ground for a few minutes and realized I couldn't get up. Without the support of my right ankle or a crutch to help me, I couldn't stand.

"Please," I quietly said as I held out my right arm for her to pull up. She thought nothing of it and as soon as I was standing she disappeared up the embankment with her friends.

"Don't forget to water your horses," the same loud deep voice shouted. "Water your horses before we leave."

I wasn't very happy with my horse Icky and I didn't care if he got a drink of water or not. Yesterday he was a champion and today he was, well, just plain icky. I bent down and rewet my bandana and splashed water all over my face once more before I left the shade of the trees.

The sun's glare was blinding. My swollen eyes squinted as the heat pierced through my sunglasses and shade hat. For a moment I had forgotten how hot it was and how brutal this morning had been.

Icky was behaving and resting quietly underneath the tree where I had tied him. His head was lowered and his eyes were shut. "Okay," I said, "I'll give you a drink." He opened his eyes and raised his neck.

I walked him down to the edge of the creek. He didn't fight me or raise a fuss. He calmly bent his neck forward and lowered his head deep into the cold water. He closed his eyes as he drank. I felt sorry for him.

He was hot, thirsty, and tired. He reminded me of how I felt. "I'm sorry Icky," I said as I patted him on the neck. "You take your time."

As Icky drank I unwrapped a peppermint candy and popped it into my mouth. He heard me unwrap it and pulled his dripping muzzle out of the water. "Do you like candy?" I asked as I unwrapped another piece and offered it to him. First he smelled it and then he grabbed it with his wet lips.

It was so small that he wasn't sure what to do with it. His neck bobbed up and down as his tongue tossed it around in his mouth in an attempt to keep it from falling out. His erratic head movements brought a smile to my face.

"I guess you like candy," I said as I unwrapped and handed

him another piece. He lifted his head up and then straight down almost in a nodding motion, as though saying, "Yes."

The riders on the front line were moving and I could hear the herd as they became restless.

"Let's go Icky," I said as I walked him back up the embankment and into the hot sun. His mouth was still playing with the second piece of candy when I checked and tightened his cinch and mounted up.

I glanced around to see who stayed back this afternoon. It was hard to recognize people because their faces were hidden deep beneath their hats and sunglasses. I had learned to recognize them by the colorful hats that they wore.

Robert was easy to spot because he was the only one here who was not wearing sunglasses.

I didn't see Jane or Gloria. I was looking forward to sharing some more crazy stories with them. Maybe they had gotten tired of me and moved forward, to the front line.

"Robert," I shouted as I closed the gap between his mule and Icky, "wait up!"

He turned his head and glanced at me as he stopped his mule. "I thought you were a goner, earlier today, Mary. Where did you disappear to, at lunchtime? I looked all over for you." I cautiously positioned Icky close to his mule. He didn't pin his ears back or even raise his head up.

"Is your horse going to bite my mule again?" he asked in a loud voice as he widened the gap between us. "No," I said, "I got rid of my mean horse at lunchtime, this is my new horse. I named him Happy. Isn't he handsome?"

Robert stared at my horse for a few seconds, then he moved his mule a little closer to me as a puzzled expression filled his face, "Are you all right Mary? That sure looks like the same horse that you rode this morning—what did you say his name was? He sure looks the same to me."

"No," I said, "yhat was Icky, this is his twin brother named, Happy." I tried to keep a straight face as I made up a story about getting a new horse at lunchtime.

I wasn't sure if Robert was buying it or not. He gave me his undivided attention as I playfully teased him. He was so easy to talk to and fun to be with.

Without his sunglasses on I could see deep into his eyes and watch the constant change of facial expressions as he tried to figure me out.

"I saw you come down that hill," he said as he slowed his mule and turned his head to look at my face. "I really thought that you were going to die, Mary." He hesitated a few seconds and in a tender, caring voice said, "I don't know why but I was frightened. I don't want to lose you."

"You were frightened?" I shouted. "I was petrified! I saw my life flash before me. I swear, Robert, I can't believe I'm still alive."

Robert reached over and as his hand touched my arm he gently squeezed it. "What am I going to do with you, Mary? You've been on my mind all day. I was hoping staying away from you this morning would help me—it hasn't."

Robert's frankness worried me. We both had purposely stayed away from each other, all morning long. It had'nt seem to help. Our attraction to each other was growing and we both knew it.

How are your friends?" he asked as a serious look filled his face. "What friends?" I said. Robert's voice deepened as he said, "The two women that you rode with all morning. Weren't they your friends? I heard you guys laughing together. I thought you were old buddies."

"Well, yes, they are my friends—I mean, no, I just met them this morning." I took a deep breath and said, "I guess we're friends—where are they? Have you seen them?"

While I was still thinking out loud Robert trotted off to the right, after three horses that had just broken away from the herd.

He chased the horses back and then disappeared with them into the herd. I thought about joining him but a little voice inside of me talked me out of it.

The wrangler couple who I had met yesterday was now riding in the back with me. I hadn't seen them this morning and I was glad to have the company.

The woman stayed on the left side of the herd and her husband stayed on the right. Any horse or mule that I missed or was too tired to chase, they went after.

Our pace slowed as we entered a long narrow canyon. A few minutes later it opened up onto a flat, level bluff that overlooked miles of tree-covered hills and green valleys below it.

There was nowhere to go except, straight down. I remembered seeing a picture just like this from a brochure I saw about the Grand Canyon. I distinctly remember throwing that brochure out because I am deathly afraid of heights and I remember making some comments on how crazy those people were, riding down those narrow paths.

The mules stopped and slowly formed a single line. One by one they stepped out onto the long narrow path that zigzagged down the cliff.

I watched them as they disappeared down the side of the mountain. I can't do this, a panicky voice inside of me said. Where was Robert? I wanted his sure-footed mule. Wait a minute, he offered me his mule this morning and I laughed at him. Did he know I was afraid of heights? Or was he just tired of his mule? Right now it didn't matter. I wanted to trade animals.

I looked around the bluff for him. I saw lots of colorful hats, but none of them was his. He must have already headed downhill.

My heart started racing as I thought about all of the terrible things that could happen to me. I was worried about getting too close to a mule and flying off the cliff, or Icky tripping and flying off the cliff, or even sliding off of my saddle and flying off the cliff.

Stop panicking, a little voice inside of me kept repeating as my heart raced. It's a piece of cake.

Cake, I thought, I would love a piece of cake. I was out of adrenaline. My body was running on empty and I think I was losing my mind, as I thought of how fun it would be to fly like a kite all the way down to the bottom.

Icky must have sensed how much of a nutcase I was becoming. He remained calm and carefully chose his footings as he followed the herd out onto the narrow trail. I sat deep in my saddle and leaned as close as I could to the mountain, as we slowly zigzagged back and forth down the steep canyon walls.

I couldn't get Robert out of my mind. Even in the terrible wind last night, all I could think about was his tender touch and soft warm lips. When I thought about my husband Steven, I saw Robert's face. Every bell and whistle inside of me had gone off a million times, warning and reminding me, that I was married. The more I thought about him the more I wanted him.

I pulled my thoughts off of Robert and focused on my own surroundings. I was on a steep, narrow path that was headed straight downhill. I needed to watch the ground directly in front of my horse's front legs as he carefully picked his steps and I needed to keep a sharp eye on the mules, both in front and behind me.

Our line of close to one hundred and fifty animals snaked down the mountainside in a moving column that could be seen for miles.

Every time a horse or mule would stop, it would cause a domino effect that played havoc with our movement.

Our path was too narrow and steep to go around the stopped animals, so whoever was closest to them got the job of keeping them moving.

Echoes of our piercing voices filled the air and the valleys below us as we all took turns hollering and whistling at the horses and mules.

When a mule stopped or slowed his pace, even for a few seconds, a mule next to him would bite or try to kick him out of his way, in an attempt to get ahead. Some of the animals were more aggressive than others. They all wanted to be first in line and it was a relentless pursuit.

If you had the misfortune of being close to them when they were on the attack they would bite or kick your horse just like the other mules they were fighting. The mules kicked almost without warning and very fast.

Icky and I wanted nothing to do with any of them. Yesterday he proved to me that he knew their game, very well. I gave him his reins all the way down the mountain. He knew when to stop and when to take a quick step backwards or left or right. He kept me a safe distance from the three mules directly in front of us. All I could do now, was hope that none of them would get the urge to stop or challenge each other.

Robert was only six or seven horses in front of me. He looked quite relaxed as his sure-footed mule glided down the mountain. His face was hidden beneath his hat and if I didn't know better I would have sworn that he was sleeping.

I, on the other hand, was a nervous wreck. I was overwhelmed with the thought of falling to my death. I rambled about nothing and kept patting Icky on the neck, in an attempt to slow down my racing heart and rattled nerves.

Icky must have know how frightened I was for he gave me one hundred percent and he didn't trip once all the way down the mountain.

As we reached level ground I closed my eyes and let out a couple of long, drawn-out, sighs.

We were in a snaking riverbed full of rocks and soft sand. In the center of it was a wide, shallow, flowing stream.

I was glad to have flat soil beneath my feet. I got off of Icky and walked him over to the water. He didn't drink. He was more interested in the thick, green clumps of grass that sporadically followed the stream. He ripped them up and didn't stop chewing on them until I pulled his head out.

Nobody around me whispered a word. Most of them were looking up at where we had just come down from; the rest were looking up at where we were going.

Our silence was interrupted by the noises and outbursts from the horses and mules as they fought over the small patches of grass.

As fast as I had gotten out of my saddle I had to get back in. I fed Icky another peppermint candy as I double-checked his cinch, then I swung my injured leg over back into the saddle.

As the animals' feet plowed through the shallow stream they churned up rocks and water. It splashed all over the bottom of my pants and boots as Icky cautiously and slowly crossed it.

The path in front of us was straight up, just as steep as the path behind us, except we were headed up it, not down.

The horses and mules didn't want anything to do with climbing up a mountain. They were all very content chewing sweet grass and walking around in the soft sand. I let Icky continue munching on the grass as I watched riders from the front line, chase the herd all over the place.

As fast as they chased a horse or two up the trail another one would come running back down. The mules didn't care if there was a path or not; as soon as they realized that they were headed up a steep path, they left the trail and ran back down all the way to the water.

"Get those animals moving!" the wranglers kept shouting "Keep them moving!" another one hollered over and over again.

After fifteen minutes of watching most of the herd go up and then run back down to the water a couple of times, it was pretty clear that the front-line riders needed a little help from us, "inexperienced" back riders.

Robert and two of the men who had ridden in the back with us this morning were still watering their horses and talking. I pulled Icky's head out of the grass and walked him downstream closer to the men.

"I hope I'm not interrupting anything," I said as we approached them. All three of them looked up and towards me. "Not at all," one of the men replied. "We're watching those, 'experienced' riders, chase horses," the other man said with a grin on his face.

"Do you think we should help them?" I asked as I parked Icky right next to Robert's mule. "I've had enough," Robert said. "Without sunglasses I'm not doing anything else today except walking this mule."

"Oh come on Robert," I said. "Let's show those, 'experienced' riders how it's done."

"I'm with you," one of the men said in a deep, loud voice. "Let's get them." He kicked his horse hard as he ran through the water towards the loose animals.

Icky's ears flew up and he pulled on his reins as we watched the horse run away. "My horse is ready," I shouted in an excited voice. "Let's go get them, Icky."

Instead of walking cautiously through the water like we had earlier, I kicked Icky hard, letting him know it was okay to run as fast as he wanted through the water. Water splashed over his neck and all the way up to my face as his legs raced through it.

"Wait for me!" I heard Robert shout. I slowed Icky down a little bit and waited for Robert to catch up. "I've got the right side," I shouted as he and the other man rode up. "We'll get the left," they both shouted back. We all tore through the water and ran back and forth getting the herd to move.

Each time the water splashed my face, adrenaline shot through me like lightning. It was an awesome feeling and I didn't want it to end.

In a matter of minutes the four of us had cornered and pushed the rest of the herd forward into the hands of the front riders. They kept the momentum going and forced the animals, one by one, up the steep path.

I could tell by the expressions on people's faces that they were enjoying chasing the herd. Everyone was reenergized.

Icky and I got in line at the back of the herd and followed them up the mountain, as adrenalin flowed.

Chapter Eleven

Earlier this morning Matt had told us that today we would cross one of the last accessible wagon trail routes in the United States.

As we headed up the mountain, we followed a trail of stone that was deeply etched and scarred with the imprints of wagon wheels from the countless loads of heavy wagons that had crossed over this vast steep terrain.

Between the increase in elevation and the steep angle of ascent, we needed to stop about every half an hour and let our horses catch their breaths. Everyone was leaning forward in their saddles and we all did whatever we could to help our horses as they slowly picked their footings and climbed.

I kept glancing back behind me looking at the mountain we had just come down. My horse back at the stables wouldn't have made it halfway down it, let alone back up this side.

It's hard to believe that heavily loaded wagons were actually pulled up and over these mountains. The hardships and pain that our forefathers must have endured are unimaginable. The ruts in the rocks left a glimpse of their drive and endurance.

I thought about the families who crossed here and the Indians that they encountered. If we were attacked right now we wouldn't have had a chance—we were sitting ducks, all in a line on a steep endless trail.

There was nowhere to go, backwards or forwards. If you were under attack while pulling a wagon up here, I don't think you could have saved it because it must have taken the blood sweat and tears of every man, woman, and child to pull and push the wagons up these steep, rocky mountains.

Adding the wrath of Mother Nature from snowstorms to heat waves was mind-boggling. It was hard to fathom the sacrifices and determination these people endured.

I felt privileged being able to walk in the same tracks that my forefathers had.

Every time we stopped to let our horses catch their breaths, we stayed on them. It felt awkward stopping at such steep angles and not being able to move because we had horses or mules only inches away, both in front and behind us. I could see Icky's nostrils as they flared open as he caught his breath.

As we climbed I thought about what Robert had asked me and what the young girls at lunch had said to me. Something wasn't adding up. Where were Jane and Gloria? The more I thought about them the more I got a sinking feeling in my stomach. I tried to make it go away. I couldn't. Something was wrong.

I wanted to talk to Robert or anybody who knew Jane or Gloria. I couldn't. We were in single file and all of us had between five and ten horses and mules in between us riders.

Our ascent was long, steep and very slow. As the horses and mules fatigued, they stopped in their tracks, and unless a rider was directly behind them it was hard to get them to start walking again.

After a while they got use to our whistling and hollering and they ignored it. The only thing that got them moving was to hit the butt of the mule closest to the stopped animal. He in turn would take a few steps to get out of the way, which pushed him into the horse or mule in front of him, which caused a domino affect in movement with the herd.

The ground beneath Icky's feet constantly changed. First it was small clusters of rocks, then shale, and now granite. The shale shattered and splintered underneath the heavy weight of our animals. The granite was solid rock and had a smooth surface, which made it hard for our horses to get a good footing . The clusters of small rocks were the easiest to climb.

The horses usually led with their front right leg and pulled themselves up each step. By midafternoon we reached a flat clearing. The herd picked up it's pace as they spotted it.

Numerous watering troughs filled with water dotted the level ground. The herd flocked to them.

The clearing wasn't larger than a small parking lot and once all of us riders and the herd were on it, there was barely enough room to get off of my horse without bumping into another animal. I knew Icky was too tired to bite anything, so I left him alone for a minute as I looked around for someone to talk to.

It was hard to see anyone in the sea of animals that surrounded me. I saw a few hats, but none of them looked familiar.

I didn't want to stray too far from Icky, so I turned around to make sure I could still see him. He was gone.

Since the beginning of this trip we had been drilled numerous times that first and foremost we were never to leave our horse unattended.

Even though we were in a confined space the herd was constantly moving. I couldn't have been gone for more than a minute or two. Where could he have gone? Icky was short and could easily disappear behind most any animal in the herd.

My heart raced as I hastened my pace around horse after horse looking for him. The higher elevation left me grasping for breath.

"Mary?" I heard a familiar voice say. "Mary, over here!" I looked around and saw a hand swaying back and forth high in the air, above the horses' backs that surrounded me.

My heart pounded as I looked around and realized that I was stuck in the middle of a moving herd of tired and thirsty animals.

I walked as close as I dared by the horses and kept as far away from the mules as I could. When a horse pinned his ears back I took a step backwards and slowly moved away from him.

I was in an endless maze of swirling, thousand-pounded, four-legged animals that were only inches from my feet and me.

"Here, over here!" the voice was Robert's and it was getting louder. I looked back up for a split second, taking my eyes off of the animals as I tried to find the waving hand again.

A mule started to follow me. "Go away!" I shouted, as he got closer to me. All of the horses around me raised their heads and started kicking the ground. I didn't know what it meant, but I didn't want any part of it.

I shot past the back legs of two mules and ducked my head under the neck of a third. My heart was racing so fast I could barely catch my breath. I lifted my head back up and looked around. I was standing a few inches from Icky's stomach. My eyes blinked twice, I guess to make sure I wasn't seeing things.

"What's your horse doing over here?" Robert asked as he handed me Icky's reins. "Are you hurt, Mary? Your hands are trembling," he said as he held on to my right hand and looked at me a little closer.

"No, I mean yes," I hesitantly replied. "I think I'm okay." I caught my breath and said, "I'm scared half to death, but I'm not hurt, I'm okay." I lifted my hat up so Robert could see my face.

"We've got to do something about your sunglasses," I teased in a shaky voice, as I calmed my racing heart.

"My eyes are killing me," he complained. "I don't think I can last another day without them." He let go of my trembling hands and said, "Hey, Mary, you wouldn't have an extra pair of sunglasses, would you?"

"I wish I did," I said with a chuckle. "I would love to see a man in my sunglasses."

"Look at that view." Robert turned and looked down the face of the mountain we had been climbing all afternoon. "Isn't it beautiful up here?"

With Icky's lead rope firmly in my hand, I walked a little closer to the ledge. Robert noticed that I wouldn't get as close to the edge as he was. "Are you afraid of heights?" he asked as he held out his hand for me to grab.

"Yes, I'm deathly afraid of heights," I admitted. "I thought I was going to die coming down that first mountain. I would have done anything to get my hands on your mule."

Robert turned away from the edge to face me and said, "Anything?" as a grin crept onto his face. "I'm not getting any closer," I said as pushed his hand away and took a step backwards.

The nervous tone in my voice must have convinced him that I was serious. He walked away from the edge and joined me.

"Look," he said almost in a whisper as he pointed out over the edge, "Look at that."

I blinked the dust from my eyes for a few seconds and focused on the hills and valleys around us. "Is that what I think it is?" I asked as I strained and blinked my eyes hard to focus.

"Over there, there's another one over there, and there." Robert had the eyesight of an eagle. Waterfalls were cascading down the mountains all around us. I couldn't believe I hadn't noticed them before this. They were surrounded by dark thick greenery, which must have hidden them from our view as we climbed.

"Wow," I said as I watched the water race down and explode on the rocks below each one, "they definitely should put this in the brochure—it's breathtaking." Robert nodded his head in agreement as we both stood there and watched the cascading water. "How come we didn't hear them or see them?" I asked as I untied my canteen from Icky's saddle.

Robert didn't reply; he looked like he was in a trance as he studied the mountainside.

"Mary, come here, look over there." Robert pulled me a little closer to the edge as he grabbed onto and held my left hand. "I promise," he said in a soft voice, "we won't get any closer to the edge." He pointed with his right arm out in the same direction where we had been looking and then he slowly raised his hand and pointed his index finger higher and higher. "Look up there, look at that one," he said as his voice filled with excitement. "And look over there, just to the right of it, that's the mother lode."

He put his right arm down and said, "This was worth the whole trip." I nodded my head in agreement.

I wonder why they didn't mention this to us?" I said as my eyes jumped from waterfall to waterfall. This is prettier than anything I've ever seen.

As we stood there in silence and watched the water cascading down the mountains Robert put his left arm around my waist and slowly pulled me close.

I thought about how calm and relaxed I was in his arms. How could I have been so frightened and scared only just a few minutes ago? Nothing I thought about made any sense.

The herd was moving away from us. We both noticed it at the same time. "I'm late again," I said as I quickly tied my canteen back onto my saddle.

"I'm moving to the middle of the herd," Robert shouted as he disappeared into the thick of the herd.

As the herd thinned out I could see more of the riders left to bring up the back of the herd. I recognized the wrangler couple and a few of the folks that I had started out with this morning.

I carefully checked out every person and hat around me. Jane and Gloria were not here and I hadn't seen Beth and her mom, Sara, since this morning. Where was everybody?

I wanted to ask everybody back here if they knew where Jane and Gloria were, but I didn't have time. When the herd started moving so did we, all in different directions.

Robert had mentioned to me earlier that he had seen Beth and her mother at lunch. He said that they were looking for me when he stumbled upon them. They were with two women that they had befriended who use to live close to the same town where they lived in Ohio. He said they never stopped talking about the coincidence, the entire time he was with them.

We had to be at an elevation of at least seven thousand feet up, yet the sun was still blistering our skin and blinding our eyes.

I adjusted my chinstrap and pulled my hat down lower on my forehead, in an attempt to hide or find some reprieve from the glare and heat.

In the distance a dark green tree line followed the top of the next mountain directly in front of us. It was miles away, but I was hoping we were headed for it.

Icky seemed rested and walked with his head up. His nostrils weren't flaring as he walked. My heart had stopped racing and I was calm. I guess I was rested, too.

Over the course of the last three days bringing up the rear of a heard had been a challenge beyond my wildest dreams. With each new day there were brand new highs and lows.

Being last in line had to be incredibly brutal on the riders in the Old West. You were the last to get off of your horse and probably the first to get back on. You were last to get food or water and with all of the dust you ate you were almost certainly the one who needed it most.

I wondered if they got better pay or if that's where they got placed when they were first hired. This wasn't corporate America, but I could see the similarities about seniority.

The front riders and herd were already halfway up another steep hill before the rest of us riders in the back even moved. The line of animals and riders stretched out half ways up a mountain.

From my position I could see most every rider, horse, and mule as they turned and zigzagged back and forth up the steep terrain. The further up the mountain they climbed, the smaller they got.

I glanced at my watch—it was already past 4:00 pm. I had no idea where we were headed; all I knew was that I was very tired and I was hoping we would be there soon.

While sprinting past the mules earlier I had put more pressure on my injured ankle than I wanted to. It was throbbing, so I rested it gingerly in the stirrup, being careful not to put any more pressure on it than I had to, as I rode.

Riding up hill all day, hour after hour was taking its toll on my body. I had to constantly lean forward and place as much of my body's weight as I possibly could on Icky's front legs. It helped him keep his balance as he struggled with the uphill climb.

Earlier, when I got off of him at the level plateau, I couldn't stand up straight. My back was as stiff as a board and nothing I tried helped to loosen it up.

If a helicopter would have been close by flying over us, I would have held up a white flag and gladly given up.

A late afternoon breeze followed us. It picked up a hint of cool air as we climbed. By early evening the air had turned cold.

My jacket was neatly rolled and tied onto the back of my saddle. I tried to untie it several times; nothing I did worked. After several attempts I realized that it was impossible to untie a knot with just one hand, especially if the knot was very tight and if you were doing it from, behind your back.

The cold air swirled around my neck, sending chills up and down my spine. I thought about stopping and getting off of Icky for just a second to untie it. I couldn't—there was barely enough room on our narrow trail for him to walk.

I tried not to think about the cold air as we climbed and climbed. I thought about the past three days. Today was by far the longest time that I had ever been in the saddle.

Then I thought about yesterday and the day before that. No, I'm sure, today was by far the longest.

As I debated in my mind on which day was longer, I hadn't noticed that directly in front of me was a roaring fire throwing yellow and orange flames, high into the sky.

Icky noticed it before I did. He lifted his head up high and shook out his neck. He must have smelled it.

In the distance I could see from the light of flames our tents and our chuck wagon. I listened to the sweet sounds of pans clanging and I inhaled the smells of meat being slowly cooked over an open flame. Our camp was a welcome sight.

The front riders were already in the camp. I sat up as best as I could in my saddle and started whistling at the herd to get them to move faster. I was tired and hungry. No, I was past tired...or hungry...I was famished and exhausted and by the way Icky was moving, I could tell that he was, too. His head was hung so low I thought it would touch the ground as he walked.

When I stopped and got off of him he didn't raise it or even grab a blade of grass only inches below his nose.

I untied my jacket and quickly put it on. My body was so cold that it was shaking. The roaring fire helped me focus as I slowly and carefully put weight on my ankle.

I didn't even say, "Thank you" or "goodbye," to Icky. I zippered up my jacket and headed up hill towards the warmth of the fire. Just watching it from a distance seemed to warm my cold, aching bones.

Our camp was in a clearing, tucked at the base of tall pine trees. Our gear was in a pile and looked like a dump truck had just unloaded it.

All I could hope for was that my stuff was on the top or on a side of the pile. I didn't have the energy to dig into the mound to find it.

I walked around the heap twice. I didn't see my gear anywhere. My ankle was hurting so I gave up and I sat down on a tree stump a few feet away. I don't need this, I thought, I need a hot shower and an entire body massage.

"Mary," I heard a voice holler. "Your tent is over here."

My back made a loud popping noise that at first hurt, and then felt better as I stood up a little straighter.

The young wrangler that I had nicknamed, "Tent maker," was smiling and waving his hands in the air. I turned towards him and stood up as he said, "I'm sorry about this morning. I've got a tent ready for you and I've already put your gear inside of it."

I didn't know his name—I just said in a huge voice, "I love you, and you're hired!" He must have seen how badly I was limping for he rushed over to the tree stump and said, "You look like you've had a long day. Here, let me help you." He held out his right arm for me to brace onto as I walked.

I piled into the warmth of the tent and zipped it up. As fast as I could I unzipped my sleeping bag and wrapped it around my chilled body. I didn't move until I stopped shivering.

If a pizza delivery truck or room service had showed up right now, I would have paid them their weight in gold.

Although we still had hours of daylight left, I could see and almost feel the flames of the bonfire through the thin walls of my tent.

I slid my entire body deeply into my sleeping bag. I knew my clothes were covered in a thick layer of dust but I didn't care. My sleeping bag was soft, comfortable, and warm. I closed my eyes.

Loud laughter and excited voices kept waking me up. I don't know where the rest of these people were getting their energy from but if anyone of them had offered it to me right now I would have paid handsomely for it.

"Hot hors d'oeuvrs are ready," a couple of women continuously shouted out in proud, loud voices as they kept vying for our attention by banging on an ear-piercing metal bell.

They got my attention and I blinked my eyes for a few minutes as I watched the flames from a roaring bonfire dance and reflect on the nylon walls of my tent. I was warm and comfortable and I felt better. The smell of hot food and the familiar sound of laughter enticed me out of my sleeping bag.

My thickest jacket was still rolled up tight somewhere inside my duffle bag. I felt around for it and put it on with great haste.

When I unzipped my tent I expected cold air to attack my face. I was pleasantly surprised with the wonderful fragrant smell of pine cones and just a touch of cool in the air. I took a couple of deep breaths and slowly let them out.

The soft blue tones in the sky had deepened lending to silhouettes of towering pine trees. The ground was covered in brown pine needles and cones. Our campground was swimming in greenery.

I wasn't sure which smelled better, the pine trees or the wonderful aroma of meat being cooked outside on an open grill.

Our entire campsite sloped down a hill. The tent man had set my tent up at the top of the incline on the most level spot of the entire area.

It was already past six thirty and the sun was just starting to fade. Daylight up here seemed to last forever. Where was Robert?

Chapter Twelve

A white cattle truck drove up and, as it stopped, the wrangler driving it stuck his head out of the window and shouted, "All aboard for the pond." He raised his voice louder and said, "Anybody that wants to get clean, get on board."

The idea was appealing to me, until I turned my head around to take a closer look at our transportation. Our bus had been replaced with an old rusty truck that had splintery wood panels all the way around the back of it.

Almost everyone who was standing around the bon fire or walking around the table of hors d'oeuvrs stopped what they were doing and headed towards the truck.

Their hands were filled with glasses of wine and cans of beer and their mouths were filled with food. Everyone was laughing and carrying on conversations.

I felt compelled to joint them. They must have known something that I didn't.

I grabbed a handful of Fritos with my left hand and a cold beer with my right as I joined them.

Someone started making a loud mooing noise, like a cow, as we all piled into the back of the flatbed, truck. It was funny and it caught on like wild fire as we were forced to stand almost on top of each other as the truck filled.

We all started making long, loud, mooing noises. Everyone tried to outdo each other. Our voices got insanely loud as we mooed and roared with laughter.

"Hold on!" the drive shouted as he headed the truck down a steep rocky hill.

We all looked around at the same time for something to hold on to. There wasn't anything except for each other. All of our food and drinks flew in the air along with most of our bodies as the truck tires jumped from rock to rock getting down the hill.

We should have been frightened; instead, we kept mooing louder and louder, which brought on more laughter. Everyone was spilling everything, everywhere. We were all being tossed up into the air and we looked like popcorn flying off in every direction imaginable.

As soon as I tried to recover my balance and to apologize to the person on my left I was thrown into the person on my right along with my open can of beer. Tears were flowing from everyone's eyes as we were consumed in wild out-of-control laughter.

When our truck finally stopped, not one of us was standing. We looked like we had been playing a game of Twister with our legs and arms sprawled out and all over each other.

We took turning pushing and pulling each other up and apologizing for the food and drink on each other's clothes. Everyone was wiping off their clothes and wiping their eyes as we helped each other out of the truck.

At the end of a grassy clearing was a large pool of dark green water. It couldn't have been more than fifty feet across.

What looked odd was that it was surrounded by hotel chaise lounges sprawled out in thick overgrown grass.

A small red truck had followed us down the hill and parked a few feet behind us.

"All right," one of the wranglers said, "it's the beer truck." Two men got out of the truck and unloaded long blue coolers.

I was wearing most of my can of beer on my shirt. I drank what was left of it and walked over to the coolers.

"The good stuff is in that one," one of the men said as he pointed to a small cooler on the ground that was next to the red trucks back wheel.

The cooler I opened was filled with beer and ice. "This works for me," I said as I dug my hand deep into the ice for the coldest beer I could find.

I followed our group over to the chairs and sat down. A woman sitting on the lounge chair next to me was stripping layers of cloths off. I still had my jacket on and I was getting cold just watching her.

"Aren't you cold?" I asked as she headed down to the water's edge with nothing on but a flimsy bathing suit.

She tested the water with her right toes first and then slowly walked in. It must be a hot springs I thought as I watched her.

Wow, a huge pool of hot water! The thought was almost overwhelming. I was ready to strip to my underwear and join her.

"It's freezing!" she screamed as the lower half of her body turned around and made a beeline out of the water.

A wrangler was watching her and said in a loud voice, "I've got a cure for that." He walked over to her and handed her a small glass bottle.

"Take a shot of this stuff," he said as he unscrewed the cap, "this will warm you up."

The woman took the bottle out of his hands and took a swift drink from it. "Good stuff," she said as she started coughing, "good stuff."

The wrangler walked around the pond offering the bottle to all of us. It looked like a ritual. Everyone wiped the top of the bottle with their shirts or a towel and then they held the bottle straight up and drank from it.

"What is it?" I asked as he handed it to me. "The hair of the dog," he said as he wiped the opening off with his own shirt. "What? What dog?" I grabbed the bottle from him and read the label, "Jack Daniels."

He became impatient as I read the writing on the bottle,

"No thanks," I said as I quickly handed it back to him.

As the liquor flowed so did everyone's energy and courage. One of the older wranglers challenged a younger one to a swimming race across the pond.

The young wrangler accepted his challenge saying, "Your on, for twenty bucks."

We were all watching and listening when someone shouted, "Make it fifty." Someone else shouted, "I'll pay you a hundred dollars to swim across it."

Without another word the young wrangler dove into the water headfirst and swam out a few feet. Then he turned around and swam back to shore as fast as he could.

"Oh my God, that's cold!" he shouted as he ran up the muddy banks. "Where's the JD? I need another shot."

He was fully dressed and soaking wet, from shirt to shoes.

"Chicken!" the older wrangler said in a loud voice, as he handed him the bottle of Jack Daniels. "I knew you wouldn't do it."

The men were standing only a few feet away from me. I had a front row seat and I was enjoying the rivalry. Everyone else was getting out of his or her chairs and walking closer to watch the show.

"I'll make it two hundred," the older wrangler said in a much louder voice that echoed through the crowd.

"You don't have two hundred." "Yes I do." The dares grew and the Jack Daniels flowed as we all watched and listened.

"I've got an idea," the young wrangler said as he walked away from us. He disappeared behind the smaller truck and reappeared carrying a large blue plastic cooler.

"What are you going to do with that?" The older wrangler asked as he studied it.

"I'm going to use it like a surfboard," the young wrangler said as he tied a thick rope around the cooler.

Everyone gathered closer and watched him. We weren't sure if he was drunk or just crazy, but it didn't matter. He was full of energy and entertaining.

"Pull me across," he threw the older wrangler the end of the rope and said, "Put your truck in four-wheel drive and pull me across."

The older wrangler had a puzzled expression on his face and said, "Okay."

He drove his truck around to the other side of the pond, pulling the slack out of the rope as it crossed the water.

"When I say go," the young wrangler yelled, "step on it!" The wrangler on the other side of the pond acknowledged that he understood by raising his hand high in the air before he got back inside his truck.

The wiry wrangler sat down on the cooler and straddled it like he was riding a horse. "Go! Go!" he shouted as he leaned his weight back.

The truck's back wheels spun on the grass as the driver floored the gas peddle.

"E-Haw!" the young wrangler screamed as the floating cooler hauled him into the water. "Faster!" He kept yelling, "Go, go, faster!"

I wished one of us would had a movie camera. We were laughing, clapping, and shouting at him, encouraging him, to hang on. "You can do it!" "Hang in there!" "I'll make it three hundred dollars!" someone else yelled.

The cooler bobbed left and then to the right in the murky water as the truck picked up speed. It was working, and the cooler was floating.

The wrangler kept shouting "E-Haw!" and "Yahoo!" as he twisted his body to keep his balance.

"I think he just invented a new sport," I shouted in a loud voice as I repeatedly clapped my hands. "This is better than reality TV." Someone else yelled. "He's crazy." A woman standing behind me said, "No," and another woman said, "He's just young." We all nodded our heads in agreement and kept on clapping and encouraging him.

About halfway across the pond the rope broke. "No!" the wrangler yelled. "Get another rope, hurry, hurry!"

The older wrangler stopped his truck and got out. He took his hat off and scratched his head as he said, "Well I'll be damned, it worked."

"Don't just stand there, throw me a rope. I'm freezing!" As the cooler stopped dead in the water it bobbed to the right. The wrangler twisted to the left to keep it upright. His weight shifted and the cooler rolled over.

We all stopped shouting as we watched him fall off into the cold water. He splashed his arms in the water for a few seconds keeping himself afloat and then he turned and swam towards the other side of the pond where the older wrangler was standing.

"Hurry up," the older wrangler shouted. "We've got to get these people back for dinner. "Hurry up!" He walked down the muddy embankment to help the younger wrangler out of the water.

We all clapped when he reached down and helped the tired wrangler out of the water.

The sun had finally set and a cold breeze sent all of us rushing to find and put on an extra layer of clothing. I was glad to have my jacket.

"Where's the heater in this thing?" I heard the young wrangler shout out from the front seat of the red truck as I headed back towards the white cattle truck.

Driving down here two people sat in the comfort of the front seat with the driver. I hurried back to the truck so I could be one of those two people for the trip back up the hill.

I held on and listened to the crowd behind me as they mooed and laughed all the ways back up the hill.

Chapter Thirteen

My clothes and face still had an inch of dirt on them. A table I hadn't noticed earlier had large, oval, ceramic bowls set out on it, along with rolls of white paper towels. Directly below it were metal buckets filled with water.

I don't think most of our group saw them. I hurried over to the first bowl and before I filled it with water I stuck my finger in the bucket to see how cold it was.

The water was hot and it felt inviting. I wasn't sure if we were supposed to wash up out here or take this stuff to our tents. I tucked the bowl under my right arm and picked up the bucket of hot water with my left.

The weight of the bucket and the higher elevation had me gasping for breath as I reached my tent, only a short distance away.

The hot water soothed and relieved me and revived every inch of my body. It was hard to believe that such a simple pleasure could do so much. I couldn't remember the last time I had taken a sponge bath and I know it didn't feel this good.

When my body was clean I indulged my foot and ankle by soaking them in the bucket of hot water. In the warmth of my tent I moisturized my skin and face with a thick layer of lotion and I brushed out the snarls and dust from my hair.

I hadn't seen Robert since this afternoon when he moved

up, to the middle of the herd.

I dabbed my clean neck with perfume and I put a second layer of warm clothes on.

My stomach was growling to the point of embarrassment. I'm glad no one was around to hear it. Four days ago I was a picky eater. Tonight if they put an entire cow on my plate I would gladly eat it, or die trying. I was famished.

As I unzipped my tent I remembered to grab a small flashlight to light my path back here tonight. I was determined not to trip or fall again. I buried it in my jacket pocket.

Darkness had fallen and the air had turned cold. Flames from a huge fire were shooting a good ten feet up, high into the air. It shed light all the way to the far corners of our campsite. Folding beach chairs were surrounding it and the flames illuminated an array of colorful hats and jackets.

I zipped my jacket up tight and followed my nose to the lanterns burning bright around the chuck wagon. There wasn't a person or cook to be seen. I patiently waited for a few minutes and then I grabbed a plate and piled it high with everything from barbeque chicken to corn on the cob and a baked potato.

Most of my life I had been a salad freak—I ate salads with everything. I stared at it for a few seconds. I couldn't put it on my plate. For some weird reason it looked green and boring. I passed it up and grabbed another piece of chicken.

If there was a chair close by I would have sat down right here and dug in. I put silverware and napkins in my back pocket and grabbed a cold beer with my empty hand.

I didn't wait to sit down to eat. As I headed over to join the crowd I bent my neck down and bit into a piece of chicken. It was dark out and I was starving and I didn't care how bad my manners were. The sauce on the barbeque chicken was layered all over my face and fingers long before I sat down.

"Is anybody sitting here?" I didn't wait for an answer. I plopped down in a chair and buried my face in my plate.

"Isn't that good chicken?" a woman sitting directly to the right of me asked. "I'm not sure," I said. "I'm stuffing it in my mouth so fast that I'm not sure I'm tasting it."

"Is that you Mary?" she asked as she lifted her head up from her plate. "Gloria, is that you?" It was dark and she was bundled in layers of clothing. The shadows on her face disappeared and she became more visible as she turned her face towards the light of the fire.

"Where have you been?" I asked as I studied her face. "I've been looking for you and Jane all afternoon."

"What a ride, wasn't that great today?" a familiar voice said from a chair directly to the left of me. I turned my head to see who it was. It was Jane.

"Where did you guys go today?" I asked in between full mouths of food. "Did you both move back to the front line? Was it something I said? I thought you guys liked it in the back with me."

Gloria lifted her right arm up and pulled her jacket sleeve up as she said, "Do you want to sign it?"

"Is that a cast?" I could see something white. I just wasn't sure if it was a lightly colored sweater or a cast.

"So," I took a few seconds to think about the last time I saw both of them today. "So," I repeated, "what happened?"

"She is such a wuss," Jane said. "Gloria, you know it, you are such a baby." "Mary," Jane said, "I was embarrassed to be with her."

"Where?" I asked as I licked the barbeque sauce off of my fingers. "Is it broken?"

"It's only cracked," Jane said, "and the way that Gloria carried on you would you would have thought they cut her arm off." "Admit it, Gloria, you are such a baby."

"Well, that's nice of you to stay with her," I said as I turned to my left to face Jane.

"What the hell are you talking about?" Jane said as she raised her voice, "I wouldn't have stopped riding for her. I stopped riding for this." Jane held her left had up. It was dressed in white.

"You broke your arm too?" I couldn't believe my eyes. "No,"

she said, "I broke my wrist, and," she said as she raised her voice again, "I didn't complain or act like a baby."

"Yes you did," Gloria said as she stood up. "You were worse than me."

"No I wasn't—stop lying, Gloria, you know you're such a baby."

The two of them kept throwing barbs back and forth at each other. I wasn't sure that I wanted to be seated in between them. As I listened to them, my mind flooded with questions.

"Wait a minute," I said as I held my hands up calling a time out. "When did all of this happen? How come I didn't see you? How did you get to a doctor? Where are your horses?"

Each time they would stop sparing for a second I would ask another question. What I pieced together was that earlier today when I was holding on for dear life with my sliding saddle, they both had their own problems with their own horses. They both had been thrown in one of the canyons only minutes apart while they were chasing the mules up the steeper terrain.

When Icky fought me to run with them I thought maybe I should have let him go. Now I realized that I had done the right thing. The way they flew by me on horses I knew they were much more experienced riders than I was. If I had taken off with them I'm sure I would have gotten hurt.

I thought about everything that had happened to me today and then I took a good long look at Jane and Gloria's casts. I felt good and very proud as I thought about how I had survived another insane day without being thrown or falling off my horse. All of my aches and pains slowly drained away from my beat-up body as I thought about how well I had actually done today.

I interrupted Gloria and Jane again. This time I wasn't sure if I should ask them but my curiosity got the best of me as I said, "Are you going to ride tomorrow? Can you ride tomorrow? And, will Matt let you ride tomorrow?"

Both women leaned forward in their chairs past my silhouette so they could see each other's faces.

"This isn't going to stop me," Jane said as she held up her

left wrist. "Well, don't think a cracked arm is going to stop me,"
Gloria said as she held up her right arm. It was settled.

I kept my mouth shut as they glared at each other. "Excuse
me," I finally said as I broke the silence, "I need dessert."

All three of the cooks were back behind the tables. "I hope
you don't mind," I said as I cleared the chicken bones and corn
cob off of my plate. "You weren't here so I helped myself."

"Did you make that cake just for me?" I teased as one of
them sliced a piece of angel food cake and offered it to me.
"Do you want strawberries or whip cream?" another one asked
as she held up a can of whipped cream. "Both, pile it on," I said
as I held my plate out. She covered the cake with gooey strawberry sauce and put a dab of whip cream on top. "More,
please," I kept repeating. "Perfect," I said as I admired my vol-
cano-shaped dessert. "Thank you."

"Are you really going to eat all of that?" the woman pouring
the strawberry sauce asked as I turned to go sit back down.
"Yes," I said, "and if there is any left I probably will have
seconds.

When I turned back around to head back to my chair the
mountain of goop and cake shifted on my plate and started to
slide off. I quickly grabbed it with my other hand to stop the
movement. I wasn't watching where I was walking and I
slammed into someone. "I am so sorry," I said as I took my eye
off of my plate and looked up.

It was Robert and I had plastered his jacket with strawberry
sauce and whipped cream. "I am so sorry," I repeated as I
looked at his jacket.

"I was coming to get dessert." He calmly said as he looked
down at his jacket. I hadn't planned on wearing it, I just wanted to eat it." He scooped up some whip cream off of his jacket
with his finger and put it in his mouth. "Not bad," he said,
"Did you make this yourself, Mary?"

The right side of his jacket was swimming in sticky strawberry sauce and whip cream. I couldn't tell if Robert was upset
or not. He just stood there and licked the sauce off of his jacket.

"Here," I said as I put my plate down, "let me get that stuff off of you." I picked up a couple of napkins and started to wipe off his jacket. The napkins were thin and started falling apart and sticking to his jacket as I tried to clean it.

The three women cooks stopped working and watched me as I made the mess bigger. Robert just patiently stood there while I worked on his jacket. When I realized I was making the mess bigger I stood up straight and started laughing as I said, "I'm so sorry, I think I'm making it worse. Do you have another jacket?"

Robert looked down at his jacket which now had a layer of white napkin embedded in it and said, "No."

"I've got an idea, follow me." I walked over to where the buckets of hot water were earlier. "Mary," he said, "it's okay, I'm dirty from today so a little more mess doesn't hurt."

"No, you don't understand," I said as we got to the table where the basins and paper towels were earlier. "it was here a little while ago, they must have moved it."

"Moved what?" Robert looked around the table. "What are you looking for?"

I still had a bucket of water in my tent. It wasn't hot but I was betting that it was still warm. "Follow me," I said again as I headed up the hill towards my tent.

"If I didn't know better I would say you're trying to get me alone." Robert said as he started to follow me. "Now, where are we going?"

I took my flashlight out and turned it on. "I'm not falling down tonight," I said as I shined it a few feet in front of where I was walking.

"I have a large bucket of warm water in here," I said as I stopped in front of my tent. "Give me your jacket, I'll clean it."

"No," Robert said, "tt's too cold out here, forget about it, Mary." I didn't listen to him. I unzipped his jacket and made him take it off. He only had a white tee shirt on underneath it. He immediately huddled with his arms to keep warm.

I unzipped my tent and crawled in. "I'm not staying out here in the cold," he said as he crawled inside the tent right behind me and zipped it up.

I clicked the switch on my small battery-powered lantern. "Be careful," I said as his shoe kicked the bucket of water and almost spilled it. He sat down and crossed his legs over each other in a yoga position. "Wow, you're really limber," I said as I looked down at his legs. "Where did you learn to do that?"

Robert was shivering and trying very hard not to show it. "I'm sorry," I said, "here, put this on. It will warm you up. I handed him a pink sweater. "I'm not wearing that." He pushed the sweater away and said, "You know, I dreamt about you last night, Mary."

For some stupid reason I said, "Was I any good?" Robert was silent for a few seconds then in a slow whisper of a voice he said, "Yes, you were very good." I stopped cleaning his jacket and looked up. "I thought a lot about you, too, last night," I said, as I looked deep into his eyes.

"Your eyes are really burned," I said as I gently touched his face with my right hand. "Let me put some medicine on them." "Do you have something that will stop the burning? My face hurts so bad I don't know if I can lay on my pillow tonight."

"Yes," I said as I continued to softly touch his face, "I've got medication and drugs for everything. I brought more medicine than I did clothes."

"Come over here lay down on my lap. Robert stretched out and slowly laid his head in my lap. I pulled out my moisturized towelettes and gently wiped the dust and dirt off of his face.

"Thank you, Mary, that feels good." He closed his eyes and tenderly rubbed my back with his free hands. When he lifted his arms up over his head to touch my back his tee shirt stretched out, showing the well-developed muscles in his chest and arms.

"You're all muscle, aren't you?" I said as I felt his left shoulder and arm. He remained quiet as I put a thin layer of pain reliever around his eyes and on his burnt nose.

He let out a long sigh of relief and said, "This is the best I've felt all day, thank you, Mary."

"Stay," I whispered to him as I gently played with his hair.. "Stay with me tonight."

Robert opened his eyes and tugged on the front of my shirt, pulling my neck down closer to his face.

My heart started to pound as our lips touched. "I'll warm you up," I whispered in his ear as I softly kissed it. I rolled over and laid on top of him. Alarms and bells were going off inside of my head. I ignored them. My heart and every inch of my body told me that this was right and meant to be.

I kissed him deep and hard as he rolled me over onto my back. He quietly and softly kissed my neck as he unzipped my jacket and unbuttoned my shirt. My body was on fire. I wanted him. He suddenly stopped and said, "No, no, Mary, not here."

I caught my breath and said, "Is it me? Is it wrong?" Robert rolled off of me and looked deep into my eyes as he said, "If we still have these feelings for each other tomorrow night, once we're back in the real world, then I'm looking forward to making love to you all night long." He slowly ran his fingers through my hair as he gently kissed my lips again and said, "I want it to be perfect and I want it to be right."

Chapter Fourteen

They've got to be around here somewhere," a loud voice said. " Mary, are you in one of these tents? Are you sure the cooks said that they walked this way?" "Yes I'm sure and you're getting way too cranky. Why don't you go take another vicodin?" "Shut up!" "No, you shut up."

It was Gloria and Jane. I pulled Robert back down to my sleeping bag and I started to giggle. He held his hand over my mouth as his face filled with a huge grin. We both grabbed for the light switch and somehow managed to turn it off.

"You don't think she snuck off with him, do you?" Jane said as she walked right by our tent. "I hope she did," Gloria replied. "He had a real nice-looking ass. Oh, the hell with them. I need another drink. I'm going back to the fire and I'm going to party hardy."

"With whom?" Gloria asked. "I don't care" Jane, said. "I'm not picky. I'll take that real skinny cowboy, over there. Sometimes they're a real good ride." "I dare you." "You're on." As they walked away we heard Jane say, "Where did you say the vicodin was?"

Robert and I could barely contain our laughter. We kept holding our hands over each other's mouths as our laughter exploded.

"Did you know they both got thrown from their horses

today?" I asked in a whisper of a voice as he pulled his hand slowly away from my mouth so I could speak.

"I wasn't sure, but at lunch today that's all everybody was talking about." Robert hesitated a few seconds and then said, "You mean you didn't see them thrown? I thought you were the one who yelled, 'Rider down.'" I thought about what Robert had said and then I thought about the young women and their conversation earlier today at lunch. My mind drifted back to the terrifying screams that I heard as someone shouted, "Rider down!" It was hard to believe that two simple words could play so much havoc with our emotions and adrenaline. I didn't want to ever hear them again.

Robert and I laid side by side in the darkness and talked. "This sleeping bag is really comfortable. What is it made of?" "Goose down feathers. Have you ever seen that many stars?" "So this is really from a goose?" he asked as he felt around it with his hands. "I don't know," I said. "I bought it because it was rated minus twenty degrees and it was lightweight."

"What do you do for a living?" I asked as I picked his hand up and felt it. "You have baby soft hands—I'll guess you're a pencil pusher." "What's a pencil pusher?" he asked as he felt the palm of my hand. In a matter of minutes we shared our life's stories, hopes, and dreams as we stared at the stars above us.

"Wait a minute," I said as I turned the lantern back on. "I never ate my dessert." "Are you really hungry?" Robert asked as a puzzling expression filled his face.

"Yes, I'm still hungry,. I hope nobody ate it." I buttoned my shirt up and put on my jacket. Robert shook his head back and forth as though he had no idea what to think or say as he said, "Okay, let's get dessert."

As I unzipped the tent I stopped and turned back to face Robert. "Thank you," I said, " you're quite a gentleman—thank you very much." Then I softly kissed him on the cheek.

"Thank you, Mary," he said as he held on to my arm. "What are you thanking me for?" I asked as I looked deep into his eyes. "For being you." He pulled me back inside the tent and wrapped his arms around me so tight I could barely breath, and then he kissed me long and hard.

I pulled away from him and said, "Wow, I think I need a cold shower. I'm going to seduce you right here and right now, if you kiss me like that again." My heart was pounding as I stood up and said, "I'm going outside to cool off."

The cold air raced across my face as I stepped outside. It felt good and it slowed my racing heart. "It's gotten a lot colder. I'm going to get another shirt on." Robert said as he headed down hill to his tent. "I'm going to get my dessert," I said as I headed downhill towards the food tables. "I'll meet you at the fire," I said as we walked away in different directions.

As I approached the tables where I had left my dessert one of the woman cooks said, "Hello, there, did your friends find you?" She looked around for Robert and said, "I found some soda water for your friend's jacket. Does he still need it?" "No," I said as I tried to keep a straight face, "I think I permanently ruined his jacket."

The tables were clean and empty. "Oh, yes," she continued, "I put your dessert in a cooler so the dogs wouldn't eat it. It's in that blue one over there." "Thank you," I said as I hurried towards the cooler.

"Listen up, folks!" Matt's piercing voice got my attention as I headed over to the fire. His hands were straight up high over his head and he was standing close to the blazing fire. "Tomorrow we won't leave here until eight o'clock. If all goes well, we should be home by 4.00 pm. Our victory dinner has been moved from 8.00 pm to 6.00 pm.

"One more thing, folks—this is important, listen up. We might hit some weather on the south side of the mountains tomorrow, so bring your heavy jackets and rain gear."

He put his hands down, and in a more friendly voice he said, Folks, this is my uncle, Pat. He's gonna to wake you folks up, aren't you, Pat?" "Or," he added as he playfully slapped the short white-haired man on the back, "or, put you all to sleep."

A young man who couldn't have been older than eighteen walked over and sat down next to the older man. He was carrying a saxophone and as he got closer to the fire the shiny chrome on his instrument picked up the colorful reflections. As his music flowed the notes came to life and danced in reflections of golden colors on his saxophone.

After a few minutes both men stood up and slowly walked around the crowd taking requests for songs.

I sat back down in the same chair that I had eaten in earlier. Jane and Gloria's chairs were empty. I looked around for them. I still had a lot of questions that I wanted to ask them.

Even in the light of an almost full moon it was difficult to recognize anyone more than a few feet away from me. An occasional flare up from the fire added enough light to clearly see a face or two. All of us were bundled up in layers of warm clothing from head to toe.

Robert appeared from the darkness and said, "Do you mind if I sit here?" as he stood next to the chair that Jane had sat in earlier. "Why would I mind?" I asked him as I looked up.

"I just wanted to be sure," he said as he plopped down in the chair so hard I thought he would fall through it. "What a day," he said with a long sigh. "Sure about what?" I asked as I dug into my dessert and watched the musicians.

"Here, have a swig of this stuff." A hand appeared out of the darkness with a glass bottle in it. "A couple of swigs of this stuff and all of your aches and pains will disappear."

Robert almost dropped the bottle as the wrangler let go of it. The voice said, "Pass it around," as it vanished back into the darkness.

"Why not?" I said as Robert handed me the bottle. I took a tiny sip and started coughing as I swallowed it. "You people actually drink this stuff?" I said in between coughs.

I handed the bottle back to Robert. He took three big swigs from it and handed it back to me again. "I don't think Jack Daniels and strawberry shortcake mix." I said as my half-closed eyes passed the heavy bottle to a wrangler sitting a few feet to the left of me.

As the bottle disappeared into the darkness of the crowd, I could hear everybody's voices as it was passed to them. "What's this?" one person asked. "Give him another shot," a giddy, loud voice yelled out. "That's smooth," another deep voice said.

The crowd reminded me of a bunch of teenagers at a

bonfire passing bottles of alcohol around and daring each other to take another drink.

The music and the liquor flowed. My energy returned and in between yawns I started clapping to the music. Maybe it was from the liquor or perhaps from the huge amount of sugar I had just consumed. For some reason, I didn't feel tired anymore and I would have gotten up and danced if my ankle would have let me.

The Jack Daniels bottle was half empty when it was passed around back at me. I unscrewed it, smelled it, and closed my eyes as I took a mouthful; it burned my throat as it went down. "That will warm you up," Robert said as he watched me. "It's as smooth as it gets."

I passed the opened bottle back to Robert. He didn't wipe the top, he just turned it upside down and drank it. "You really like that stuff, don't you?" I asked as he passed it on.

"In my younger days, yes," he said as he nodded his head. "I drank a lot of it when I was on the rodeo circuit." He leaned a little closer to me and quietly said, "I'll be honest with you, Mary, I haven't had that stuff in twenty years. I hope I can find my way back to my tent."

"I think you're already drunk," I quietly whispered as I leaned closer to him and said, "Are you sure you don't want to go back to my tent?" Robert sat up, a little straighter in his chair and said, "Let's dance."

"I can't," I said. "My ankle is still really sore. I'd love to, but I can't."

"Go, go, go!" The people on the other side of the fire were getting louder and louder as they all yelled, "Go! Go! Go!"

We all picked up our chairs and shifted them so we could see what was happening.

Two women were climbing up onto a dilapidated picnic table. It groaned and wobbled as they climbed up.

"Play us an Irish jig," one woman shouted as she attempted to stand up. I recognized her voice it was Jane.

"Bring it on!" the other woman yelled as she unzipped her jacket and twirled it around and around high up in the air.

"Robert, look," I said. "That's Jane and Gloria. The musicians started playing a much faster song. The crowd started clapping in rhythm to the music.

Jane and Gloria held on to each other's shoulders as they balanced each other and kicked their legs up, high into the air.

The crowd went crazy. Everybody around them stood up and started dancing. Most of them were pretty tipsy and half of them ran into each other as they hooted and hollered and stomped their feet, cheering the women on.

The old table that they were dancing on was swaying left and right as they hopped around on it. They both stumbled a couple of times as the table kept shifting. It didn't deter them—they just laughed louder as they held each other up.

Most everybody around me was still seated in his or her chairs. We were all content to stomp our feet and clap our hands to the music.

As the song ended, a man shouted out another request towards the musicians. He helped Jane and Gloria off of the table.

When the new song started, he leaped onto the table. The crowd roared as he found his balance.

"Take it off!" an older woman yelled as the man started dancing. "Take it off!"

I glanced at Robert. He caught my eye and winked at me. He reached over and squeezed my hand.

These people were all a little crazy. Most of them had been thrown or hurt by their horses. Every one of them was bruised and sunburn. None of them had a full night's sleep in four days. Yet there wasn't a person amongst them who was feeling sorry for him—or herself. They were all clapping, dancing, and laughing.

I wondered if in the Old West, after surviving through an impossible day, they had magical moments like this. I hoped so, because it was exactly what was needed to rekindle our   spirits and drive.

A cold blast of air swirled around my ears sending chills up and down my neck. I didn't want to miss a minute of the entertainment, but my eyes and body had convinced me that it was time to get some sleep.

I stood up and bent down to quietly say good night to Robert; his eyes were closed. I thought about waking him up and walking him back to his tent until I realized I didn't know where his tent was.

"Good night," I quietly said to the few people watching me as I stood up. I turned on my flashlight and headed to the warmth of my tent.

The music and laughter must have lasted until the wee hours of the morning. I passed out the second my head touched my pillow.

At four in the morning I woke up in a panic. I thought I was late. It took me the rest of the night to convince my racing heart, that it was okay, to sleep in, past four in the morning. In only three days I had conditioned myself, to get up and move fast long before dawn.

Chapter Fifteen

A small bird landed on the top of my tent and serenaded me awake. I was still totally dressed from my jacket to my boots. As I unzipped my tent sunlight blinded me, but it was a welcome change from darkness.

Our campsite was extremely quiet. My ears were drawn to a wrangler chopping and adding wood to a dying fire.

I could smell fresh coffee brewing. I took a couple of deep breaths and let them out slowly. The cold air and the fragrant smell of pine trees were invigorating. I found my coffee cup and headed down the hill.

I was surprised to see trash littered all over our campsite. I didn't remember it being windy last night. I must have missed a heck of a party, I thought, as I walked through it. Where was everybody?

Two women were cracking eggs open and cleaning off the tables. "Wow," I said as I poured myself a cup of coffee, "you guys must have really partied last night, what did I miss?"

One woman kept on working while the other one looked up at me and said, "We didn't make this mess—the damned bear did. Didn't you hear him last night?"

"Bear? What bear? When?"

The other woman raised her head a few inches as she said, "I'm so tired." She took a deep breath as she said, "I don't think

I've slept a wink." "Me either." Their heads hung low as they went back to work.

I headed over to the warmth of the fire. "Good morning," I cheerfully said, as I sat down close to where the wrangler was chopping wood.

"Long night," he said as he kept splitting wood. "Did we really have a bear here last night?" I asked as I sipped my coffee.

He didn't answer me. I wasn't sure if he heard me or not, he just kept working. I would have walked around and picked up some of the trash but my ankle wasn't real happy with me this morning. I should have taken my boots off last night and medicated it.

I stayed in the shade of the tall pine trees and watch the sunrise. The hot coffee and crackling fire soothed and warmed my weary bones.

Matt had said that today was going to be an easy ride. With the aches and pains I was already feeling this morning, I was hoping he was right.

I thought about last night and the special dinner party we were all going to attend tonight.

Somehow late this afternoon we were all going to find enough energy to drive back into town, a good hour and a half away, and get a hotel room and get cleaned and dressed and show up to a dinner party at six.

Right now it sounded way to ambitious for me. A hot, very long shower followed by beer and delivered pizza sounded much more appealing.

Slathering my face all day long with sun blocker yesterday really helped. I had thought it was in vain because after a while, I felt like I was applying sandpaper to my face as I rubbed more and more layers of it onto my dirty skin. It burned with each application and I wasn't really sure if I was helping or hurting myself.

I'm not sure how fried your skin has to be to have second-degree burns, I just know that when the sun's rays touched my face it hurt and burned. My skin was on fire.

Today the redness and swelling around my eyes had all but disappeared, and when I applied a thick layer of sun blocker this morning it didn't burn or irritate my skin.

Matt had said that we were going up to a higher elevation today. I wasn't going to take any chances. I applied a second layer of sun blocker as I sat in the shade of the trees and watched the morning fire.

I took my boot off and unwrapped my ankle. The dark, black color has spread down all the way to my toes and up my shin. A wrangler walked by me and dropped more wood in the fire. He noticed my foot as I warmed it by the fire.

"That looks pretty bad. Did you have Matt look at it?" "No," I said, it looks worse than it feels; it only hurts when I walk on it." It looked pretty bad, so I put my sock back on before anybody else saw it.

No one was up but the crew and me. I drank coffee and quietly watched the sun as it slowly lit up the countryside below us. My mind drifted as I thought about how fond I was of Robert and how comfortable I was in his arms. I thought about my husband Steven and my two children. I thought about all of the decisions I was going to have to make tonight.

As the sun rose, tents slowly unzipped and weary riders stumbled out. Pleasant greetings, or, "good mornings" were scarce. I don't know how many people stayed up and partied last night, but by the way everyone was slowly moving I would guess most of them.

I wasn't a morning person either, yet in the last four days I had been transformed into one. How could I have changed this much in only four days? Was it Robert? Or perhaps it was because of all of the sugar I was consuming?

Steven, my husband, was very hyper and a morning person. When I would tumble out of bed at six in the morning he would already be up and on the phone. He would throw so much information at me before I had a cup of coffee, it would make my head spin.

Robert, on the other hand, was calm and moved at a much slower pace. I think that's part of the reason I was so attracted to him—he reminded me, of me.

As I stared into the flickering flames, I thought about all of the wonderful amenities that awaited me in a hotel, just a few hours from now.

Although I had only been away from the real world for, four days, it seemed more like months. Simple pleasures like hot and running water sounded nothing short of a miracle right now. I had never really thought about my lifestyle or how much I had taken it for granted.

When I had signed up for this trip my husband was very disappointed that I would not take a cell phone with me. If I had, Matt would have probably thrown it out or I would have dropped it or almost got myself killed while trying to ride and talk at the same time.

"Look what I found," an excited voice from behind me shouted. It startled me and I dropped my coffee cup.

"Were you sleeping?" Robert walked over and picked my cup off of the ground as he said, "Mary, are you awake?"

I slowly replied, "I must have dozed off. I was thinking about a bathtub and a real bed. I can't wait to get to a hotel."

"Look!" Robert held his hand up and said, "Look what I found." His hand was holding and displaying a pair of sunglasses.

"You found your sunglasses," I said as I yawned. "Where were they?"

"One of the cooks found them. I must have taken them off and left them on a table. Today is going to be a great day." The excitement in Robert's voice and the smile on his face pulled me away from all of my thoughts.

"Well, you're in a good mood." I held back a smile until after I teasingly said, "I thought that after all of that liquor you drank last night that you would be sick and walking around like a zombie today."

"That stuff you put on my face stopped the burning. It really worked, thank you so much, Mary. And the Jack Daniels, that's great stuff. It warmed me up and knocked me out. I slept like a baby and this morning I feel like a new man."

"You're right," I said as I stood up. "Today is going to be a great day. I'm starving—let's go get some breakfast."

"What's with all of this trash?" Robert asked as he dodged paper plates and napkins on the ground.

"I guess a bear tore our camp apart last night. Did you hear it?"

"No, I dozed off last night when the music was playing. When I woke up you were gone, so I stumbled to bed and didn't wake up until about half an hour ago."

"I thought I missed a party," I said. "I can't believe I slept through a bear tearing this place apart like this. That's the last time I'm touching Jack Daniels."

"Mary, you barely had a shot. I'm telling you, it's good stuff, it sooths the aching heart and bones."

"That sounds like an ad from television. Did you make that up?" Robert stopped in his tracks and said, "I thought you weren't a morning person. How come you got up so early this morning?"

"You know, I was just thinking about that myself. I don't know why, I guess I just couldn't sleep."

Robert took his sunglasses off and looked deeply into my eyes as he said, "Do you still want to meet me tonight, Mary?" I hesitated as I thought about his question and then I said, "Yes, do you still want to meet me tonight?" He put his sunglasses back on and without hesitation he said, "Yes, I'm looking forword to it."

He reached over and gently squeezed my right hand. The two women who were cooking breakfast were watching us.

"How did you like my coffee this morning?" one of the women asked as she held the coffee pot up to pour me another cup. "I made it extra strong?" She glanced at Robert and then winked at me as she filled my cup. "It's great," I replied. "This is my third cup." Both women were moving a little faster and seemed in better spirits.

"I'm starved," Robert said as he piled his plate with eggs and bacon. "I don't eat like this at home; there must be something in the air up here."

"Me neither," I said as I followed him around the table. "I don't think I've eaten this much meat in an entire year."

I looked up from the table and smiled as I said," Thank you ladies for feeding us so well. We really appreciate all of your hard work." Robert stopped loading his plate and added, "Ladies, it's been my pleasure."

They both winked at us as we turned around and headed back towards the fire.

"That was really thoughtful, Mary. Thank you, I wouldn't have remembered to thank them."

"Well," I said as I bit a piece of bacon, "I don't know when I will see them again. And I don't think I would have gotten through this trip without all of the brownies and sweets that they made. Small things like that are really important to me."

Robert didn't take his eyes off of me all the way back to the fire. I wasn't sure why; it kind of made me feel uncomfortable.

"How late did you stay up last night?" I asked as we sat down. "Before or after I fell asleep in my chair?" He said as he grinned. "I think it was about midnight."

"What time did you go to bed, Mary?" "I don't know," I said. "I think about the fourth time that I was tempted to drink the Jack Daniels as it was passed around. And," I said with a giggle, "I'm glad I didn't. Everybody looks terrible this morning. They're all walking around like zombies."

Robert stared at me as a serious look filled his face and he said, "You're a really nice person, Mary. You don't have a pretentious bone in your body, do you?"

"Where did that come from?" I said as I thought about what he had said. "That's pretty deep, I bet you like poetry, don't you?" "Yes, I do, how did you know that?"

Robert was popping bacon into his mouth like it was candy. "You know you'll never keep that great body of yours if you keep consuming bacon like that." I watched him for a few more seconds and jokingly added, "Why, I can feel you're arteries hardening as you eat it."

Robert raised his eyebrows and grabbed two more pieces of bacon. He lifted them above his head and slowly dropped them into his mouth. "Your cholesterol level just went up," I said as I tried to keep a straight face while watching him.

"Is that how you eat bacon up here?" A loud familiar voice asked. It was Jane—both Robert and I turned to greet her.

"Can you hold this while I sit down?" Jane handed me a plate filled with scrambled eggs. "How's your wrist today?" I asked as I handed the plate back to her. "My wrist feels fine, but my head hurts like hell." She slowly picked up her coffee mug and said, " That was quite a party last night. Where did you two disappear to?"

Robert and I glanced at each other as Jane said, "Well, you two obviously had more fun than I did—I must be losing my touch. Why, I couldn't even hook up with a wrangler last night. So I made love to Jack Daniels instead."

Although she sounded dead serious, her frankness was funny. "Jane, you put on quite a show last night. I was sure that you and Gloria were going to end up back in the hospital. You must have tripped a dozen times while you were dancing on that table."

"Yeah, that was fun. Do you guys have any aspirin?" She lowered her head and started rubbing her forehead.

"I've got Extra Strength Tylenol, will that work?" Without lifting her head she said, "Do you have anything stronger?" "No," and then I said, "Vicodin is much stronger, why don't you take some more of that?"

Jane slowly lifted her head up and said, "I already took two of those. They didn't help—wait a minute—how did you know I had vicodin?"

I picked up my cup of coffee and pretended to take a slow sip as I searched for an answer. Robert's eyes were glued to my face as I said, "Robert and I were trying out my goose down sleeping bag last night when you and Gloria walked right by our tent looking for us."

"Oh," she said, "How was it?" "How was what?" I asked. "The sleeping bag." She said in a testy loud voice, "How was the sleeping bag?"

Robert shook his head as though he had no idea what I was

talking about. I shrugged my shoulders as though I didn't either and I don't think Jane had any idea what anyone was talking about.

"Did you find those pills yet?" she asked as she lowered her head again. I smiled and winked at Robert as I said, "Hang in there, Jane, I'll go get them for you right now."

As I stood up a young, slender woman sat down on the other side of Jane and said, "You sure got us going last night . . . that was fun—what did you say your name was?"

Without lifting her head up Jane said, "My head's killing me. Do you have any aspirin?" "No, but," her voice got an octave higher and her eyes lit up as she said, "I've got something a lot better than aspirin, as long as you have food in your stomach. It's really good, it will take you anywhere that you want to go."

I listened to her and decided that whatever she had, probably would work better than what I had. I sat back down and said, "Thank you, can I help you get it?" "No, I'll be right back." She sprang out of her chair and ran back to a tent.

She stopped a few feet away from us and shouted, "Don't let anybody eat my breakfast."

The chairs around the campfire were nearly all filled by the time she got back.

Everyone was being so quiet it was almost eerie. The only noise to be heard was the sound of metal forks as they scraped plates. I was having fun communicating with Robert by simple jests and body language. He kept teasing me by raising his eyebrows and rolling his eyes. We were the only two people of this entire group who were awake and enjoying ourselves.

Even Matt was walking slowly this morning. "We're a little late, folks." He spoke so quietly I could barely hear what he said. H cleared his throat and in a much louder voice said, "I see you all survived last night." A slight grin crept onto his face. "We're a little late this morning, folks. We had a bear in camp last night. He made sure that none of my crew or I got a wink of sleep. Take your time, we'll mount up in about an hour."

"If any of you are packed and ready to go, you can walk

down to the corral and help saddle the horses." His grin disappeared as fast as it appeared. He looked like a cop directing traffic as he pointed and hollered at crew members sending them out all over the camp in different directions.

Gloria had joined us and was talking to the young woman who had brought back pills for Jane. Her head was also hung very low and her movements were sluggish.

Robert noticed her slow movement and quietly said, "Maybe they were drinking something different than we were." "No," I said as I shook my head in disagreement. "They just had a lot more." I grinned at him and said, "I'm going to stick to margaritas tonight."

"I'm out of here," I added as I stood up. "I'm going to help saddle the horses. I feel bad I didn't even thank Icky last night when I got off of him, shame on me."

The tent wrangler was already pulling out the metal pegs holding my tent down. My sleeping bag and air mattress were neatly packed beside it. "Thank you, for all of your help." I said as I watched him. "I heard you didn't get much sleep last night." He stopped what he was doing and looked up. He had dark circles under his eyes and a frown deeply embedded on his face that made him look ten years older. "Thank you," I said again as I picked up my gear and jacket.

Chapter Sixteen

Our horses were in a flat clearing, down a hill, about a half a mile away.

White flowers and waist-high green shrubs dominated my path downhill. I huffed and puffed and never thought my legs would carry me up this path yesterday afternoon. The trail was a lot friendlier this morning.

The flowers grew in and around the shrubs and were in full bloom. I stopped to smell them. They had a sweet, mild fragrance and the petals were sticky. A couple of bees quickly let me know that they were off limits.

The heat from the sun had me peeling layers of clothes off long before I made it to the bottom of the hill.

Two wranglers were lifting and slapping saddles on the backs of horses. The animals' weight shifted as the saddles landed. It looked a little harsh to me.

The horses were lined up like an assembly line. They didn't seem to mind the abruptness and quick movement of the men.

I stayed my distance from them for a few minutes while I watched them. I wasn't sure if I would fit in with their assembly line saddling.

"Do you need any help?" I finally asked in a wimpy girly voice. "Do you know how to put bridles on?" one of the wranglers asked as he slapped another saddle down hard on a horse's back.

"Sure," I replied in a much more confident voice. "Okay, there on the saddle horns." I thought a minute about what he had said. I guessed the word "okay" meant, get to work.

I walked over to the far end of the line of horses where they had started. The animals were tied only a few inches apart from each other. I was cautious and very uncomfortable squeezing in between them, to reach their bridles. If the thousand-pound animals shifted the wrong way and I could have been flattened like a pancake. I kept my ears open and a keen eye on their feet.

The horses and mules remained calm as I slowly and gently put the bits in their mouths and pulled the headstalls over their ears. I stroked each one's mane and talked to them before I asked them to accept the bit.

After seeing how harsh the saddles were thrown on, I wondered how rough the wranglers would have been putting these bits into the horses mouths.

Every one of them was incredibly receptive to my gentle touch. As soon as I pulled the bridle off of the saddle horn, they would lower their heads and open their mouths. Not an animal amongst them refused the hard metal bits.

It was amazing how quickly I bridled all of them. I caught up to the wranglers and had to slow my pace as I waited for horses to be saddled.

The wranglers groaned as they picked up and lifted the heavy saddles above their heads before they plopped them straight down on the horses' backs. Then they buckled and tightened all of the loose leather in fluid motion as though they were just simply tying a shoe.

Back home it took me about half an hour to get my horse saddled. These guys were doing it in about five minutes.

Icky recognized me when I put his bit into his mouth. He lowered his neck and almost laid it on my shoulder as I gave him a neck massage. By the way he was reacting I could tell that this was quite a welcome treat for him. If I had a horse brush with me, I would have spoiled him rotten. He actually closed his eyes as I massaged his mane.

"You're going to spoil that horse," One of the wranglers hollered. "That's a good thing," I shouted back. "They need to be spoiled."

I walked over to where the last of the animals were being saddled. They were all mules. I had never put a bit on a mule before. Their ears were long and soft to the touch. They were much more alert then the horses and I could tell that each one had its own distinctive personality.

One played with his bit after I put it on him. Another kept his ears pinned back the entire time I was around him. I nick-named him "Grumpy."

The wranglers were young and thin and men of few words. None of them wore gloves and all of them wore cowboy hats.

They were perfect gentlemen and consistently said "Yes, ma'am" or "No, ma'am," whenever any of us talked to or asked them a question. They weren't like any young Californians I knew. I wondered how many of them were from other states.

After I got the last bit in the mule's mouth, I walked back over and hid in the shade of the tall pine trees. The sky was dark blue and clear and the air was crisp and clean.

"Hi!" A man walked over and extended his right arm to shake my hand. "I'm Hank and that's my fiancée, Tammy. It's so pretty up here—would you mind taking a picture of us on our horses?"

I had seen him at camp a couple of times and I recognized his fiancée—we met two nights ago. She had mentioned that she was from New York. Neither of them sounded like New Yorkers and they both were in very good shape. I pegged them to be in their early thirties.

"Sure," I said with a smile. I looked around for the perfect setting. "Over there," I said as I pointed to a patch of dark green grass with snow-covered mountains as my backdrop.

"Perfect," I said as I positioned their horses so I could see their faces. "Lift your hats up, I can't see your faces. . .good. . . hold it." The picture was so pretty it looked like a postcard. The dark greens and colorful cloths and the snowy mountain looked too perfect to be real.

"Please, take one of me. I'm still upset that I couldn't bring my camera, please." I was having fun telling people to raise their hats or to hold their horse's head higher. I felt like I was playing the game, "Simon Says": "Everybody move a few feet to the right. . . no. . . you in the back, move to the left." Actually, I had no idea what I was doing, but I sure sounded like I did. Before I knew it, I had gone through two rolls of film and I had made a dozen new friends.

Over the past three days I was the only one in our entire group who carried a camera when we were riding. I brought ten rolls of film with me and gladly clicked whatever anybody wanted me to whenever I had a free hand or moment. The word must have spread around. I think I had become our group's company photographer.

"Mount up!" Matt's powerful voice was back. "Mount up, folks!"

I carefully tied my satchel and camera back onto my saddle. Icky was calm and didn't move a muscle when I checked and tightened his cinch.

The last three mornings as we let the herd loose they fought each other for positions in line. Today was different. They were all calm and content to walk butt to butt without a fuss.

Icky woke up as he heard and saw the herds' movement. "Not yet," I said as I turned him away from the herd and kicked him in the gut, reminding him who was boss. He immediately stopped pulling on his reins and patiently waited his turn.

I was happy to see that Robert, Jane, and Gloria had decided to ride in the back with me today. The wrangler couple that I rode with yesterday was also back here.

I never knew who would stay to bring up the back of the herd. As the horses and mules moved out, so did most of the riders. I think most of us really weren't sure what part of the herd we were going to ride with until we were caught up in the actual movement of the animals.

Once again we headed out in single file. First down a long

set of rolling hills dotted with tall, shady, pine trees. Then we took a sharp curve left and zigzagged up the side of a steep mountain.

As our assent sharpened, we had to stop about every half an hour and let our horses rest. I could tell that the air was thinning by the way Icky was breathing. Yesterday as we climbed, his nostrils flared. Today his entire midsection was visibly moving in and out as he grabbed for air.

The trail was just as brutal on his feet. Large rocks formed our path like an endless set of stairs.

Each step up had to be carefully chosen. Icky led with his front right leg and followed with his left. When his front legs were securely set in place he would lunge forward, pulling his back legs up the step. The metal shoes on his feet tore into the rocks as he found his footing.

Yesterday morning five horses were tied away from the rest of the herd. A wrangler was shoeing them. I didn't understand why they weren't joining us; now I knew why. Without shoes on these animals would have been lame long before our day ended.

I hadn't checked Icky's feet. I really didn't even think about them, I wish I had. If he was to throw a shoe up here I don't know what I would do. There's not way I could physically walk up this steep of a terrain.

The way the horses were huffing and puffing I half expected them to pass out. Their labored breathing was muffled by the loud clanging noise beneath their feet as they struggled up the rocks.

Whenever our terrain opened up into a flat clearing, large enough for all of us to rest, we would get off of our animals and let them catch their breaths.

Each time we stopped we were instructed to drink water, even if we weren't thirsty.

Matt had put the fear of God into us about altitude sickness and how the thinning air could cause us to hallucinate and or pass out. We were told that drinking water every thirty minutes or so would help.

My canteen was empty long before we stopped on flat ground where we could get off of our horses and refuel. When we finally stopped to rest, I urged Icky forward towards the mule who was carrying our water.

Two mules blocked our movement and cut us off. We were on a long, rocky clearing that water was flowing through and around. Shallow pools of it formed small ponds. The horses and mules made a beeline for them. Icky fought me as I headed him away from it, in a different direction towards water for my canteen.

I could see the mule carrying our drinking water. He was nibbling on a small patch of grass a short distance away. A wrangler was untying the heavy plastic bottles that were lashed to both sides of his back.

Icky fought me; he was thirsty and wanted water. I kicked him hard and forced him closer to the mule. I wasn't about to get off of him and walk uphill. He would just have to wait till I got a drink, first.

My canteen was small, about the size of a plastic water bottle. This was the third time I was filling it today.

"Fill her up," I said as I handed the wrangler my bottle. "Yes, ma'am," he said as he lifted a heavy, round bottle of water like it was a feather pillow. With amazing accuracy he slowly filled my small bottle without spilling a drop. My back ached just watching him as he lifted the awkward, heavy bottle high in the air and carefully poured it out.

I would have broken my back if I had lifted and held up that heavy of a bottle as patiently and for as long as he did.

"Ma'am, is that your horse?" The wrangler put the bottle down and pointed past me. I turned around. Icky was already a good ten feet away from me. He had positioned himself in between two mules and was walking step for step with them. If I didn't know better, I would have sworn that he was sneaking away and they were helping him.

"Icky, stop!" I yelled in an angry voice. "You don't even like mules!"

"Yep, that's Icky," the wrangler said with a chuckle. "Did

you see that?" I turned back towards the wrangler. He lowered his hat and pretended he didn't even hear me.

"I can't believe this!" I yelled out. I knew Icky was thirsty and my ankle was too sore to chase him. I watched him walk away. I figured he wouldn't go to far.

I slowly followed him and his two new buddies. As I followed them, my sore ankle reminded me, with every step, that I should have never let him out of my eyesight.

Although I was upset, I wasn't mad. I was fascinated with my horse. Was he this smart? He knew I wouldn't get in between two mules, and I knew he didn't even like mules. A smile crept onto my face as I limped after him.

His lead rope was dragging on the ground. I figured I could step on it and grab it and pull him away from the mules.

When I got close enough to grab it, I heard Matt shout out, "Mount up, folks! We're behind schedule, folks, mount up."

The front riders got into position as the herd started to move. Oh my God, I thought, I'm going to get trampled.

Icky and the two mules stopped to drink water. He was still tightly wedged in between them. His lead rope was underneath his stomach, dragging on the ground.

I took my hat off and in a loud angry voice shouted, "Get out of here!" as I waved it at the mule closest to me.

He lifted his head up from the water for a few seconds and then he dropped it back down ignoring me.

"Who's that rider over there?" someone yelled in a loud voice. "Get on your horse." A deeper, louder voice shouted, "Get on your horse, now!"

My heart was racing and I still couldn't reach Icky's lead rope. The herd was swirling around me. Icky and the mules didn't move. All three of them kept their heads buried in the water.

"Mary, what are you doing?" Jane stopped her horse and positioned it alongside of me. She whistled and hollered at the herd to keep them a safe distance away from me as they crossed our path. "Hurry up!" she kept shouting. "Get on your horse!'

"I can't! I kept shouting back at her. "I'm afraid to get in between those two mules. I don't want to get kicked or bit."

"That's better than being trampled," she shouted as she whipped her horse with her reins, forcing it to spin in a tight circle. Her horse's head stopped only a few inches away from one of the mule's necks.

She kicked the mule hard in the neck with her right boot, as her horse tried to back away from it. She kicked her horse forward, forcing it almost on top of the mule. The mule pulled his face out of the water. "Look out!" I shouted. "His ears are pinned back, he's going to kick!" "You stupid mule," she yelled in an angry voice, as she kicked him again.

I was too close for comfort, but I had no safe place to go. The mule swung his neck around and snapped at Jane's leg. Jane kicked him again and landed a direct blow on his nose as he turned to bite her again. He kicked his hind legs straight up, high in the air as the force of her boot smacked him.

He backed away from Icky and closer to Jane. It was far enough to expose Icky's lead rope. Without hesitation I ran in front of the mule and grabbed onto the rope. Icky still had his face buried in the water.

My quick movements startled him. He sidestepped to his left, smashing into the mule on the other side of him. The mule pulled his muzzle out of the water and lunged with his mouth wide open at Icky's neck. Jane backed her horse up as I tightened my grip on Icky's lead rope.

Icky pinned his ears back. He was ready to fight. "No!" I yelled. "No, stop it!" I yanked on his lead rope. For a second it distracted him. I yanked on it again.

I took a step closer and used the rope like a whip to slap the mule. "Get out of here!" I shouted as I hit him.

The herd was all but gone. The mule backed away from the water and kicked straight at us, before he took off towards the herd. His buddy next to Jane looked up and ran after him.

"Jane, are you all right?" I knew she was hung over and with a cast on her wrist. I felt bad that I had put her in this scary of a situation.

"What a rush!" she shouted as she checked out her leg. "Did you get bit?" I wanted to walk over and take a closer look at her leg. I didn't have time.

"I'm sorry," I said as I threw my leg over Icky's saddle. "What for?" she said as she lifted her head up. "That was fun."

The herd had disappeared and a wrangler was riding back towards us at a full gallop. I could see Gloria; she was following the wrangler.

"What did I miss?" she shouted in a loud voice, as she reached us. "Not much," Jane shouted back. "Just some stubborn mules and Mary's stupid horse."

I turned Icky around to face Jane. "Are you sure you didn't get bit? That mule looked like he had part of your pants in his mouth. Are you okay?" She didn't answer me.

"Beat you back to the herd," she shouted as she kicked her horse hard for a fast response. "In your dreams!" Gloria yelled back as she kicked her horse into movement.

"Slow down!" the wrangler yelled as their two horses left us in the dust. "Can you ride?" he asked me as he yelled at them over and over again to slow down.

"Yes," I said. Before I could blink, we both took off at a full gallop, chasing Jane and Gloria. I kept Icky a safe distance behind him as I followed in his tracks.

Our path took a sharp curve left and narrowed as we approached a long canyon. Their loud laughter and dares were echoing off of the steep canyon walls directly in front of us.

"You are such a wuss, I would have beat you if our path hadn't narrowed." "In your dreams," Gloria shouted back. "You never could ride. Don't you remember the rodeo last summer?" "You had to bring that up, didn't you? I don't even know why I ride with you. If my horse hadn't thrown that shoe I would have kicked your ass." "In your dreams," Gloria kept repeating, each time in a slightly louder voice.

Hearing their voices echoing around the canyons as they teased each other brought a smile to my face. These two women were best friends and their own worst enemies.

"I won," Gloria, shouted as she turned her horse around to

meet us. "She cheated," Jane, yelled, as she slapped the white cast on Gloria's arm. "That hurt," Gloria, yelled as she backed her horse away from Jane's.

"Don't run these animals like that again!" the wrangler shouted out in a deep angry voice as he slowed his horse down to a walk. He was mad and he let them know it. He stopped his horse and glared at them both as he eyeballed their horses. Then he urged his horse forward and rode away.

"Mary," Gloria said in a whisper of a voice, "you told us it was okay to run. What's his problem?"

"Don't look at me," I said, "Icky and I get into enough trouble, all by ourselves."

I looked at the white cast on Jane and Gloria's arms and as a grin filled my face I said, "At least we all have a souvenirs to take home." I pointed at their arms and held my leg up and pointed at my ankle.

"Bring it on!" Jane shouted out in a loud, proud voice. Her words echoed off and around the steep canyon walls. We all started laughing as we heard it.

"Thank God for pain pills," Gloria said as she popped something in her mouth. "This Vicodin is good stuff."

"Wait a minute, this isn't fair," I said as I frowned. "You guys get pain pills and real drugs. How come I only get aspirin?"

Gloria held out her hand, offering me some Vicodin, "No, thank you, but do you mind if I take them for later? I might need them tonight."

Jane positioned her horse close to Icky and said, "Mary, what did you say to me this morning about the Vicodin? My brain was a little hazy then."

"What are you talking about?" Gloria asked. "You promise not to tell?" I asked, as I raised my voice.

"Tell whom?" Jane said in a loud voice that echoed around us. "I don't even know your last name." Gloria shook her head as though in agreement with Jane.

They kept glancing back and forth at each other and then me. "We get it," they both blurted out at the same time. "You hooked up with Robert last night, didn't you?"

"No, no I didn't. I'm really confused. He's everything that my husband isn't. I'm going crazy trying to figure out why I'm so damned attracted to him."

"So, was he good? How long did he let you ride him?" They bombarded me with questions that were all, at best, blunt. I found their frankness refreshing.

I spilled out my guts to them and told them about the plans Robert and I made for tonight. It was nice to have someone to talk to. They both were good listeners and they both had an endless list of advice.

Men were simple to them; they used them and spit them out after they were done. Jane must have slept with half of the men in New Mexico. Gloria admitted trying to sleep with the other half.

They wanted nothing to do with children or settling down. They were living for the moment, and proud of it. They were unique in every sense of the word.

We laughed and teased each other as we told stories and relived the crazy fun of our youth and past. My life seemed so simple and tame compared to theirs.

Chapter Seventeen

In the blink of an eye, clouds rolled in and the sun vanished.

A large, icy raindrop slapped me on the back, sending chills up and down my spine. "What the . . .?" I looked up. Another raindrop hit my cheek, then my eye. I pulled my hat lower, tighter to my face as a heavy rain began to fall.

"Where the hell did this come from?" Gloria loudly yelled out. "Where's the thunder and lightning? Back home we at least get a warning." "Damn! The rain is cold up here," Jane added.

All of our raincoats were tightly rolled up and attached to the back of our saddles. Thin leather straps that looked like shoelaces held them down, tied, securely in place.

As I rode, I tried to untie mine. The leather was wet and so were my gloves. "This isn't working," I complained as I looked up to see if Gloria or Jane were having any better luck—they weren't.

"I'm stopping," I hollered as the freezing water pelted my clothes. I knew we weren't supposed to stop for, "anything," but I was freezing and my teeth were chattering. "Stop!" I shouted as loud as I could as Jane and Gloria kept on riding. My voice was lost in the downpour.

I held Icky's reins with my left hand as I tugged on the knots with my right. They wouldn't budge. I took my glove off and tried again, nothing worked. My right hand started to shake as the cold water hit it. I needed to use both of my hands.

Icky kept swinging his head around looking at me as I stood next to his rear end. I dropped his reins and grabbed the other end of the knot with my left hand. "All right!" I shouted as one of two knots finally loosened up.

As I reached over his butt to untie the second knot, I startled him, and he bolted forward. "Oh, no!" I shouted. "Stay Icky, stay! Whoa!" I grabbed for his reins and missed them.

My jacket was still halfway attached to the saddle. I grabbed ont o it as Icky moved away from me. It was slippery, but I got a good grip on it. I was hoping the knot keeping it tied on my saddle would hold and that I could stop him.

"Easy boy, easy boy," I said as I held tightly on to the jacket as he started to walk away from me. I yanked on the jacket to stop his forward movement. It slowed him down and I could almost reach his reins, they were only a few inches from me. I was afraid to let go of the jacket in an attempt to grab the reins. If I missed, he would be gone, along with my jacket.

A loud clap of thunder sent my heart racing even faster. I grabbed at the reins with my right hand. I touched them but I couldn't hold on to them; roke away from the saddle and flew at me.

Icky was free and he knew it. He broke into a trot as he ran away. "No! No, stop!" I screamed as my heart pounded out of my chest.

I hurriedly wrapped my shivering body in my raincoat and pulled the hood tight to my face as I zipped it up. I put my wet gloves back on over my shaking hands and tucked them deep into my jacket's pockets.

My horse was gone. I was alone, somewhere in the mountains and being pelted by freezing rain. A terrible feeling crept over me.

The dampness and cold air worsened the pain in my ankle. I walked as fast as my injured body would let me; each step was excruciating.

I fought back tears, I wanted to scream, I wanted to go home. My emotion, ran wild as I tried to block out the pain and catch up to my horse.

"Mary, where are you? Can you hear me?" I sniffled and stopped walking to listen. "Can you hear me?" The voice shouted again.

The rain slowed to a drizzle and the sun reappeared as fast as it had disappeared. I plopped down on a flat rock to catch my breath. The sun felt good. I looked up and let it dry my face.

"She's over here," someone shouted. I should have stood up and waved my hands. I didn't. I was out of breath and my body felt like it weighed a thousand pounds.

"What are you doing? Are you hurt?" When I heard Gloria's voice, my eyes filled with tears. I was embarrassed and upset with myself. I took a couple of deep breaths to hold the tears back as I gathered my thoughts.

"Did you loose your horse again?" she teased as she stopped her horse a few feet away from me. She was pulling Icky, he was directly behind her.

"Does everybody know?" I asked as I wiped a tear from my eye. "No, just Jane, and she's in worse shape than you are."

"What? What happened to Jane?" I took another deep breath and stood up. The sun was already shining in full blaze and the sky was clear except for a few dark puffy clouds.

She held out Icky's reins as she slowly said, "Are you sure you're not hurt?"

"Only my pride," I said as I limped over to grab the reins. "We better catch up." Jane turned her horse around and urged him forward. "Everybody is held up in a clearing up ahead— we're stopping to have lunch there."

I checked Icky's cinch and wiped off the beads of water on his saddle. He let out a loud moaning noise as I plopped my bottom into the saddle.

"Let's go," Gloria said as she took off up a steep embankment. I didn't hesitate. I urged Icky forward and stayed on her horse's tail. "How far is it?" I asked as our horses slowed up the steep slope.

"I don't remember," Gloria replied as she looked around the countryside. "It looks different now."

"Don't say things like that, I'm already a nervous wreck," I shouted back at her. "You're joking, right?"

My heart had stopped racing but my thoughts were still mixed up and moving a thousand miles an hour. "Where did you say Jane was? Did you say she got hurt, again?"

Everything had happened so fast that I wasn't sure if it had been real. Had I been daydreaming? Matt had warned us about altitude sickness. Did this really just happen?

"Gloria," I shouted out in a loud voice, "what just happened?" Gloria glanced back at me and said, "Mary, you're not making any sense, you need to drink more water."

On her cue I drained the rest of my canteen. It didn't help. I didn't feel any better or different. I was as confused as ever.

"There they are!" Gloria excitedly shouted as she pointed towards a long, green valley, "I'm starving."

Lunch—I hadn't eaten lunch yet? It had to be later than lunchtime. Matt had said today would be an easy day. I wanted to feel a soft pillow. I wanted to soak in that tub I had been dreaming about. It couldn't only be noon.

The herd was grazing in a long, narrow valley blanketed in dark green grass. Wranglers and riders were sitting and lying basking in the sunlight.

Gloria and I tied our horses to the closest tree limb we could find by the mule carrying our lunches.

"Where have you been?" a wrangler asked as he handed us our lunch. "We're leaving in five minutes."

We both dug into our brown bags and plopped down on the dirt. I stretched out my wet pants and let my legs bask in the sun. Everyone around me was unzipping their jackets or taking them off.

I inhaled my peanut butter and jelly sandwich in four large bites. I popped cookies in my mouth as fast as my teeth could grind them. A few people walked by me and asked me if I would take pictures of them. I shook my head, no, while I kept on eating.

My canteen was empty and my very dry lunch left me really thirsty. The mule carrying the water was in a clearing about a hundred feet away. A wrangler was already reattaching the water bottles back onto the mule.

"Wait!" I shouted as food flew out of my mouth. "I need water." I swallowed what was left in my mouth and limped over to the mule.

The wrangler had heard me and was untying one of the water bottles. "Thank you, thank you so much." I felt like hugging him, but I thought that everyone would have thought that I was losing whatever sanity I still had left.

I was losing it, whatever, "it," was. I just said, "Thank you," again as he patiently and slowly filled my canteen.

"Are we almost home?" I asked, not sure that I even wanted to hear his reply. "A couple more miles up, then straight down," he replied as he reattached the bottle to the mule's side.

I wanted to ask him what, "straight down," meant. The part of my brain that was still functioning said, no, no, I don't want to know.

Everyone around me was retying their jackets to the back of their saddles and checking their cinches.

My clothes were still damp, so I decided to keep my jacket on. If we were still going "Up" as the wranglers said, I wanted to be prepared.

Jane and Gloria were already on their horses and walking them towards the back of the herd. I looked around for Robert. He was nowhere in sight. I turned Icky around and followed the women to the back of the herd.

In my haste to eat I hadn't noticed how beautiful and picturesque my surroundings were. The sky was painted in layers of deep blue hues. It flowed down onto the tips of towering pine trees that were nestled in a valley of thick grass that was so dark green and level you would have thought that someone had just manicured it.

As I looked around I realized why everyone was asking me

to take a picture—there wasn't a view within my eyesight that wasn't postcard perfect.

As we headed out we rode under the arms and shade of tall pine trees. They were so dense that not even a sliver of sunshine touched us. I was glad I had left my jacket on.

Our green surroundings slowly turned white and got colder as our trail narrowed and we climbed above the tree line.

We followed along the edge of a mountain that carried us higher to the tallest peaks of this entire range.

We were at the top of the world. I didn't hear a bird or see signs of any squirrels or small animals. Everything around me was white and frozen in time.

The clanging of our horses' hooves turned into a crunching noise as their feet plowed through the snow as it deepened. At this point I was glad to be in the back. I felt sorry for the animals in front that had to work much harder clearing the path of snow. They left us a deep cleared trail that was easy to follow.

Above the tree line the sun was shining in a full blaze. The snow seemed out of place. I wanted to stop and play in it. Was it cold? How come it wasn't melting? I thought about getting off of my horse and touching it. "Drink water," a little voice inside of me kept repeating. "Drink more water."

As I stared at the snow my thoughts became twisted as they swirled around in my mind.

I wasn't thirsty and I was tired of drinking water. Right now a cold margarita and a snowball fight sounded great.

How were we going to get back to our base camp by late this afternoon? We were on the top of a mountain at least eleven thousand feet up. It took us a day and a half to get up here.

What did the wrangler say to me when he filled up my canteen? Straight up then straight down, or was it straight down then straight up? I couldn't remember.

None of it sounded like fun. A real bed and a real shower seemed light-years away.

Icky pinned his ears back as our path once again narrowed and we formed an endless single file line. I looked around us and realized that we were smack in the middle of a long line of mules, my least favorite place to be.

"Leave them alone," I said as I patted him on the neck." We're almost home, let's get home, Icky." I knew he heard me because he twisted his left ear towards my voice as I spoke.

The mule directly behind us wanted to be with the mule directly in front of us. Icky let him know that he wasn't going to pass us, at least not now. He repeatedly lifted his tail up and slapped it hard, constantly hitting the mule in the face.

Our path was cold, slippery, and strewn with jagged rocks. If the mule charged us now, it could be disastrous. I kept my eyes peeled at the uphill, uneven surfaces in front of us and hoped that Icky could keep the mule from biting him or trying to pass us.

The snow thinned and disappeared as our path curved to the right and headed into a long set of canyons. Both Icky and I were hoping that the trail would open up into a clearing. We were looking forward to getting away from the mules. It never did.

As we followed the snakes and curves of the canyons, a wind picked up and whistled with a high-pitched, screeching noise. It was an eerie sound and it made me feel very uncomfortable. It echoed around the canyon walls and followed us as we rode.

We were still riding in single file when our trail finally leveled off and dropped, carrying us back down towards the greenery and trees.

I thought that going downhill would be a lot easier, especially on Icky. I was wrong. I could feel his back leg muscles shaking as he slowly and carefully chose his footings.

The mule behind us was annoyed at his slow movement. He was still determined to catch up with his buddies who were now quite a distance in front of us.

I wasn't about to push Icky. We were zigzagging down a mountain and if he slipped or stumbled one or both of us could have fallen off the ledge.

I caught myself leaning as close to the mountain as my saddle would let me.

I knew it didn't help Icky's balance, but it made me feel better. The sheer drop off the cliff kept my heart racing. I kept thinking about a hot bath and cold margaritas in an attempt to slow it down.

The clanging noise from the horses' metal shoes was suddenly shattered by a loud, terrifying, high-pitched scream. It shot through and echoed around the canyons, and sent my heart racing even faster.

Every animal in front of me as far as I could see stopped in their tracks and lifted their head and ears straight up. So did Icky.

A few seconds later I heard a deep voice yell, "Rider down!" at the same time a panicky high-pitched voice screamed, "Rider down! Somebody help her!"

I hated these two words and I had hoped that I would never hear them again. I tried to calm my racing heart as I listened to them echo around the canyons.

I was on a narrow ledge halfway down the side of a mountain. The movement in front of me stopped. I was trapped. There wasn't enough room to turn around and go back up.

A terrible feeling crept over me as I looked over the steep ledge. I was scared stiff. Don't panic, your almost home, I'm sure we'll start moving again. Just close your eyes and relax and stop looking over the edge. My thoughts were racing just as fast as my heart. I closed my eyes and froze in the saddle as my adrenaline flowed.

"Mary," a voice shouted, "move those mules forward." I couldn't see who was yelling at me, but he sounded serious.

"I can't," I shouted back, "all of the mules in front of me are stopped. I can't."

"Kick him hard!" the deep voice hollered back, "Do it now!"

"Kick who?" I didn't know what he meant. I wasn't about to kick Icky. No way, not on this narrow ledge, no.

Before I could gather another thought, I felt Icky's back legs move. I glanced at the mule behind me. His teeth were only inches from Icky's butt. Icky was trying to kick him with his right back leg.

"No, Icky, we'll fall off this narrow cliff—don't kick him!" I yelled in a loud, panicky voice. Without thinking, I kicked Icky hard in the stomach as I leaned back in the saddle. He bolted forward and before he could catch his footing we slammed into the butt of the mule directly in front of us.

Adrenaline shot through me like lightening as my heart was pounding out of my chest.

I grabbed the saddle horn and held on with every ounce of energy I had. We surprised the mule. He swung his head around to get a better look at us.

Icky recovered his footing and bit the mule smack in the middle of his butt. The mule leaped forward and landed on the mule's butt directly in front of him. It created a domino affect, and in a flurry of biting and kicking the mules started moving again.

I slowly loosened the death grip I had on the saddle horn. My left arm and hand were shaking from holding on so tight. I took a couple of deep breaths as I blinked for a few seconds to make sure I was still alive.

Icky stayed a safe distance from the mules in front of us as we once again started our steep descent.

In the shade of the trees ,the ground beneath Icky's feet darkened. It was difficult distancing each downward step. Sometimes it was only a few inches to the next safe step. Other times I had to lean my entire body back, positioning as much of my weight as possible on Icky's back legs, giving him the leveraging he needed to jump down to the next step. I gave him his reins.

I kept thinking about the blood-curdling scream I had just heard. I wondered who it was. I wondered if she was all right. I had so many unanswered questions. I was hoping I would remember some of them tonight at dinner.

I glanced at my watch, it was nearly three o'clock. Wait a minute, wasn't that the time Matt said we would be home? Were we lost?

Most of today we rode through heavily wooded forest. The trees blocked the view of horses and riders alike. I could hear people from time to time as the wind shifted, but I rarely saw anyone except the mules in front and directly behind me.

As the tree trunks thickened our path widened. It was a welcome change. We still had to ride in single file and our descent was still quite steep, but I felt a little safer not having to ride along the edge of a mountain.

I would have felt a lot better if I could get away from all of these mules. And have an extra set of eyes in the back of my head.

Chapter Eighteen

A roar of thunder shook the tree limbs above us. I glanced up and my face was pelted with hard cold rain. It stung and chilled me at the same time.

I tucked my arms and head as tightly as I could inside my jacket as the heavy downpour started. I was hoping the branches of the thick pine trees above us would take the brunt of Mother Nature. They didn't.

A loud popping noise began drowning out the deafening thunder. It was an odd noise. I had never heard anything like it before. I peeked my head out of my jacket and cautiously looked around.

Marble-sized pieces of ice were racing from the sky and exploding as they slapped the ground around us. I tucked my head back into my jacket and curled my body closer towards my saddle.

A second later something slapped my back so hard I almost lost my breath. It must have hit Icky, too, for he tried to lunge forward the instant I was hit. What just hit my back?

It couldn't have been hail. It was too big for hail. I wiped a layer of water off of my sunglasses to get a better look. Something brown the size of a baseball flew by my left leg and smashed into the ground.

The mules in front of me were as confused as we were. They

were crowding each other, moving in different directions and tucking their heads and necks as close as the could to each others.

A familiar fragrance filled the air. I bent my head down to take a closer look at what was falling from the sky. What was that smell? It was a pinecone. It was raining pinecones.

Is this possible? I thought as I stared at the pinecone. Could it really be raining pinecones? None of this was making any sense.

They hurt when they hit —that part was real and Icky and I wanted nothing to do with them.

The mules behind me decided it was time to get past us and join their buddies in front of us.

They recklessly climbed up a steep embankment and ran a few feet before they slid back down, bringing rocks and mud back down with them.

I held Icky back as they came tumbling down only a few feet in front of us. Mud and rocks bombarded us. I felt like I was in a war zone dodging bullets. My back was still stinging from whatever had hit me a few minutes ago.

"Get close to the tree trunks!" I heard someone yell, or I thought that's what I heard.

A set of large boulders cantilevered over our path a short distance away. It was high enough and long enough to offer us some shelter.

The ground beneath Icky's feet was already swimming in mud and it moved like Jell-O, as Icky's feet stomped through it.

I tucked my body as close to Icky's body as I could as he slowly walked and slid in the mud; he hesitated with every step.

I kept hearing voices but I couldn't see a thing. Right now, all I could think about was finding shelter. I don't know who was more scared, him or me.

The overhang of rocks was only a few feet away. Icky was walking so slowly I wanted to get off him and pull him to it. My better judgment told me to stay on top of him.

The ledge that the rocks formed was shallow—only a few

feet deep and much longer then it looked from a distance. I slid off Icky and pulled him under it. He refused and stayed in the downpour. "You stupid horse, get in here," I repeatedly yelled as I pulled and yanked on his lead rope.

My boots slid in the mud as I tried to pull Icky inside. I almost fell down. "Have it your way!" I shouted as I loosened the tight grip I had on his rope. "Stay out in the rain!" The thunder roared and drowned out my voice.

Although the ledge was shallow, it was quite long and there was plenty of room for Icky and even a couple of mules.

Water was racing to the ground and splashing everything in its path. Even under the safety of the ledge it was reaching and splashing onto my boots and the bottom of my pants.

The ground was alive, moving in a pool of bouncing pinecones and slushy ice. I was safe and out of the line of fire for the time being.

Icky was nervous and kept sidestepping to his left and then back to his right as the ice and the cold water slapped his body. I wrapped his lead rope around my hand and kept a tight grip on it.

I could see the pack of mules. They were huddling close to the trunk at the base of a tall pine tree. They all had their heads tucked low to the ground and their bodies were hugging each other.

Where was everyone else? Robert and a wrangler were bringing up my rear. The last time I saw them was a couple of hours ago. They were riding about ten horses and a couple of mules behind me.

Had they found shelter? The pack of mules was blocking the trail down the mountain, so I knew that they couldn't have gotten ahead of me.

One minute the hail would slow as though stopping and a second later it would become deafening as it crashed through the trees and dislodged everything it touched in its path. Small branches and pinecones were raining from the sky.

I was thankful that I had found shelter. I was still safe and relatively dry. I couldn't imagine being out in this weather, even with rain gear on.

The ground was cold and muddy. I could feel the pounding rain as it splashed all over my boots. I was glad that I had put a thick layer of waterproofing protection on them. Hopefully it would work and keep my feet dry.

A mule and rider appeared up at the top of an embankment that Icky and I had just come down.

"Robert!" I shouted as loud as I could. "Robert, is that you? Here, over here!"

I left the safety of the shelter and waved my free hand high in the air. I kept my face lowered and my head covered. "Over here!" I repeatedly shouted, "Over here!"

I couldn't see the rider's face. I was just hoping that he would see my hand and join me.

Icky and I were only a few feet off of the trail and I knew that his horse would have to walk right past us.

As his mule cautiously walked down the muddy hill, another rider appeared riding about ten feet behind him. This has to be Robert and the wrangler I thought, as I shouted, "Robert, there's shelter over here!"

Both riders were leaning forward in their saddles with their heads tucked tight to their chests and neither of them was wearing a jacket. Why didn't they have their jackets on? What was wrong?

"I found shelter!" I yelled as they sat up a little straighter in their saddles and looked over in my direction, "It's dry in here, come over here!" I shouted.

"Get back on your horse!" a deep surly voice loudly yelled. "Get back on your horse, now!"

I knew he was shouting at me but I didn't know why. I stopped waving my hand and stepped back under the overhang.

What was wrong with the wrangler? Why was he yelling at me? I was much safer in here, and why didn't he have his jacket on? Maybe he is delirious, I thought.

I peered outside again as their animals approached me. "It's dry and safe in here," I shouted. "Why don't we just stay in here until this storm blows over?"

In a deep, loud voice he quickly replied, "No, ma'am, please get back on your horse now." I could barely hear him because of all of the thunder and crashing noises around me.

I pointed towards the mules as I said, "Look, the mules are blocking the trail."

"Aren't you freezing? It's safe and.dry in here." The wrangler turned his horse around towards the mules and started hollering at them in a loud, intense voice.

He kicked his horse hard in the gut and yelled, "Haw!" As it leaped forward, its front legs started sliding. The mud played havoc with its feet as the horse tried to regain its balance. He was slipping and sliding in a pool of brown, sloppy muck. Its front legs buckled beneath his belly, throwing the wrangler forward, onto his neck.

Robert and I looked on in horror and watched the wrangler as he struggled to stay on the horse while trying to, pull it back up onto its front feet.

"I'd rather be crushed by this ledge than thrown into that mess," Robert cried out as he jumped off of his mule and joined me. He was soaking wet and his face was as white as a ghost. His body was shaking and as he got closer I could see his teeth chattering from the cold. I glanced at him for a second as he dashed back out and untied his jacket from his mule and rejoined me.

I kept my eyes focused on the wrangler. His horse's head slammed into the ground. "Damned!" I heard him yell as his knees hit the muddy soil. His right hand still had a tight grip on his horse's reins.

His horse's legs were shooting out in every direction as it panicked and slipped and slid while trying to stand back up.

The wrangler was dangerously close of being rolled on or kicked by his horse, and he knew it. He was scrambling with his arms and legs, desperately trying to get up and away from the thousand pounds of kicking mass that was inches away and almost on top of him.

"Robert, here, hold these." I threw Icky's lead rope at him.

I didn't look back to see if he caught it.

Freezing water slapped my back and head as I left the safety of the shelter. Adrenaline shot through me like lightening as my boots sunk deep into the mud. I had no idea of how I was going to help the wrangler but I knew I had to try.

The mud held on, tight to my boot, like a suction cup as I plowed through it. I felt like I was moving in slow motion. My injured ankle reminded me with every step, that this was all, very real.

I wanted to yell out to the wrangler and let him know that I was on my way to help him. I couldn't. I didn't even know his name.

Everything above me was falling on and around me and the ground beneath me was swirling in wet motion. My arms helped my balance as I pulled myself forward up a slight hill; the short climb seem to take forever.

I didn't want to get near the back of his horse or its legs. I need to go up, higher above it.

The wrangler was already layered in mud and looked like he was stuck in quicksand. Every time he attempted to stand up, the ground beneath his knees or boots gave way, sending him falling back, crashing to the ground. He was struggling and I could tell by his slower movements that he was tiring.

"Throw me the reins!" I shouted. "I'll pull your horse uphill."

His horse was lying on its stomach, half buried in a pool of mud. The more it kicked and twisted, the deeper it sank in.

The wrangler had made it back up onto his knees and threw the reins at me as he briefly looked up in my direction.

I was only a few feet uphill from his horse and the reins landed close by my right leg. They started sliding back downhill. I stomped my left boot at them and missed. They slid down, back towards the wrangler and stopped on a jagged rock by his horse's head.

Against my better judgment, I went after them. I dug my left boot deep into the mud for support. My right ankle twisted as the muddy ground beneath it gave way. The pain shot through me like a slashing knife. My ankle gave way and I fell to my knees.

My heart jumped into my throat as I realized that I had landed almost on top of his horse's right legs. They were up in the air and wildly moving everywhere. Mud splashed in my face as I grabbed for the reins. It was cold and it sent shivers up my spine.

"Get away from my horse!" My body was sliding right into the path of his horse's legs. "Mary, get out of there!" "Get away from my horse!" Both Robert and the wrangler were yelling at me.

They weren't helping my situation. I knew I needed to get back up the hill, I just wasn't sure how to do it, I was still sliding. My right ankle was throbbing and it refused to dig in any deeper. My left leg slid and as I pushed my boot deeper into the mud. It hit something hard. I propped my boot and leg against it. It worked, I stopped sliding.

The reins were only inches away from my right hand. I bent down and grabbed them. I've got him!" I shouted out. "I've got the reins!"

A pinecone crashed into a cluster of rocks right next to my leg and on impact it shattered and exploded into a million pieces that flew at my face. I tucked my head tight to my chest and without looking up I braced my left leg on the rocks and slowly headed back up the incline.

With each step I pulled on the wranglers horse's reins. His neck was now bent, uphill, facing me. I wasn't sure of what I was doing, but it seemed to be working.

As I pulled the horse's neck uphill his front legs followed. He used his neck to stabilize his body as he attempted to stand. His back legs were still slipping and sliding as he made another attempt to get back up on all four legs.

I glanced back at him for a second. It was working, he was almost standing, and so was the wrangler. "Throw me the reins," he shouted as he held his hands out high up in the air.

"Mary, get Icky!" "What?" I didn't have Icky—what was he talking about. I looked up and back towards the wrangler. He still had his hands in the air shouting, "Let him go, throw me the reins!"

I watched his hands as they pointed to my left, and he yelled," Get your own horse!"

Icky was loose and walking away from Robert and the wrangler. "You stupid horse!" I screamed as adrenaline shot through my body. "Get over here!"

I threw the wrangler his horse's reins and hurried to catch Icky. Once again I felt like I was moving in slow motion. Luckily for me, so was Icky. I was so mad at him that I broke into a fast sprint and cut him off. He was headed towards the pack of mules about a hundred feet in front of me.

"Whoa!" I shouted as I reached down on the ground grabbing his lead rope. "Easy boy, relax Icky, it's just me." Icky's neck was bent low to the ground, trying to hide it from the downpour. I turned him around and headed him back to the safety of the ledge.

The wrangler wasn't very away from me and he was headed back toward the shelter. He was moving really slow and he was limping.

"Are you hurt?" I shouted as I closed the gap between us. He didn't reply or even look up in my direction, he just kept walking. I wasn't sure if I should ask him again.

Robert had his arms tucked tightly to his chest. His body was still shaking. He had wet mud all over his clothes, I felt sorry for him.

I tucked my head into the safety of the ledge and this time Icky didn't fight me he calmly followed me inside.

"This is crazy!" I screamed out, in a loud angry voice as I brushed ice and mud off of my cloths. "I'm so mad that…"

It felt good to yell, it felt good to be angry, I had had enough and I yearned for a soft pillow and a hot bath. What was I still doing up here? I was freezing, tired, and dirty.

"This definitely was not in the brochure!" I screamed out in a long, drawn-out angry voice, at the top of my lungs.

My anger echoed around the rocks as the wrangler joined us

and calmly said, "What brochure?"

I hung my head down low as though I had been defeated, and in a slightly less frantic voice I said, "The brochure that doesn't mention flying pinecones, getting up at four in the morning, and…" I thought about what I was saying as my racing heart slowed.

"And," I said, in a much slower and calmer voice, " I… am… going to rewrite that stupid brochure."

Both men were staring at me as though I had lost my mind. It made me feel a little bit uncomfortable. By the looks on their faces I guessed that they both had already had enough of me. I stopped talking and glanced outside, watching everything above and around us come crashing down.

"This is a first for me," the wrangler said as he broke our silence. "What do you mean?" I asked, not even sure, if I wanted to here his answer.

"Ma'am," he said as he threw me a quick glance, "we don't have this kind of weather in Texas, it doesn't rain pinecones there."

"So…" I hesitated a few seconds as I thought about what he had just said, "so, you've never done this before?" "A frightened look filled my face as I waited for his answer.

"No ma'am," he simply replied as he zipped his jacket tighter.

"How about you?" I turned to face Robert. "Have you done this before?" "No," he slowly replied as his teeth started to chatter. "What brochure are you talking about, Mary?" he added as a confused look filled his face.

I was short of breath, in pain, and freezing to death, yet for some strange reason I felt the need to stay calm and talk. Having two grown men around me was comforting.

I lowered the tone in my voice as I shared stories with them of my younger, crazier days. And then I compared them to the craziness of the last four days from this trip.

Both of the men chuckled a couple of times as they listened.

"I think I'm going to rewrite this brochure and call it:

Thriller-seekers insanity ride.'"

"Why?" the wrangler asked as a grin crept onto his face. "Aren't you having fun, ma'am?"

An ice-covered pinecone slammed into the ground a few inches away from all of us, spooking our horses. "No!" I shouted. "This in not my idea of fun!"

All three of us tightened the grip on our horses' lead ropes as we peered outside.

Pinecones weighted with frozen water were falling and crashing around us. They exploded and shattered as they hit the ground and rocks. The noise was deafening. I felt like I was in a war zone.

"And," I said as I raised my voice and pointed outside, " this, is going to be in my thrill-seeker brochure." Both Robert and the wrangler nodded their heads in agreement as we watched the sky fall and explode around us.

"Listen," The wrangler said. "Quiet—listen." I strained my ears. I didn't hear a thing. "What?" I asked as I glanced toward Robert. "Shhh, quiet," he said in a whisper of a voice.

I threw a puzzling glance at Robert, hoping he could enlighten me. He shrugged his shoulders and remained quiet as he paid attention to the wrangler.

"The hail and rain are stopping," The wrangler said in a louder voice. "I think its over."

As the wrangler took a step outside of the overhang, a piercing rumbling noise shook the ground below us and echoed around us.

"What is it?" I asked as a bad feeling crept over me and sent my heart racing. I tightened my grip on Icky's lead rope as I listened to a deep rumbling noise that was shaking everything around me.

"Get out of there!" The wrangler yelled. "Get on your horses, now!" The tone in his voice was alarming. It scared me. I didn't hesitate. I yanked Icky away from the ledge and jumped on his back. I didn't bother tying his lead rope or checking his cinch. Robert followed my lead.

"Look!" the wrangler shouted as he pointed up above the ledge. "Get out of there, now!" I didn't have to look up or behind me, I could already feel debris as it flew at and hit me. Icky was already in motion. I held on.

The hill above us had become a wall of moving mud and rocks and it was headed straight for us. The noise was deafening as boulders smashed into trees and crashed into rocks as they flew downhill.

Icky broke into a fast gallop. I think he was as frightened as much as I was. Mud and debris were flying everywhere. I tucked my body as close as I could to my saddle as I hoped that Icky wouldn't slip or trip in the muck below and flying at his feet.

The mules huddled around the trees sensed the danger and were fighting each other to get down the steep narrow trail. They were directly in front of us and they were blocking our only way down, off of this mountain.

The wrangler hollered and yelled at them to get out of our way. They were panicking and kicking each other as they ran up and slid back down steep embankments.

The wrangler untied his lead rope and in an angry loud voice yelled, "Haw! Haw!" as he whipped them, out of our way. I followed his lead and used the end of my reins to do the same.

I was moving so fast that everything around me was a blur. I wasn't sure if I hit a thing, I just kept whipping anything that got close to me. I held on tight and hoped that Icky and I wouldn't get bit or kicked as we charged the pack and pushed them out of our way.

Chapter Nineteen

I screamed and yelled at the mules with every ounce of energy I had. My voice cracked and turned into a screeching noise as my throat went dry. Icky carried his head high and kept his ears pinned back as we pushed the mules out of our way, forcing them up steep embankments and down vertical drops.

I never looked back to see if Robert was behind me. I was hoping that he was safe. My eyes were focused on the wrangler directly in front of me and I had no intention of letting him out of my sight.

As we dropped downwards, our surrounding became more visible and the sky cleared. We slowed our horses down as the horrific rumbling noises behind us faded.

My adrenaline was still racing as I glanced behind me. I was glad to see that Robert was safe and only a short distance away. The pack of mules brought up his rear and was stretched out in a long line behind him. I took a couple of deep breaths and slowly let them out as the terrified expression on my face faded.

The soft mud beneath our feet quickly hardened as the sun's rays came back out in a full blaze.

I was caked from head to toe in cold, wet mud. For the first time on this trip, I welcomed the warmth from the sun. As the mud dried on my face, I could feel my skin tighten. My clothes became stiff as the mud slowly dried and added an extra layer on them.

We all remained silent as we slowed our horses down to a walk. We were so quiet you could have heard a pin drop. I wasn't sure why we walked in silence—perhaps we were all still scared to death or still trying to figure out, in our minds, what had just happened. I personally was straining my ears listening for that frightening rumbling noise to start again. I was ready to take off in a second.

A bluebird landed in a tree a few feet from me. The movement of the tree startled me. I was still on pins and needles. He announced himself with a couple of loud chirps as a few of his buddies joined him.

Their racket interrupted our silence and was a welcome change that helped calm all of our racing hearts.

I turned around in my saddle to face Robert. He looked as bad as I felt. His neck was hung down low and his hat covered his face. His red-checkered shirt was now a pale gray color along with the rest of his clothes.

"Do you think this is where the first mud baths started? I asked as a smile returned to my face.

Robert lifted his head up. He coughed and cleared his throat as he untied the bandana around his neck. "You're a nutcase, Mary!" he shouted as he cleaned the mud off of his sunglasses.

Robert's voice was soothing; today was already, way too long. I felt a burst of energy as I realized that I was still alive and finally headed home.

"Yes!" I shouted in a loud voice so both the wrangler and Robert could hear me. "I have become a nutcase, and, " I added with a giggly voice, "I'm going to rewrite the brochure and it will say 'mud baths included at no additional charge.'"

I knew that both men had heard me for they both grinned a few seconds as they looked down at their muddy clothes.

"How much further? I asked as I closed the distance between the wrangler's horse and mine. "How much further do we have to ride?"

The wrangler turned his head to face me and slowly said, "I

don't know, ma'am." He cleared his throat as he talked.

I glanced at my watch. It was four o'clock. Is it really only four o'clock? I shouted in a loud angry voice, "I want a bath. I want to feel a real bed. I'm tired and I want this trip to end!" Both men watched me and remained silent as I yelled and complained out loud.

Their silence got me to thinking. I pulled my hat down, hiding my face, once again from the hot sun and I started to think.

Where was the rest of our group? Were we lost? Why were Robert and the wrangler so quiet? Did they know we were lost and they didn't want to tell me?

"Drink your water," a little nagging voice inside of me kept repeating. "You're almost home, Mary, relax,." another voice kept reminding me.

The wrangler in front of me kept stopping and looking around. At first I didn't pay any attention to him. I was glad to follow him, but a bad feeling was creeping over me. I did my best to ignore it as I started to carefully watch the wrangler.

After all, we were still heading downhill and the sun was still shining and warming my tired, aching bones.

I stared at my canteen from time to time as we rode. I hadn't had a sip of water since lunch and I wasn't about to. I had seen enough water today to last the rest of my life.

I looked up. There wasn't a cloud in the sky. The pine trees thinned and then disappeared as we dropped to a lower elevation. Thick oak trees and knee-high green shrubs were now guiding us downhill.

The wrangler was about ten feet in front of me. He stopped and got off of his horse. "Is there a problem?" I asked as I caught up to him. His silence brought back that bad feeling in my stomach. I didn't need him to answer, I knew something was wrong.

I stopped Icky a few feet behind his horse. I remembered how much he had yelled at me for getting off of my horse earlier, so I stayed seated as I watched him. Robert's mule was directly behind me.

"That's where we need to get," the wrangler said as he pointed down towards a large green valley.

"How do we get there?" I foolishly asked as I looked down the steep slope in front of us. "I don't see the zigzagged path."

"Yeah, that's the problem," the wrangler replied as he took his hat off and wiped his forehead. "You two know how to ride, right?"

The bad feeling growing in my stomach got a lot worse as he took his sunglasses off and said, "We're going straight down, it looks steeper than it actually is."

I bent my neck out a little further over the sheer drop and said, "No way!" Robert stepped his mule close to the edge and looked over. "I don't see the trail, where is it?"

"Didn't you hear him?" I said in a loud, panicky voice. "There is no trail—he wants us to go straight down. "I'm not going," I said as I shook my head "no" and backed Icky away from the edge.

"I can't find the trail and this is the best spot I can find to get off of this mountain." "Then you go. I'm staying here. I'm not dying today."

Robert studied our surroundings and in a calm voice asked the wrangler, "If Mary and I stay here, can you go get us help?"

"Yes, sir, I could, but I can't. I couldn't get back up here before nightfall."

"I'll take my chances up here," I said in an angry voice, "I'm not going down that mountain. You'll have to shoot me first!"

"I wouldn't do that, ma'am. Now please get off of your horse and tighten your cinch as tight as you can."

I looked over at Robert to see what he was going to do. He stayed on his horse and was still studying our surroundings. "Why don't we try to zigzag down? That area over there looks a little less steep."

"Yeah, I was going to try that. If we all had mules it would work. These horses' front legs would buckle at our first switch-back."

"Oh," Robert calmly said as he got off of his horse and

tightened his cinch.

"There has to be a better way. I'm not going, can't you call for a helicopter or something?"

Both men turned towards me and just stared at me. "Ma'am, it's not as steep as it looks. All you have to do is sit deep in your saddle. We'll let the horses do all the work, they'll lock their front legs and sit back down on their butts and slide down."

"It's a lot of fun. All you have to do is give them their reins and lay as far back on their butts as you possibly can."

"Fun! This isn't remotely what I call fun! I yelled out. "You are insane I'm not—going!"

"Ma'am," the wrangler said as he stepped closer towards me, "would you like me to tighten your cinch for you?"

He had circles under his eyes and a deep frown on his face. I could tell by the tone in his voice that I was going over this cliff one way or another.

I got off of Icky and tightened his cinch. Then I tied his lead rope around his neck. He didn't know what was happening, but he kicked his leg out behind himself as I tightened his cinch he was uneasy. I knew that he sensed something was wrong.

In one last attempt I said, "What about the mules how will they get down?"

Robert and the wrangler looked at the mules and then back at me. I felt like I was being ganged up on.

"Mary," Robert said in a calm voice, "do you want to ride my mule? It's okay with me, I'll ride your horse."

A little voice inside of me said, Your not going to let two men show you, are you? Another little voice inside of me said, Let's go home.

"Just follow me." The wrangler put his hat back on and without another word he kicked his horse hard in the gut. His horse hesitated and stepped back away from the ledge. He leaned forward and spurred his horse hard in the stomach. The horse's legs flew out in front of him and headed downhill.

I was next. My stomach was churning and my heart was pounding as I inched Icky closer to the ledge. He stretched his neck over the edge as I kicked him hard, urging him forward. He wanted nothing to do with the ledge. He fought me and backed up as fast as he could, slamming hard into Robert's mule.

"He doesn't want to go." I cried as I urged him forward again. "Mary, hurry up!" Robert yelled. "The mules are right behind me, go!"

Every inch of me was shaking as I kicked Icky again. Against my better judgment I leaned forward, closed my eyes, and with every ounce of energy my legs had left, I kicked him again.

As we flew over the ledge I opened my eyes up and leaned back as far as I could in the saddle. Icky's front legs landed spread apart and they immediately locked at his knees. His back legs scrambled to stay standing. I had a death grip on the back of my saddle. I held on.

I think Icky's heart was racing faster than mine. "Easy, boy, " I managed to say in a semi-calm voice. I think I was saying it more to myself than to him.

The wrangler's horse was only a few feet in front of me. His hind legs were kicking up rocks and throwing them at us. I should have waited a few more minutes and put more space between us.

Icky's front legs looked like skis as they slid downwards through dry red clay and rocks. I tried my best to lean with him as he threw his neck left and right for balance.

The pack of mules behind us had caught up and was passing me on both sides. They churned up rocks as they slid, throwing them at us. The rocks pelted Icky's body as the mules passed us. I tucked down as low on his back as I could hoping I wouldn't get hit. My head was practically on his butt.

His back legs dropped to the ground, throwing me even further back, as he fell to his butt. I thought I was going to roll off his back. I reached forward and locked my right hand around the saddle horn and tried to pull myself forwards, up and away from his rear end. The downward motion pulled me further over the back of his saddle.

"Not today!" I yelled as a rush of adrenaline shot through me. "I'm not dying today!" I slowly released my left hand from the death grip I had on the back of my saddle and threw it forward, frantically grabbing for the saddle horn.

As I locked both of my hands around it, my body stopped sliding backwards. I held on and pulled myself forward and realized that I had dropped my reins. I could see them as they bounced around on Icky's neck. I didn't want to let go of the saddle horn to grab them, but without them I was no longer in control.

I knew I had to grab them, I just didn't know how. If I sat up a little straighter in the saddle, I would be thrown forwards into or over Icky's neck. If I let go of the saddle horn, I would fall back and roll off of his back and be trampled by Robert's mule. This was my worst nightmare and I wanted it to end.

I don't think I took a breath the entire way down. I sat up a few inches straighter in the saddle and got a better look at my surroundings.

Icky was sliding, straight down the mountain while sitting on his butt. He used his neck to balance his body as his front legs stayed locked and led the rest of his body in the fall.

I didn't have time to panic or worry; those thoughts were behind me. I kept my eyes peeled on his neck and followed his movements, adjusting my weight as he slipped and slid. I locked my legs around his stomach and squeezed him so hard that my leg muscles were shaking and straining to hold on.

He kept trying to stand back up on his hind legs. As his body slid, the ground around his feet broke loose and fell with us. Mules sliding all around us added to the growing shower of rocks that picked up speed and were now flying at us like bullets.

They hit my legs and thighs and stung. I closed my eyes and held on as I listened to them slam into and slap Icky all over his body. My heart was racing so fast I thought it would explode.

Halfway down we hit a cluster of level boulders. As Icky scrambled to regained the use of his back legs, he tried to turn around and go back up the hill.

"No!" I screamed in a panicky voice as he lifted his head up for a split second and tried to turn around. I grabbed at and caught his reins and pulled his neck back around, urging him forward and back downhill.

We were dangerously close to tipping over sideways. "No Icky!" I screamed as loud as I could. "Let's go home!" I let go of my tight grip around his midsection and kicked him. He fought me as I yanked on the reins and kicked him again.

Robert was shouting something at me. I didn't dare turn around to see or hear him. I kept my focus on moving forward and down to the green valley below us.

Almost immediately Icky's back legs collapsed and flew under him as he fell back down onto his butt. As the valley got closer, tears pooled in my eyes. A rock ricocheted off of Icky and slammed into my right thigh. It turned on a faucet of tears. I tried to fight them as they ran down my face.

I wasn't sure if they were tears from fear or joy, they just kept flooding my face and clouding my sunglasses. Don't loose it, Mary, I kept saying to myself as the rocks flew around me, you're almost home.

The valley below us was level and filled with dark green grass. I could almost feel the soft grass as I watched it get closer, home. I was almost home.

The wrangler directly in front of us had distanced himself from me. I was glad. The last thing I wanted to do was crash into him and his horse.

Thick brown brush slowed the mass of moving rocks as we reached the valley. Icky was able to gain his balance and almost immediately stood back up, as his feet hit solid ground.

I released the death grip I had around his stomach and let out a sigh of relief as we reached the valley floor.

Chapter Twenty

I was numb and energized at the same time. Every inch of my body was exploding with adrenaline. I was alive and I had made it down a mountain that only in my dreams I would have thought was possible, and I was almost home.

I looked up, I don't know why. I think I was looking for an angel. Icky decided to do a full body shake at the same time. He shook himself off just like a dog getting out of the water, from head to toe. I almost fell off as he bounced me around in the saddle. My adrenaline spiked and I tightened my grip on his reins and grabbed on to the saddle horn at the same time.

Robert's mule passed me on the left. "What a rush!" he shouted out in a high-pitched, excited voice.

He slowed his mule down and with a little less excitement in his tone he said, "Mary, what is your horse doing?"

"I don't know," I said as I bent my head lower, so Robert couldn't see my wet face. "I'm just trying to stay on him. I think he's trying to shake the mud and dirt off."

The enthusiasm in Robert's voice and the excitement written all over his face brought me back down to earth. I wiped the tears from my eyes and in a weak, shaky voice I shouted, "Come on, Icky, let's go home!"

He was still shaking his rear end and tail out. He wouldn't move. I sat tall in the saddle and kicked him twice. He reluctantly stopped his lateral movement and took a step forward.

The wrangler had stopped about fifty feet in front of us. He had turned his horse around and he was watching us. He was also pointing up the mountain about a half a mile to the left of us.

Robert and I looked up. In the distance we could see the rest of our group zigzagging down the mountain.

Tears filled my eyes as I realized that, they were safe and we were safe and we all were headed home.

"That was worth this entire trip!" Robert shouted. "What an adrenaline rush!"

I remembered that he had said the same thing when we jumped into the river two days ago.

"You're an adrenalin junkie, aren't you?" Before he could answer me, I pointed towards the rest of our group slowly coming down the mountain and in an angry loud voice I said, "Look, that's normal, this was insane. We could have been killed!"

"Mary, life doesn't get any better than this." He took off his sunglasses and as he studied my face he said, " Mary, don't you feel, really, I mean, really alive right now? Wow, that was incredible!"

Nothing Robert was saying made any sense to me. He was insanely excited over this experience. I, on the other hand, was still trying to slow my racing heart and hold back tears. The tone in his voice and the gleam in his eyes were unmistakable; he loved the thrill and excitement and the adrenaline rush that came with it.

Now I understood why grown men voluntary jumped onto barebacked bulls and horses. They did it for the rush, and what a rush it was. I could tell that Robert loved the insanity and I knew he missed the thrill and the excitement of the rodeo.

I took my sunglasses off and as I studied his face I said, "You miss the rodeos, don't you, Robert? You came on this trip because you're bored. You're tired of teaching and you want to get back on the rodeo circuit, don't you?"

Robert stopped his horse in its tracks and slowly turned his head to face me. He didn't say a word; he just watched me as Icky and I walked right by him.

The wrangler joined us and said, "I wasn't off by much. Now, wasn't that fun, ma'am?"

First I wanted to scream at him and say, "Your fired!" Then I wanted to shout out, "You're a total moron. You idiot, I almost got killed!"

I bit my tongue as I listened to Robert and him talk about our free fall; it was easy to tell that both of these men loved every minute of the experience. Maybe it was me. How come I wasn't as excited or thrilled over this experience?

I didn't bother to answer or scream at the wrangler. I was just glad to be down on level ground and safe. I remained quiet and watched the animated expressions on both of the men's faces as they relived the steep descent.

The three of us rode side by side as we backtracked to meet the rest of our group, who were now on their final cross back and almost to the valley floor.

As we rode I listened to the men and thought about being home. Where was home? Where was I right now? How long had I been here? For some strange reason I thought that I lived here. This place and all that it had thrown at me, now, felt like home.

Icky knew he was close to home and he picked up his pace as we met up with the rest of our group.

Jane and Gloria saw us and hurried their horses over to join us. "Why didn't you take us?" they both shouted as they reached us. "That was awesome," Gloria added.

I realized that they were talking about us flying down the mountain. "So you guys saw us?"

Matt galloped ahead of the rest of our group still coming down the mountain and stopped a few feet in front of the wrangler.

"What the hell were you thinking?" We all turned and listened as his loud voice echoed around us. In a deep angry voice he yelled, "You're fired! Go pick up your pay and get off of my property!"

"Wait!" I shouted, as he turned his horse around to leave us. "It's not his fault." Matt stopped his horse and turned his neck around to face me. Anger was written all over his face. Mine was still covered in mud.

"I fell off of my horse and," I hesitated as I took a deep breath, "and this wrangler saved my life." The wrangler turned and looked at me with a confused look on his face.

"I was thrown too," Robert said as he pulled his mule closer to Icky. "The sky opened up and the mules went crazy."

The wrangler remained silent as his eyes darted back and forth, watching Robert and I as we spoke.

"He doesn't deserve to be fired," I added in a calm, more sincere voice, "He saved our lives." I was lying through my teeth and doing my best to make it sound good. If Matt would have asked me how I fell off or for anything specific about falling off, I wouldn't have been able to answer him.

The rest of our group had caught up to us. Matt grumbled something under his breath and trotted away from us, heading back towards the front line.

I looked around and said," Anybody ready for margaritas?" I held my right hand up and held it out for Robert, he slapped it in a high five, and said, "No, I'm going to drink an entire bottle of Jack Daniels; margaritas are way to tame for me tonight."

"I'm with you, Mary," Gloria shouted as she moved her horse forward. "A couple dozen of margarita's will work for me."

"You can't drink that many. "Jane argued. "Bet me!" "Deal!" Gloria shouted back as she rode away from us and headed after two mules that had stopped to eat grass.

"Hey, Mary, how come you're so full of mud?" Jane rode side by side with me as we headed home. "Did you and Robert really get thrown?"

"Robert!" I shouted. "Why don't you tell Jane and Gloria about our little adventure?"

Robert rode over closer to us and said, "Which one?" Then

as a grin filled his face he said, "Maybe after that first bottle of
Jack Daniels, maybe."

The herd was restless and picking up its pace. They knew
that they were close to home and their long day was almost
over.

I glanced at my watch, it was after five o'clock. "I'm ready
for a hot bath, cold beer, and pizza. I don't think I have the
energy to go out to a restaurant. Aren't you guys tired?"

Gloria had rejoined us and with enthusiasm in her voice
said, "Nothing a few drinks won't fix, bring on the men!"

"We earned this, it's time to party," Jane added. "She can't
drink that many margaritas. I could make some money off of
her tonight. This is going to be fun."

The excitement in both of the women's voices convinced me
that I was going to this party, no matter how tired or bad I felt.

Over the past four days I had learned to trust twenty-five
crazy new people who I now was proud to call my friends. I was
looking forward to sharing stories with them and enjoying
some long overdue laughs and hugs.

We followed the fertile green valley only for a short distance
before the herd came to a dead stop.

All of us bringing up the rear instinctively spread out to
keep the herd contained. A wrangler from the front of the herd
suddenly appeared riding towards us, at a full gallop.

Icky's ears flew up as alarming thoughts raced through my
mind. Were we lost again? Is another rider down? Did Matt figure out we were lying?

The wrangler slowed his horse down and shouted,
"Everybody go forwards, everybody needs to go to the front
line, now."

Jane and Gloria were on the other side of the herd to my
left. I watched them as they put their horses in motion and rode
past the herd, heading for the front line.

Robert and a few other riders were on my right side, behind
the herd. They took off and headed past the stopped animals
towards the front row.

I was the only one left at the back of the herd. The wrangler galloped closer to me and slowed his horse down as he said, "Ma'am, all riders need to go up front, now."

"Why?" I asked as our horses walked side by side, "We're home," he said as a smile filled his face.

"Are you sure we're not lost again?" I said as I watched the smile fade from his face. "No, ma'am, we're home. You need to go to the—"

Before he finished his sentence, I loosened Icky's reins and yelled, "We're home, Icky, let's go home!" Icky bolted forward. He knew he was close to home and he had every intention of getting there first. "Easy boy," I said as I pulled back on his reins, keeping him from breaking into a fast gallop.

All of the wranglers and riders had formed a long line holding the herd back. As I caught up to them I could hear Matt shouting, "Keep your backs up straight and walk your horses. There is a crowd watching us and waiting for us."

I watched everyone in front of me sit up tall in their saddles and straighten their clothes as they proudly walked their horses towards the barn and fences in front of us.

Excitement filled the air as everyone walked his or her horse in perfect stepped harmony holding the herd back. We had all survived and we were all very proud and glad to be home.

I slowed Icky down to join everyone; he jerked and pulled on his reins. "Oh no you don't!" I shouted as I yanked back on his reins. "Don't run! Who is that over there? Slow your horse down, you'll stampede the herd!" I heard a lot of shouting from a lot of different voices. I think they were all aimed at me.

The ground was green and level. Icky wanted to run and it sounded like a good idea to me. I gave him his reins and without hesitation he flew past two horses on my right. "Wow, you're really fast," I said as I pat him on the neck.

"Mary!" I heard Matt yell. "Slow down!" "Stop running!" another deep voice shouted. "Pull back on your reins, slow that animal down!"

I pulled back on Icky's reins, slowing him down. We were now way in front of the herd and everyone else. "What are you doing?" Robert shouted as he caught up to me. Jane and Gloria were on both sides of him. "Having fun!" I shouted in an excited voice. "Last one home buys the first round!" Gloria shouted as she kicked her horse forward.

"You're on!" All of us shouted as we took off after her. I could hear men's voices yelling and hollering at us. None of us turned around to look back—we didn't care. This was our vacation and for the first time, I was really having fun.

"What's Matt going to do, fire us?" Gloria shouted as she tried to gain a lead on all of us.

We could see a fence and a wood cabin in the distance. We yelled and shouted at each other as we pushed our horses to their limits.

Icky was the smallest of the three animals and he was determined not to let anybody pass him. Somehow he found a fifth gear and flew by both Gloria and Jane. Robert surprised us all as his mule, for the first time this entire trip, broke into a fast canter. I slowed Icky down a bit as Robert caught up to us. "Now this is what I call fun!" he shouted as he passed me.

None of us dared to look behind us. We didn't care about the herd or anybody else right now. The wrangler's voices faded as we distanced ourselves from them and the rest of the herd.

I caught up to Robert and rode side by side with him at a fast gallop. Gloria and Jane pulled up alongside of us and shouted, "Is this the best you can do?"

They were laughing and shouting back and forth at each other, "You're buying."

"No, you're buying." They showed us how well they could ride as they teased and pointed back and forth at each other while riding their horses as fast as the animals would carry them.

Robert and I were more cautious and kept our animals at a comfortable controlled gallop. We watched as Jane and Gloria widened their lead.

Gloria passed Jane and every opened ear in this valley could hear her, as she hooted and hollered about her victory.

"Shall we show them how it's done?" I gave Icky his reins

and let him go. He flew past Robert's mule. "Go, Mary!" I heard Gloria shout. I could hear Robert's mule as it closed in on me.

"Not today!" Robert shouted as he started to pass me. "Go Mary!" Both women were shouting at us. "Go Robert!"

"Come on, Icky, you're not going to let a mule beat us, are you?" I leaned forward and urged him on. He surprised me and flew past Robert's mule.

A small crowd of families and wranglers had gathered at the fence. They all started clapping and cheering as they watched Robert and I race to the fence. It was close, but Icky was determined not to let a mule past him. We took third place.

I don't know where Icky had gotten this last burst of energy from—for that matter, I don't know where I got mine from, but I did know that it felt good, real good, knowing that I was home.

The herd was about five minutes behind us. The four of us stayed mounted and joined the clapping as the rest of our group and the herd entered the corrals around us.

"What did you do to your face?" a well-dressed woman, decked out in jewelry, asked me as I got off of Icky, and walked him past her. I looked down at my shirt and pants. I had forgotten that my face and clothes were layered in dry mud.

"Oh," I said as I touched my face, "it's a new facial mud mask, it comes free with the trip." "Really," she said as her eyes lit up. "Does it work?"

Robert overheard me and with a serious look on his face said, "Yes, Mary is going to write the next brochure for this company." He lightly brushed mud off of my forehead and cheeks and added, "She is looking forward to telling everyone about the free mud."

"Do they offer massages too? I'm here to pick up my nephew and he didn't tell me about any of these things, or, I might have went on this trip with him."

Robert and I were having a hard time keeping a straight face as the woman touched my face.

"Sam, over here, I'm over here. How was your trip?" The

woman, high heels and all, walked over to a young man just getting off of his horse.

Robert leaned closer to me and softly kissed my ear as he whispered, "I still don't know what I'm going to do with you, Mary?"

I broke out in laughter as I pushed him away and in a loud voice said, "I do, and you owe me a drink."

"Listen up, folks." Matt's deep penetrating voice filled the air, "Everybody, listen up. Our farewell dinner is being moved up two hours later, to eight o'clock. Don't forget to take your belongings off of your saddles."

I didn't want to say goodbye to Icky. Over the past few days we had been through thick and thin and I trusted him with my life. I thought about buying him and taking him home. Then I thought about all of the trouble he had gotten me into.

I didn't know how to say goodbye to him. I didn't even have a carrot or a piece of candy to give him. I felt bad. "I love you Icky," I quietly whispered close to his ear as I stroked his neck and patted him. "Thank you for taking such good care of me." He knew I was saying goodbye. As I spoke to him he hung his head down, low to the ground. Tears swelled in my eyes as I bent down and put my arms around his neck and hugged him. I didn't know if I would ever see him again.

Chapter Twenty-One

L et's party!" an excited voice shouted. Husbands, wives, and wranglers greeted us as we left our horses and walked away from the corral.

My husband was three hundred miles away. I stayed with Icky a few extra minutes hugging him and saying goodbye.

I hadn't realized how many of us on this trip had left our spouses at home. From the crowd here I would say almost all of us had. Everyone was smiling and clapping or hugging. Long kisses and embraces were flying around. You would have thought we had been gone for years by the way everyone was reacting.

As I walked out, back into the real world I glanced at my watch. It was five thirty in the evening yet the sun was still shining bright high above us. The days up here were endless.

I decided to save my hugs and farewells for tonight. Right now my ankle needed serious attention along with the rest of my body. Soaking in a hot tub was all I could think about.

Without saying goodbye to anyone I grabbed my gear, carried it over to my truck, and threw it in the back.

"Mary, wait!" Robert stopped me before I could leave. "Mary," he said in a quieter voice, "Do you realize I don't even know your last name?" He slowly touched my left hand and squeezed it while saying, "Do you feel any different towards me, now that we're back home?"

Robert was way to serious, for me. All I wanted or I could think about right now, was a hot bath. "Robert," I tried to gather my thoughts as I slowly and with every emotion I had left tenderly said, "I've never been more sure about anything in my entire life "except ..." I raised the tone in my voice and purposely repeated, except, for," Robert's soft hands stroked the back of my neck and I melted as a serious look filled his face. He slowly said, "Except for what? What is it, Mary?"

"Except for my hot bath." "What? What hot bath?" As Robert thought about what I had just said, I looked deep into his eyes and I pulled him closer. "I wouldn't miss tonight for the world," I quietly whispered as I kissed him first lightly on the cheek and then on the side of his lips. "I don't know why, but somehow I've fallen in love with you and I already miss you." He pulled me tight to his chest and kissed me.

His warm lips begged me to stay but I knew it was time to go. Before either of us exchanged another word or embrace I got in my truck and drove away, leaving a trail of dust behind me as I headed down a long dirt road heading back to town.

A hot bath and soft pillow were only thirty minutes away. I thought about what I had just said to Robert. The bells and whistles to stay away from him that had been going off in my mind the past couple of days were gone. I surprised myself telling him that I loved him. What was love? How could I be this comfortable with a man I had only known for a couple of days? All I knew for sure was that I already missed him and a feeling deep down inside of me told me that he was "Mr. Right."

As I drove away I studied my steering wheel. It was a lot larger then I remembered it being. When I accelerated I leaned forward, as though I was still in the saddle urging my horse to move. I even caught myself saying, "haw" a few times as I pushed my foot on the accelerator to pick up speed. Everything around me was creaking and making noises. I felt awkward in my own truck. I turned the radio on and then back off. All of the music was way too fast and loud for me. Had I really been gone for just four days? What was happening to me?

As the dirt road ended I slowed my truck down and watched the freeway traffic as it sped across the concrete directly in front of me. The cars were moving so fast that I hesitated to join them. I reluctantly pushed my foot down on the accelerator and watched the red needle climb on the speedometer. When it hit fifty-five miles per hour, I felt like I was on a rocket headed for space and going a thousand miles per hour. I stayed in the slow lane and watched the traffic pass me as I kept both of my hands wrapped with a tight grip around the steering wheel.

I wondered if this was how wranglers from the Old West felt when they came back from a long cattle drive into the hustle and bustle of the real world. Everything around me was foreign and moving, way too fast.

I thought about how hard it would be, if not impossible, to change everything that you had become comfortable with, just to get back in the real world. I thought about my horse Icky and how much I already missed him and I thought about the slower paced lifestyle that living on the trail brought. And for some crazy reason part of me really missed the excitement and thrills that Mother Nature had constantly thrown at us.

As I crawled along the freeway in the slow lane a million questions flooded my mind. Most of them were about Robert and all of my new friends; very few of them were about my husband Steven or even my children.

How could I have changed so much in only four days? No matter how deep or long I thought, the answers eluded me.

The buildings in town looked bigger and their colors were much more vibrant than I remembered. I had reserved a room for tonight over a week ago. All I had to do now was remember the name of the hotel and where it was.

I was glad the sun was still shining, keeping me in daylight. I don't think I could have driven this far or found my hotel in the darkness.

As I pulled up and stopped by the lobby, I wondered which hotel Robert and everyone else was staying in. I thought about what Robert had said, he was right, we didn't even know each other's last names. In my haste to get to this hotel I had isolated myself from all of my new friends. Oh well, I thought, there aren't that many hotels in this small town. I'm sure we'll all find each other.

I picked up my purse and starred at it for a few seconds and thought about how bulky and heavy it actually was. I hadn't carried it in four days.

My ankle wanted nothing to do with the hard concrete beneath it as I limped to the lobby. I was glad that I was only minutes away from a hot soothing tub.

"Excuse me," I said as I hopped into the lobby and over to the front desk. "I have a reservation, my name is ..." I stopped and grabbed onto the counter to brace my right side and drop my heavy purse.

"We're full," a small oriental man said as I caught my breath. "See sign? No vacancies."

I looked around the lobby to see if I had the right hotel. There were two men and a woman all sitting in overstuffed chairs by large glass windows a few feet away from me. The lobby was small and I noticed that all three of them had put down whatever they were reading and they were staring at me. It made me feel uncomfortable.

I looked down at my clothes and started laughing. I was still layered in mud from head to toe. I must have looked like a vagrant or homeless person.

The elderly man from behind the counter repeated himself in a louder voice and again in broken English said, "No vacancies—we full."

I was sure that I was at the right hotel. I stood up straighter and with a softer tone in my voice I said, "I'm sorry, I must look a mess. I have a reservation, here are my driver's license and credit card."

The balding desk clerk kept his distance from me and slowly reached over the counter for my credit card and driver's license. He held my driver's license close to his thick glasses and repeatedly looked up, staring at me and then back down at my driver's license.

I forced a smile on my muddy face in the hopes that he would hurry up. "You Mary?" he said as he studied my driver's license. I wanted to say, "No, I have no idea where Mary is. I just borrowed these from her." I didn't. I bit my tongue and in a sweet, gentle voice I simply replied, "Yes, I'm Mary."

Over the last four days I had kept my riding gloves on, from the minute I woke up to the minute I went to bed. As I signed for the hotel room I noticed how dirty my fingernails were. They were filled with dirt and grime. It was embarrassing. The desk clerk's wife had joined him and was also closely watching me.

A hotel room never looked so inviting. I plopped my weary body down and sunk into the soft bed. I wanted to close my eyes and sleep forever. As I drifted away, thoughts about soaking in a hot tub filled with soothing bubbles motivated me enough, to pull my aching bones out of bed and head towards the bathroom.

Something fell out of my pocket and bounced around on the ground as I took my shirt off. I bent down to pick it up and must have put too much weight on my injured ankle. It screamed in pain and I fell to my knees. It was two pain pills that Gloria had handed me earlier today. "Thank you, Gloria, this is exactly what I need," I said out loud as I crawled over to the bed and used it like a crutch to help me stand back up.

I popped them both in my mouth and swallowed them long before I filled a cup of water to chase them down. Tonight was special. I was hoping that they would block my pain and that a long hot bath would make the rest of me feel like a new person.

I filled, soaked in, and emptied the tub more times than I could remember as I washed and pampered my dried-out, bruised body. If the hotel knew how much water I was using, they would have doubled my rate and I would have gladly paid it.

The deep black bruise on my right ankle had spread all the way down my foot and onto my toes. I was thankful that I had brought some soaking herbs and bubble bath; right now they were worth their weight in gold. As the layers of grime drained beneath me a sense of calm filled me. I was alive, safe, and warm. The pleasures from simple amenities like hot water and clean towels now seemed so much more important.

"Hello, Mary, are you in there?" I could hear someone knocking on my door and calling out my name. "Yes," I replied, then in a louder voice without thinking I said, "Come on in, the door is open."

"Mary, it's me, it's Robert, are you in here? I brought you a present. Where are you?"

"I'm in the bathtub." I slowly replied as I sat up in the tub. "How did you find me? Are you staying at this hotel?" Before Robert could say a word, I added, "What do you mean you brought me a present?"

"I hope you don't think this is too foolish," he said in a hesitant, slower voice, "I brought you a hot pizza and a cold six pack of beer."

"You're kidding!" I yelled, as I sat straight up in the tub, "Are you serious? How did you get a pizza this fast?" I wanted to get out of the tub and go look.

"Mary, this is a little awkward, I'll just leave everything here on the table. I'm glad you like it, I'll see you tonight at eight, okay?"

"Wait a minute!" I shouted as I heard him close the door. "Robert, get back in here!"

"What is it?" he asked as he walked back inside. "You're not getting away that easy. Would you mind bringing me one of those cold beers?"

"Are you sure?" Robert replied in a tiny voice. "Yes, and bring me a piece of pizza too!"

Just the sound of Robert's voice sent my heart racing. I was glad he had found me. My tub was layered in bubbles and if he didn't mind looking at my bruised and weary body I sure didn't mind.

"Where should I put this?' he asked as he purposely tried not to look at me or the tub. "Oh, stop acting like a baby, come on in, sit down, and let's share a cold beer."

Robert slowly walked inside the small bathroom and carefully sat down on the closed toilet seat. With his head still turned away he held out his hand with the can of beer. "Robert," I said as I took the beer from him, "you can open your eyes, it's okay. I'm covered in bubbles. "I never closed them," he said as he turned around and a grin filled his face.

Robert looked terrible. His face was bright pink and his nose was as red as Rudolph's and he still had on his muddy clothes. "You look like crap," I said as I opened the beer. "That's the thanks I get for bringing you this?" he said as he held up the slice of pizza in his left hand. He had it on a napkin and as he lifted it higher to hand it to me, it slid off of the napkin and splattered all over the floor.

We both stared at it in silence for a few seconds and then I started to giggle. "Let me have a sip of that beer, Mary, I think I need it."

"No," I said as my laughter became contagious, "Go get your own beer." "Boy, you don't have any mercy, do you?" He said as he stood up and carefully stepping over the pile of goop on the floor. "Do you still want a piece of pizza?"

"Only if it's right side up, " I joked, "or is this a new upside down kind? Right now I'm so hungry I'll eat anything. How about another cold beer too?"

Robert didn't hesitate coming back inside. He handed me a cold beer and as he sat down said, "You know, Mary, you shouldn't leave your door unlocked, it's not safe." I studied the serious look that he had on his face and as I tried to keep from laughing I slowly replied, "Robert, you are absolutely right. Why, look at what's already happened. I have a stranger in my bathroom watching me take a bath and I'm sharing pizza and beer with him. You're totally right, I'll have to be more careful next time."

The stern tone in my voice caught Robert by surprise. He sat up straighter and when he realized I was kidding he started laughing, so hard I thought he would fall off the toilet. His face lit up and then it faded as he said, "Mary, did you mean what you said when you kissed me this afternoon?" I slowly replied, "Yes," as I tried to sort out and remember what I had said.

I couldn't remember but it didn't matter. I was more comfortable with Robert than any man I had ever been with, in my entire life. I sat up above the water line exposing my bare chest and with every emotion and feeling I had inside of me I said,

"Robert, I don't know how or why, but somehow," my words came slow, "somehow I know with all of my heart, that I've fallen in love with you."

"And," I said in a less serious voice as I ducked back below the bubbles, "this is the weirdest first date I've ever had. I don't know how we will ever top it."

I was glad that Robert was here and I was delighted that I had him all to myself.

He watched me play with and build snowmen with the bubbles in my tub. It brought a smirk back to his face and he said, "Mary, do you remember telling me that I was an adrenaline junkie and that I was bored with life, this afternoon?" I turned to answer him and before I could speak he said, "It upset me, until I really thought about what you had said.

"I don't know how, but you seem to know me better than I know myself. Mary, you were right. I am bored and I do miss and need the adrenaline rushes I use to get on the bulls and broncos. I went to school to get away from all of that and now, fifteen years later, I realize that without it I'm bored. And I don't know what to do about it."

I closed my eyes and listened to Robert as he spilled his heart out to me. I'm not sure if I heard everything he said; the water was so soothing and the beer was cold I just floated in the layers of bubbles and listened to him.

Robert had hung on to and remembered every word, I had said over the past four days. I was having a hard time remembering our conversation from five minutes ago. I didn't have to memorize what he was saying to me, I knew that when I was with him I felt whole and alive and that's all I needed to know.

"Don't just sit there," I said as I opened my eyes and looked at the pizza he had in his left hand, "give me a bite. You're eating it all. I thought you bought that for me."

Robert bent down and handed me the piece of pizza that he had been nibbling on. It was greasy and almost slid out of his hand again. He managed to catch it before it hit the floor, but not before the gooey cheese and red sauce splashed all over his hands and shirt.   I could tell by the expressions on his face that he was embarrassed. I thought it was the funniest thing I had ever seen.

I laughed so hard that my body slipped and my head sunk deep into the water and bubbles.

When I came back up Robert was on his knees and at the edge of my tub. He gently wiped the bubbles off of my face and said, "Pizza delivery," as he held out his index finger layered in red sauce. I licked the sauce and cheese off of it, and as he handed me another finger he slowly and carefully said, "I can't get you out of my mind, Mary. You're all I've thought about since the minute we met. I've never been so confused and so sure about anything in my life. I've fallen for you, Mary, and I don't mind saying it out loud, I love you."

I stopped laughing and splashed Robert's muddy face with bubbles as I pulled him halfway into the tub and kissed him deep and hard.

Chapter Twenty-Two

W hat is that noise?" I asked as I pushed Robert away to listen. "Robert, what is that noise?"

I waited for Robert to answer me, he didn't. All I could hear was a loud beeping noise.

I cleared the bubbles out of my eyes and looked around. I wasn't in the tub, I was in a bed. I looked around for Robert. He was gone. I felt my face. It was dry.

I blinked my eyes and tried to focus on where I was. The noise was still piercing my brain. I sat up and looked around following the noise. It was an alarm clock that I had set for seven thirty. I tried to shut it off and no matter what button I pushed it just kept beeping. In a last effort attempt my hand followed the plug down to the socket and I yanked it out of the wall.

Where was I? Where was Robert? I glanced at my watch and then down at my bed. I was lying on top of the bedspread and my bed was still made. I must have dozed off, I thought, as I looked around for the pizza box and cold beer. My stomach growled and reminded me of how hungry I was.

I felt drugged and my body was heavy and limp. I took a couple of deep breaths trying to clear the cobwebs out of my thoughts. I looked at my watch again and realized that it was seven thirty and that I must have dozed off.

My body was wrapped in a large clean hotel towel that I don't even remember putting on. It's time to party, get up Mary, an excited voice inside of me kept repeating as I yawned and laid back down. It left good to be clean and in a soft warm bed.

As I moved around on the bed slowly stretching out every muscle I heard my stomach growl again. The little voice inside of me was right. It was time to get up and party.

I was afraid to look in a real mirror at my face. When I finally did, I was surprised to see that most of my red face had already turned brown and that the color looked really good on me. A new pair of contacts and a fresh set of clean clothes picked me up and helped to motivate me as I yawned. My mouth was really dry and I hurried a little faster as thoughts of ice-cold margaritas enticed me.

Something was gnawing at the back of my mind. It confused me. I kept yawning and pushed it away. I was getting excited and nothing was going keep me away from gathering with my new friends and reliving the past four insane days with them. I had every intention of out-drinking Jane with margaritas and out-eating anyone who challenged me.

No, what I really needed to do was get some closure and answers to a million questions. How many people got hurt on the second or third day? And who got hurt this afternoon? I still wanted and needed to thank the woman wrangler for saving Icky and I from the barbed wire. And I was dying to find out if Matt had fired the wrangler who slid us down the mountain.

A funny thought filled my head as I blow-dried my hair. I wasn't sure if I would recognize anybody or if anybody would recognize me. We had all been covered from head to toe in protective clothing and sun gear. What color was Robert's hair or Jane's or Gloria's?

Even my ankle was cooperating a little bit better. The pills that Gloria had given me were working. I was ready, bring on the party.

Outside my room the sun was still shining, but something didn't seem right. I thought about how awkward I felt when I first got into my truck earlier and I shrugged off the thought as I headed towards the restaurant. I glanced at my watch to make sure that I wasn't late. It was seven forty five. I was right on time.

I was only a few blocks away from the restaurant. I couldn't wait to get there. I was dressed to kill and I was looking forward to drinking with and hugging all of my new friends.

As I pulled into the parking lot something didn't seem right. There were only a few cars parked in front of the restaurant. Where is everybody? I thought as I looked around. There was a two-story motel across the street. Had everyone walked over from there? If so, they were a lot smarter than I was because they didn't even have to drive home.

Something still didn't make any sense in my mind. As I parked my truck and got out, a bad feeling sunk deep into my stomach. Was I late? I looked at my watch again. No, I was right on time. It was almost eight o'clock.

A flood of emotions shot through me as I pulled opened the restaurant door. It wouldn't open, it was locked. I walked over to a window and peaked inside. The room was dark and empty.

What was going on? Was everybody playing a trick on me? I tried the door again as I slowly read a sign by it that said, "Open 11:00am—11:00pm." They must have changed restaurants, I thought, as I pulled harder and knocked on the door. As I stood outside the restaurant's front door I wondered where else in this small of a town could everybody had gone.

A car drove by and slowed down in front of the restaurant as it turned into the parking lot. "Mary, is that you?" I heard a familiar voice shout, " What are you doing here?" I would have recognized Jane and Gloria's voices anywhere. I was glad to hear them.

"I was getting worried," I shouted as I walked over to their car, "Where is everybody? Am I early? Or did Matt change the time again?"

"What do you mean?" Gloria asked as a puzzling expression filled her face. "What are you doing here?"

By the expression on her face I knew that something was

wrong. I shrugged of the thought and in an excited voice I shouted," I'm here for our celebration dinner and a lot of margaritas—bring on the party!"

Jane shut the engine off and got out of the car. "Mary," she said as she walked over to where I was standing, "the party was last night. We all thought you drove home. Robert was really disappointed. He watched the door and waited for you till they closed the place down. What happened to you?"

"What?" I said in a weak voice, "But…" I looked at my watch and said, "I'm on time, it's eight o'clock."

Gloria got out of the car and joined us as she said, "Mary, maybe we should drive you to a doctor's office, you're not making any sense. We all were disappointed when you didn't show up last night. What did you say happened to you?"

"What are you talking about?" I said as I raised my voice and pointed at my watch as I lifted up my arm. "Look, it's eight o'clock, I'm on time." "The dinner and party were last night," both Jane and Gloria yelled as they raised their voices,

"Mary, it's eight in the morning, not at night."

All of my thoughts came crashing down on me and I started laughing. "I get it," I said as I laughed even louder, "you two are messing with my mind. Okay, you guys win. Now tell me the truth, they changed restaurant's, didn't they?"

Both Jane and Gloria remained silent as they stared at me. Jane finally said, "Mary, why don't you get in our car and we'll take you to the hospital. It's only a couple of blocks away from here. You don't look so good."

"So," I slowly said as I tried to figure out what was really happening, "you're trying to tell me that it's eight in the morning? I don't believe you!" I yelled out in an angry voice as I stared at my watch, which still said eight o'clock.

Both women threw each other a confused look and at the same time loudly said, "Yes, it's morning, Mary, you missed the party."

"We're starved, do you want to go out to breakfast with us?" "No," I said in a low angry voice, "I need a margarita."

"That works for me," Jane enthusiastically shouted. "The

first one is on me."

"Boy, did you miss a party." Jane walked around and got in the driver's seat. "Get in," Gloria added, as she sat down in the front seat and pointed to the car's back door.

I sat down and tried to fight off a flood of angry emotions. I had missed our party, how stupid could I have been? Poor Robert, I thought, he must think that I'm a real jerk. I felt even worse as I thought about how I had promised everyone that I would get their names and addresses to send them all of the pictures I had taken. As the frustration and anger built up inside of me I lost my appetite. I thought about a margarita. If it was really only eight in the morning I didn't need or even want one.

My thoughts kept turning to Robert as I stared outside the car window, into the daylight. I must have looked at my watch a dozen times as I tried to comprehend what had happened. The sun was shining but the sun was also shining at eight at night. How was I supposed to tell the difference? My watch didn't say morning or night, it just said eighto' clock. No matter how hard I tried to figure out what had happened, I couldn't. I felt horrible. How could I have made this big of a mistake?

"You know," Gloria, said as she turned here head to look at me, "I didn't know you had blond hair. I wouldn't have recognized you, but we're staying in the hotel across the street and when I saw somebody standing at the door of the restaurant I just had to see who it was.

"You clean up real well, Mary. I'm so hung over a margarita sounds real good. Where do you want to go?"

"I feel so stupid," I said with a long drawn out sigh, "I took those two pills you gave me and set the alarm for seven thirty. And the alarm went off at seven thirty. What did I do wrong?"

"You took both of those pills?" Gloria said as she started to giggle. "Both at the same time?" Jane joined in giggling as she listened. I had no idea what was so funny. But their laughter helped me fight off all of my angry thoughts.

"Yes, wasn't I supposed to take them both?" "Only if you want to knock yourself out for twelve hours," Gloria said as she started laughing even louder.

Their laughter was contagious, "Thanks a lot," I said as I started to giggle. "Now I feel even dumber. I don't think anyone will believe me when I tell them that I missed my own party because I drugged myself. I don't even believe me."

A smile returned to my face as I shook my head like I was going crazy and I said, "Yeah, let's have another party. Bring on the steaks and margaritas. I deserve them both."

"Wait a minute," I said as I thought about the dream of Robert and I in the bathtub. "Do you guys know if those pills cause weird dreams?"

Gloria turned back around and she raised her eyebrows as she said, "How weird?" "Really weird, and it seemed so real. I dreamt that Robert came over last night, when I was in the bathtub. He had brought me a cold six pack of beer and a hot pizza. He joined me in the bathroom and we ended up in the tub together."

"That doesn't sound weird—that sounds like fun," Jane said. "What kind of pizza?"

"I don't know," I said as I blushed and started to giggle. "He dropped most of it on the floor and I licked the rest off of him. It seemed so real. I actually could taste the pizza."

"That's not a weird dream, that's a horny dream," Jane said as she stopped for a red light at the only signal light in town.

"I've never done it in the tub. Was it fun?" Gloria asked, as she rolled her window down and looked outside. Before I could answer her she said, "Look, Mary, look over there, isn't that Robert?"

I stared out the window and looked in the general direction that she was pointing at. "I don't know," I said as I watched a man walking towards a car. "I forgot what he looks like, I'm not sure."

"Mary," Gloria said as she shook her head, "you need some serious help. How could you forget about a man that was in your bathtub? I know that's Robert and we're going to stop him before he leaves town. Floor it, Jane," she said in a much higher voice.

The light was still red. "What are you doing?" I yelled as Jane plowed through the red light. "Are you crazy? You'll get us all killed!"

Both women ignored me and Gloria stuck her head out the window and yelled, "Robert, is that you?" A couple of people turned their heads and watched us.

"Stop it, you're embarrassing me'" I said as Gloria shouted out again.

"You don't know her very well," Jane said as she turned the radio on and started singing loudly with the music. "You get used to the embarrassing parts," she shouted even louder as she drummed her hand up and down on the dashboard to the rhythm of the music. I could barely hear her over the radio and Gloria's voice.

The man Gloria was shouting at has stopped walking and was watching our car. Gloria was already halfway out of the window as she shouted, "We found Mary! Robert, don't go, we found Mary!"

"We're going to get arrested," I complained as I watched her, "Gloria, get back in the car, before you break another arm!"

Jane slowed the car down and turned into a parking lot where the tall man was standing.

He followed us to our car as we parked. "Hello," He said in a warm friendly voice, "Good morning." It was Robert I would have recognized his voice anywhere. He seemed taller and was neatly dressed in slacks and a buttoned-down shirt.

"We're going out for margaritas," Gloria shouted out, loud enough for everyone within a mile to hear. "Come on, get in the car, Robert, we found Mary, let's go!"

Robert leaned over and took a peak at me. "We all thought you drove home—what happened, Mary? Are you all right?" I could see the pain that I had caused Robert, it was written all over his face. I didn't know what to say, but I knew I couldn't say it in front of these two crazy women.

"I'll be right back," I said as I got out of the car, "I've got to talk to Robert." "Hurry up!" both women barked as I stood up and looked into Robert eyes. Everything felt awkward. I didn't

even know what to say. I held out my hand to see if he even
wanted to be around me. He grabbed it and we walked away
hand in hand back over to where his car was parked. I still
couldn't find the words to tell him how deeply I felt about him
and how sorry I was that I had ruined last night. All I could do
was squeeze his hand and look deep into his eyes. I was hoping
my eyes would express my feelings. I knew my words couldn't.

"Do you remember when I asked you, if you believed in
fate?" he asked as he tenderly touched and studied my face.
"Yes," I slowly replied as I gently leaned my face on his warm,
soft hand. "I'm sorry," I said as tears pooled in my eyes.

"This was fate, not us," he said as water filled his eyes. "I
already miss you, Mary, and no matter how hard I try to deny
it, this was not meant to be." Robert bent over and kissed the
tears rolling down my cheeks.

"Would you two get a room?" Jane shouted. "Hurry up!"
Gloria yelled, "I need that margarita."

We both turned to look at them and as our eyes met for the
last time we embraced and kissed, as though there was no
tomorrow.

Robert was right and we both knew it. Somehow twelve
hours in time a twist of fate had stopped us and it was time for
us both to go home. As I fought back tears, I let his hand go
and turned away.

"Mary," Robert said before I walked away, "I'm glad that
you're safe. I was really worried about you last night."

I'd never been so emotionally torn in my life. I wanted to
scream like an angry teenager and yell out, "It's not fair!" I
knew that Robert was the man of my dreams and I knew that
I had just lost him. Somehow a twist of fate, a moment in time,
had stolen him from me.

Everything inside of me felt wrong and a piece of my heart
and soul died as I watched him drive away.

"He did have a cute ass," Jane said as I limped over to the
car and got back in.

Gloria and Jane took me out for the breakfast I will never
forget. I ate a steak the size of a football and actually had a

crowd gather around me as I polished it off.

"Well, little lady, you sure can eat beef, why, I don't know where you're putting it with that girlish figure of yours. My name is Mark, good morning."

As another younger wrangler came over and looked at my empty plate, Jane bent over and whispered, "This isn't fair, Mary, you had your chance, he's a hunk and he's mine." "Ma'am that's pretty impressive eating for a skinny little thing like you, can I buy you another one?"

I winked at Jane and said, "No, thank you, this is my celebration dinner, but my two friends still have a real good appetite, if you know what I mean, and after they drive me home, I'm sure they would have room for round two."

"Are you sure you can't stay a couple more days?" Jane asked as we all walked out of the restaurant and back to the car.

"Those two cowboys said the fun starts here at ten tonight and they'll be back with a bunch of their friends. We're going to stay for a while and party with them."

I was tempted to stay and join the party I missed last night, but in my heart I knew it was time to go home. And I figured if I hung out with these two crazy women long enough I would have either a broken bone or wake up in bed with a total stranger. I was glad that they had befriended me and I was truly going to miss them.

"Gloria!" I shouted as I got back in my truck. "Are you guys going on this trip next year?"

She glanced over at Jane and as she hung half of her body out the window she slowly said, "We don't know, maybe."

"How about you, are you going next year, Mary?" I pulled my body out of the window and sat down on the open window frame as I said, "I don't know, maybe."

We both laughed and waved goodbye as we drove off in different directions.

I unlocked my hotel room door and slowly looked around the room. I half expected to see a pizza box and empty beer cans.

I plugged the alarm clock back in and watched it as the bright red letters on it flashed seven thirty over and over again as it screamed "wake up."

"Yes, Robert, I believe in fate," I said as I unplugged the alarm clock, and tears swelled in my eyes. "I hope a twist of fate brings us back together."

I dropped the key next to the alarm clock and headed for home.